Dec

# Genetha

Roy Heath is from Guyana. He
England at the age of twenty-four to read
Modern Languages at London
University. He has been teaching since
1959 and is at present a schoolmaster in
a London comprehensive school. He
was called to the English Bar in 1964 and
to the Guyana Bar in 1973.

He has published short stories and
essays in Guyana; his first novel, *A Man
Come Home*, was published in 1974. His
other novels include *The Murderer*,
winner of the *Guardian* Fiction Prize in
1978; *Kwaku*; and the trilogy *From the
Heat of the Day*, *One Generation*, and
*Genetha*.

*From Nav + Flip.*

Roy Heath

# Genetha

FLAMINGO

Published by Fontana Paperbacks

First published in Great Britain
by Allison and Busby Ltd 1981

This Flamingo edition first published
in 1984 by Fontana Paperbacks,
8 Grafton Street, London W1X 3LA

Reproduced, printed and
bound in Great Britain by
Hazell, Watson & Viney Limited,
Member of the BPCC Group,
Aylesbury, Bucks.

I return to the edge
Where the sea gnaws always

– Christopher Aird (Guyanese poet)


"Shall my heart go
As flowers that wither?
Some day shall my name be nothing?
At least let us have flowers!
At least let us have singing!"

– Poem from the Aztecs

# BOOK 1

## 1. Recollections

Genetha was left to brood in the house when her brother Rohan went away, driven by the fear of incest after their father's death. Night after night, on coming home from work, she went over the events since her family had come from Agricola to settle in the north of Georgetown, back to the area of her mother's birth: the dismissal of Esther, the servant who had done all but suckle them; her father's reproach that she lacked compassion because she would not entertain the idea of taking Esther back to live with them; the discovery that he had brought the former servant to the house and paid her as other men did. . . . And every night the recollections brought the same panic fed by some demonic energy.

Rohan had told Genetha that he could not remain when he found out that she had become intimate with Fingers, a young man from one of the deep yards that spread like scabs over parts of the town. She had believed that his poverty was no impediment to their association since Fingers was Rohan's best friend, so she was not prepared for her brother's fury. She was never to discover the true reason for his departure.

Rohan had gone away as if he had the right to. And she, in the same way as her mother had been until death, was tied to the house like a dog to a post.

The war between Genetha's loneliness and her vague fear of allowing an intrusion in the family home reduced her to tears on her waking up in the empty house. She came to dread the morning with its clamour of bells interspersed with the pounding of dray wheels, and the muffled sounds of night-time.

She became furtive, if her neighbour was to be believed.

"You're getting like my son. Secretive, like my son," the woman once said when she caught Genetha scurrying to the back of the yard to avoid her. "But you don't have any reason. He's got debts."

Genetha talked to her for a while through the walaba paling staves and even forced a smile when the neighbour asked her to laugh a little.

"You've been through a lot," she told Genetha, in an effort to

1

console her. "But I had a hard life too! When your father died it was a sort of deliverance, wasn't it? It *was* a deliverance."

"No," retorted Genetha sharply.

Undismayed, the neighbour persisted. "You can entertain now, at least. You didn't have a chance to live your own life."

Genetha bowed her head. If the neighbour were younger she might have told her of the morning dray-carts and the evenings when shadows kept thronging at the doorway, like the visitors on the stairs after news of her father's death had spread.

"You need friends, Miss Armstrong. You give your life for your father and he went and died. And for your brother and he gone away. They wouldn't let you have friends and look how they left you in the lurch!"

Genetha was no longer offended. She would not have dared speak to the neighbour like that, and God knows her son did enough to be gossiped about. But she was not offended, for the neighbour was older and had no malice.

When Genetha left the neighbour she locked herself in, switched off the light and took off her clothes. Then she wandered about the house for a few minutes in her nightdress before delivering herself up to her secret vice, which consisted of taking a poisonous concoction that went to her head, left her arms heavy and numb and in the end vouchsafed her visions filled with purple clouds. Marion, one of their servants of long ago, had taught her brother the secret of visions and he, in turn, had passed it on to Genetha, who remembered well the forbidden euphoria of that late morning when they were on school holidays and going from house to yard and from yard to house, frantic with boredom, and the break in the monotony that came with the new-found indulgence. After that long August the secret lay dormant, for Rohan had discovered cricket and left Genetha to the insipid games of girlhood. Now, as in that far-off August, she indulged herself endlessly, having summoned up her brother's presence with copious tears.

As always she sank on to the floor after standing defiantly before the looking-glass, weighed down by her numbed arms and visions of blood-stained beds. But the short period of nausea was soon followed by a feeling of contentment and then by an indescribable sadness as she rediscovered her whereabouts, the long sky-light through which filtered the gently bleeding night and the feeble rays of a handful of stars.

2

There came an unexpected respite for Genetha when the neighbour's misfortunes were made public in a distraint by the bailiffs, who "levied" on her late one Friday morning. Her furniture was piled high on the pavement and tallied carefully by one of them, dressed meticulously in jacket and well-pressed trousers. Her son, no doubt the cause of his mother's shame, was seen by the curious – who had gathered in front of the house in spite of the sun – to be smoking nonchalantly at the window, looking on as if it were someone else's disgrace. In the end he was obliged to give up his seat at the instance of the second bailiff, who remained in the house.

Genetha, home for the midday meal, went over to offer her neighbour tea and had to endure a flood of invective, directed ostensibly at her but meant for the ne'er-do-well son.

The experience, unforeseen despite the son's trail of past misdeeds and his notorious skill at persuading those who dealt with him to part with their money, had a salutary effect on Genetha. She resolved to stop taking the mild poison and to renounce the favourite recollections of her brother and the time when her parents were alive and a destitute aunt lived in the room under the house.

On Sundays she went to church and took a Sunday-school class of children between the ages of seven and eleven; and once during the weekend ventured over the river on a taxi ride past the house of girls on New Road where her brother used to visit. She got out at some nameless village on the coast and walked along the ploughed fields above which wheeling gulls squawked endlessly.

Time and time again she came back to take the taxi ride until the villagers began waving to her, believing that she was looking for a plot of land to buy. Two of them even took her to the dye-pits which were about to be uncovered now that the sun was low and invited her into their houses afterwards where their wives admired her bodice all covered in braid. She in turn wondered at the soles of their feet, which had the tapir-like thickness of those who had never worn shoes.

There was soon an end to her excursions after she had explored the length and breadth of the village; but at least they had exorcized her panic; and now boredom had settled in its place, a healthy boredom that afflicted most of her class.

Genetha found herself watching the young men go by as her

3

mother had done even after she was married. Unabashed, she gazed at the odd passer-by who stopped to urinate against the corrugated fence at the corner, uninhibited by the presence of a father or brother. And now that she was alone it dawned upon her to what extent her behaviour used to be regulated by them. The mask she had worn on their account she still wore, but only when she was out of the house and her behaviour was subjected to the examination of others. Yet all around her she saw the way other women had changed, how they smoked and drank, how they took advantage of their status as working women to go out with more than one man or to leave their men if they were married; how they flew in the face of convention with that aplomb of a youth who had drunk for the first time. But some unseen hand guided her conduct outside, and even her father would have approved of the show of propriety and the proper opinion those who knew her held of her.

Then came February, when the window panes melted in their frames, and the brilliant nights. And once more her recollections pressed upon her, the childlike obsession with pictures, the afternoon when in a fit of jealousy she had deliberately left the gate open and Rohan, then only two years old, had wandered into the road and was nearly run down by a horse and carriage. She recalled the castor-oil doctor who always gave a word-for-word commentary of a one-horse race he had witnessed on the race-course when he was a youth and then cleaned up on the gambler's spinning-wheel by putting a five-dollar note on the ace of spades. She recalled the woman who lived on the edge of Agricola, in a house overlooking the back-dam, who, according to her father, shaved in secret. And her story book with a blue, pellucid sea, and her disappointment at the first encounter with the curling waves that died on the sand; her father's anger when he found that a new pair of trousers had been destroyed by the moths, in spite of the precaution of naphthalene balls which gave to the wardrobe a scent that came to characterize for her the better side of domesticity; and the long stay in her mother's parents' home, after her mother's death, when her father grudgingly gave his consent for her to be taken away, even though he was overcome with grief and wanted nothing better; and her grandparents' house where there was constant talk of superior things, like saffron and potted orchids.

At the back of her grandparents' yard was a swing on which

she used to spend much of the afternoons after the ritual of the main meal, which everyone called *breakfast*, at eleven in the morning. She could not believe that such a wondrous toy remained unused, that the neighbourhood children did not flock into the yard to gaze at one another soaring up to the roof-top and falling back in an arc.

And then came the loss of her father on that afternoon when dust spun in the late sunlight. A single accident achieved what a long illness did not, when the sick-room smelled of bay-rum and damp from the yard. Everything threatened: the coming dusk, the indistinct voices. A single accident that prevailed over the long months when sickness hammered on the walls. In that night filled with people Rohan had remained calm and the old women who came to tend the corpse never tired of caressing the weathered head while outside the wind scattered leaves like monstrous insects. Genetha had been warned about death and had covered the mirrors, as was the custom. So many things she had learned about death since her childhood, but it had been different. All she could remember was the sense of loss and the leaves scattering as if dealt by mysterious fingers.

February passed; then came April and early May with much rain and grey days. Genetha felt less oppressed, and the routine established after the neighbour's misfortune was elaborated by regular visits to her father's sister and her grandparents' house.

After a time people no longer enquired about Rohan, just as they stopped asking after Esther a year or so after she was dismissed. The shopkeepers, like the neighbour, grew accustomed to the fact that there was a house in the street with one occupant, as they had grown accustomed to the sight of Genetha shopping for the household when for years Esther had haggled with them with the assurance of one who controlled the family's purse-strings.

Every Saturday afternoon she looked up her grandparents in Queenstown, in the house where her father had courted her mother and learned of the gulf that separated him from her family. Genetha's mother's two sisters never failed to remind him of his origins in a hundred and one little humiliations. And for that reason he did everything he could to keep their family and his apart after his marriage. Rohan hardly knew them and Genetha's tenuous connection with the household really began with that stay in the wake of their mother's death. After that she

5

did not dare speak of those relations in her father's presence and only dropped in to visit them on occasion, when she found herself riding past on her bicycle.

Now, with the Saturday afternoon visits established as a routine, she got to know them better, even though she remained on her guard, carrying deep within her a residue of her dead father's resentment.

"When are you getting married?" her elder aunt was in the habit of asking, for the sake of conversation.

"No one's proposed yet, Aunt," she always replied.

"I can't believe that, dear," her younger aunt would put in. She was like her father, Genetha's grandfather, gentle and warm.

And sometimes her grandmother, kindly but distant, would smile at her as if she were still a child. She and her husband seemed to be one in their decrepitude, with their backs stooped in the same way. They had aged together, and so suddenly that now her father's monstrous curses seemed charged with absurdity.

Her two aunts were preoccupied with marriage.

"Has Rohan written lately?" asked the younger aunt once.

"Not lately, Aunt," replied Genetha.

"I suppose he'll at least write when he gets married," observed Deborah, the elder aunt, always the more officious.

"I hope so," said Genetha dryly, seeking to quash a subject that never failed to pain her.

"The family before everything else," went on Deborah. "The individual is nothing. The family's everything."

"Yes, Aunt," said Genetha dutifully, not certain what she meant by "family". The word was widely used to include even cousins far removed, to the sixth and seventh degree, because they were "blood".

Whenever Genetha happened to speak of her father she was met with a frigid silence. And once her other aunt, her father's sister, who used to live in the room under their house, told Genetha that those two fine aunts of hers in Queenstown had once remarked that their sister, Genetha's mother, *tolerated* Armstrong, her own husband.

Genetha recalled this remark when her older aunt said, "Your mother was a fine musician before she got married, Genetha. Did you know that your mother was a fine musician before her marriage?"

6

"We knew. We all knew," replied Genetha. "Father knew, too," she added deliberately, with unwonted boldness.

"You must miss him, dear," said Alice, her younger aunt, in a conciliatory voice.

Genetha looked at her, astonished that she should be required to respond to a remark like that so many months after her father's death. Her younger aunt mistook her silence for grief and started smoothing her dress.

And yet Genetha was drawn to these two ageing women, whose hair was streaked with silver since, disdaining the new style, they could not bring themselves to dye it. The same tranquillity that had fired her mother's nostalgia for the house long after she was married had begun to infect Genetha. Had she been able to visit without being obliged to make formal conversation, she would have come when the spirit took her and lingered as long as it suited her.

If the Queenstown relations did not approve of Genetha's father they would not have approved of his sister either, because she used expressions like "take out your photograph" for "take your photograph" and "keep noise" for "make noise", and for all the other reasons they never approved of him.

Genetha found her father's sister pleasant enough, but there was something lacking in their relationship, that something which distinguished maternal aunts and uncles from paternal ones and placed the former on a higher plane in the scale of affections. Genetha's visits to her paternal aunt were made out of duty, while the visits to the Queenstown house, even when they were casual, were the result of a deep need.

"You can't keep away from your grandparents' house," her father's sister once told her, and in an effort to compete with her dead brother's in-laws had a bracelet made for Genetha of eighteen-carat gold. But the niece's exaggerated delight on receiving the present only increased her bitterness. Though she had occupied a room under the family's house for years, in contrast to their mother's sisters who had never even condescended to visit them since they came to live in Georgetown, that had brought her no closer to them.

Her paternal aunt's obsessive conversation, consisting of little else save her opinion of the Queenstown aunts and her dead brother's injustice towards her, had the effect of reducing the frequency of Genetha's visits. And as these visits became rarer

7

so her aunt concentrated even more on the subject of the ageing women in Queenstown and on her brother who once robbed her of two houses, the remnants of a fortune. In the end Genetha stopped going altogether, daunted by her aunt's resentment.

All this happened within a year of Rohan's going away to take up a new post in the Essequibo. And in that year Genetha had learned to live alone.

## 2. A Dog in Heat

Before Genetha had taken up with Rohan's friend she had gone out for a while with Michael, and it was to him that she now turned for male companionship. Their relationship before, up to the moment when it was interrupted, had not been happy. They used to go to religious meetings together, continuing a tradition in his family that went back two generations. The fervour he displayed at these gatherings surprised Genetha, who was always acutely embarassed by his silences. But, as he explained, his was a deeply religious family which practised what the Church preached.

Michael did not approve of her clothes, by most standards conservative, nor of her love of the cinema, an incipient vice he denied her after they had gone out together for a few weeks. Convinced that she was unattractive, Genetha did her best to please him. Mistrusting the model of marriage her parents had presented her, she relied on her own ideas of what her role as a potential wife ought to be. When Michael boasted of the number of professional people among his relations she concealed her revulsion and listened dutifully.

Against her expectations she grew to like him, but noticed that as he became certain of her affection and loyalty he set about imposing his will on her with unexpected ruthlessness. She was to go here, could not go there; she ought not to eat this and should drink that or that bush tea because it cleaned you out. And the one shortcoming he was unable to forgive was her inability to show enthusiasm at religious meetings. Her Methodist background had inculcated in her the habit of restraint, and at best she managed to sing hymns that were not to be found in the Methodist hymnal.

Genetha would not give Michael up, despite all this, believing that his uprightness was the uprightness of her dead parents.

8

Her brief association with Fingers, Rohan's best friend, had been partly responsible for her brother going away: if she had learned anything she had learned that the flesh was not to be trusted, that the spirit must maintain its ascendancy above all. On a visit to the Courantyne when still a little girl she had accompanied an East Indian woman to a Kali Mai Poojah ceremony and was mesmerized by the disc of burning camphor in the priest's hand; to her the dazzling flame at one and the same time promised warmth and threatened disfigurement, a chastening fire that nevertheless aroused in her for the first time a longing for an unknown contact. Michael was sobriety, the mid-point between two fires that spun as one in the priest's hand.

Michael's refusal to countenance any experience that he deemed improper made Genetha suspicious of confiding in him. The guilt she felt at possessing the secret of visions and at indulging in the euphoric poison had to be borne alone.

But Michael was not entirely without experience; more than once he had, in his peremptory way, made one of his mother's servant girls take down her drawers when everyone else was out, and he had contemplated her featureless body for several minutes on end like the traveller who, for the first time, casts his eyes on a stunning landscape of desert and brush. Yet despite Genetha's vulnerability he had remained aloof, seeming to want nothing from her in that way. In the past when she had suffered from Michael's virtuousness she turned to Rohan's friend; but now she would not make the same mistake again. After all, there were women who had been courted for as long as ten years before they married.

He always came after dark, like a rider in the mist, hardly making a noise as he pushed his cycle over the bridge. People in the street would not have credited the innocence of their association and Genetha's neighbour remarked to her son that since her father's death she had gone to the dogs. Could he remember the daughter of the sea captain, who lived in Light Street? While he was away for months on his schooner she behaved correctly, never giving tongues a reason to wag. But soon after his death she began to carry on like a dog in heat and any newcomer was welcome.

Genetha's doctor urged her to wear glasses and Michael strongly advised her to follow his counsel. When she declared herself willing to risk further deterioration of her eyesight, Michael's

9

fury was incomprehensible. He accused her of never following advice, even though Genetha hardly dared to ignore his. She gave in and for a few weeks took on the habit, which she firmly believed disfigured her. But Michael's repeated assurances to the contrary made her suspicious of his motives in condoning the doctor's views. She abandoned the habit abruptly, and, in what was until then her only act of revolt, refused to discuss the matter any further with him.

So they grew to know each other and she went to meet him with hurried steps when he came visiting at night with his ponderous observations as to the state of the world and his mask well adjusted like the revellers of the twenties on the eve of a new year. She loved him and opened her heart to him; and he in turn told her of his resolution not to take advantage of her.

One Sunday as Genetha and Michael were listening to the service on the radio she saw Rohan's friend strolling by in the presence of a young woman and involuntarily gave a start and rose from her chair to look at them until they went out of sight.

Michael must have seen the despair in her eyes for, uncharacteristically, he interrupted the voice on the radio to ask:

"What's wrong? You're not listening."

"No . . . it's someone I saw passing."

Michael represented the genteel side of her upbringing. Rohan's friend, on the other hand, was the forbidden face of Georgetown and Agricola which surged up out of the alleyways and cook-shops and blew down the necks of decent women who walked the pavements alone.

The mole on Michael's chin suddenly seemed offensive, like a floor strewn with toenails, and the conviction that she loved him was suddenly intolerable.

"What's wrong with you?" he persisted.

"Nothing," she said sadly, ashamed at the things swarming so close to the surface of her composure.

"Listen to the service, then," he declared impatiently.

Genetha was overcome by that same despair that overtook her when Rohan went away to live on the Essequibo and from which the neighbour's distress had wrenched her. Rohan's friend had pricked her flesh and opened a wound she thought had healed, but for the sight of him in the company of a woman.

At the end of the service Genetha could not bear the silence, that void that could last all night because Michael was sparing

10

with words. She found herself saying whatever came into her head, unable to stop although she knew he was judging her.

". . . and d'you know that in Barbados there's such a shortage of wood that the coffin-makers go to the cemetery the night after the funeral to steal their own coffins?"

"What's the matter with you?" Michael asked. "What's got into you?"

She could not answer. Then, after a short while she said, "You tell me something for a change, Michael. We're together so much and we don't have much to say to one another."

"What do you want me to say? I'm happy. Nothing's happened, so what can I say? Aren't you happy?"

"No, Michael."

And from that night their relationship began to wither. He came and went as before, but they grew impatient with each other. He accused her of being less compliant than before and believed that she really took his silences to heart. So each night he came armed with a tale to tell, about his home or work, or about something he had heard during the interminable hours he listened to the radio.

One night just before he was about to go home she said, "I'm not coming to the meeting tomorrow night, Michael."

"Don't be foolish; of course you're coming."

"I'm not coming to the meeting. I don't want to come. I don't want to come any more. Not tomorrow night, anyway." The last few words were spoken in a murmur, for she was still uncertain about standing up to him.

Michael was nonplussed. "Very well," he said. "Goodbye."

He got up, took his hat from the hat stand and was about to go out. At the door he turned and with trembling voice said,

"You're no Christian! I can't marry a woman that blows hot and cold like you."

It was the first time he had ever mentioned marriage, as far as Genetha could recall. She did not answer him. Michael thwarted his urge to do something positive. If only *she* would say something. He had never felt so humiliated and remained rooted to the spot, twirling his hat in his hands.

"Say something, damn it!" he exclaimed, half-imploring, half-dictating.

"Michael, I . . . I thought I loved you; but now I . . ."

He stared at her, unbelieving. "Since when?"

She remained silent.

"I can't stand here all night. Since when, I asked?" he repeated.

She was loath to answer him. "I don't think I ever loved you, Michael."

Michael sat down in a chair opposite her, never taking his eyes off her. "I don't believe you."

She leaned forward and put a hand on his arm.

"I want to be alone, Michael. Since Boyie went away I don't know where I am."

Her use of Rohan's fond name increased Michael's dismay.

"I don't want to be alone," he declared. "It's not natural to want to be alone. Only yesterday my mother said she wanted to see you. You don't understand: I can't stop seeing you now."

Overcome by a strange sense of power Genetha put her hand on his arm once more, but he drew away with a violent gesture and got up.

"You're one of these women who lure a man then imprison him for months, even years; and when at last he's got peace of mind you slam the door in his face. What d'you expect me to do? Knock on somebody's door and say, 'Have you got a daughter who I can see and be friends with?' This isn't a village where you know everybody. I've never been so lonely in my life as since I've come to town."

He sat down once more.

"People say you're eccentric," he continued, twisting the hat energetically in his hands, "because you don't make friends easily. Only God knows what I've been through. When I started going out with you I told myself how lucky I was to meet someone clean, someone decent who doesn't only think of men. At home I don't speak of anything but you. My mother and my aunts are tired of hearing what you wear and what you say. . . . O my God!" He bit his lips and closed his eyes.

"Don't touch me!" he cried in despair, as Genetha came towards him.

A few moments later he got up and with great dignity held out his right hand.

"Goodbye," he said in a firm voice.

"Goodbye, Michael," Genetha said in turn, shaking his hand weakly.

He left, closing the door quietly behind him.

12

Genetha went out to eat. The night was warm and couples were walking arm in arm. She took it into her head to go past the house where her aunts and grandparents lived. It was in need of painting. Someone was at the window and as Genetha looked up the person stared back but did not recognize her. It was several weeks since she had gone to visit them and on an impulse she nearly went in, but changed her mind and walked past slowly. She found herself walking in New Town, Kitty. Why? she reflected. Only once had she been there before and the impression then was of wretched houses and poorly lit streets. It was odd that Georgetown should stop at Vlissingen Road with its smooth asphalt and massive trees, and that a different world should lie beyond.

She turned back to go down Lamaha Street and walked on without knowing where she was going; and when at last she found herself in front of the Astor cinema where a queue had formed for the night show – the "theatre" as it was called – she joined it. There was a certain excitement in rubbing shoulders with the crowd that slowly gathered, and as the queue started moving she was impatient with anticipation. She was going at night-time to see a film! And she would get home after eleven, like hundreds of others.

## 3. A Humble Mortal

The next time Genetha saw Rohan's friend she smiled at him warmly. As she had anticipated, he came back to the house, to see Rohan on business, he declared. She offered to make him a meal and he was so tongue-tied he answered her questions awkwardly. When she complained that the tap was dripping he jumped up and came to her assistance. In no time he had dismantled it and made a makeshift washer from a piece of rubber he found lying about the house. As she watched him working and admired his body he looked round and saw her staring. From then on he was more at ease, his words came more readily and he no longer avoided her eyes. In fact she began to avoid his, which were frank and smiling.

When the meal was ready the two sat down at table. From force of habit Genetha joined hands to say a prayer which she shortened on his account. He ate like a stevedore and at the end got up to pour himself a glass of water from the clay goblet in

13

the kitchen. He then came back to the table where he stood watching Genetha, who was chewing the last mouthful carefully. Then pretending that he had to go to the kitchen once more he excused himself, but on coming back remained standing behind Genetha's chair.

She neither looked round nor said anything, but continued chewing her last mouthful. He eased his hand into her bodice and began stroking her left breast, while she went on chewing, bent over her plate. Unbuttoning her bodice and letting down the straps of her brassière he lifted out her breasts with both hands. Genetha continued chewing, from time to time looking down at her bare shoulders and exposed breasts, cupped in his hands; and when she was naked to her hips she raised herself slightly from her seat so that he could pull off her dress and petticoat. Sitting on the chair, clothed in nothing but her panties, she felt like weeping and fell to thinking of the night before her father's accident, when she sat reading to him from Ecclesiastes, a passage she knew by heart:

"For the living know that they shall die; but the dead know not anything, neither have they any more a reward; for the memory of them is forgotten. Also their love, and their hatred, and their envy, is now perished; neither have they any more portion for ever in anything that is done under the sun. Go thy way, eat they bread with joy, and drink thy wine with a merry heart. . . ."

Genetha opened her mouth wide and accepted her lover's mouth. His left hand was on her breast and his right hand was on her leg. She yielded with her mouth and with her arms and with her shuddering loins. They copulated on the floor, by the dining table; and the cat at the foot of the chair blinked once before falling alseep again.

Long after he went, she lay naked under the blanket listening to the crapauds croaking, to the hum of a distant traffic and the voice of her reflections.

Her father and brother's conduct had goaded her into setting out on the road to freedom; but soon afterwards her father had died and Rohan went away, precisely because of her show of independence. Then came the discovery that she had not yet learned to use her freedom, that her belief in the strength of men was so deeply rooted – a conviction confirmed by Michael's single-minded egoism – she needed the resentment of the men

14

in her family to impel her towards her goal. "Men are so strong!" she had once heard her mother say; and the seed of that remark had grown into a massive trunk which towered above the trees of her illusions. She remembered how Michael had nearly broken down when she confessed to having no love for him; how she looked on, refusing to accept the reality of his weakness, and how, as his vulnerability was exposed by the fear in his eyes and the way he twirled his hat in his fingers, she quivered with elation. Then Fingers came with the brutal affirmation of her father's and brother's egoism. But she persuaded herself that so long as she was certain of his loyalty she would accept him for what he was.

However willingly Genetha gave herself to Fingers he believed her to be aloof. He did not realize that she had never been so happy, that the people she worked with noticed the transformation, as did the neighbours and the shopkeepers.

"She getting it, dat's why," one of them said to a customer who remarked how well she was looking.

"Since the men gone away the chile don't got to work so hard," was the opinion of another, who went on to say how she remembered well the night the family moved into the district.

"Is 'cause she getting it, I tell you. Is 'bout time too," insisted the first.

"Funny, funny family."

"You din' know she mother? Is she husband send she to she grave."

"An' the son. I only know he when he grow up, but I hear that when he was a boy they couldn't control he. Between he an' he father they drag that poor woman to the grave. She had rings under she eyes like that; big, big like that, bigger than the rings under Quashie eyes."

The customer made a gesture denoting the size of the rings, to which her companion replied, screwing her face in a gesture of pity and shaking her head eloquently, "Tut, tut, tut. Like that, eh?"

"Rings like that?" asked another customer, who had moved into the district after the death of Genetha's parents. "Death was a deliverance then. I hear she family only live up the road, y'know. Yes, in Queenstown. Somebody tell me that since she marry she husband she sisters din' have nothing more to do with

15

she. So I hear. I in' know if is true."

"My Eversley say it's in the blood," said the woman acquainted with the size of the rings under Mrs Armstrong's eyes.

"What's in the blood?" asked the second speaker.

"Women."

"Well, I know 'bout the father. . . ."

"The son is the same."

"Oh?"

"I mean he's more discreet, but is the same."

Fingers tried to teach Genetha how to dance and paid her compliments about the clothes she wore and went with her to the shops to help her choose her shoes. If he was not enthusiastic about anything she bought, she gave it away or exchanged it.

He was again out of a job and Genetha helped him to look for one, but employers were not encouraged to take on a man skilled at nothing except billiards. In the end Fingers was offered work at the ice factory; six weeks later, however, he gave notice because the factory was too cold. Genetha found him his next job at Sprostons foundry, where the foreman was a slave driver, according to Fingers. Eight weeks under a man like that was enough.

Genetha instinctively knew that he would tolerate no serious interference in his way of life. Her strategy was a long-term one; she would strengthen their relationship and accustom him first to the bondage of domestic life. Then she would set about changing him. There was time.

One night the minister of the A.M.E. Zionist Church which she used to attend with Michael paid her a visit. Fingers was out playing billiards and Genetha was sitting near the radio, picking the rice for the next day's midday meal.

"Let me put you at ease about my visit, Miss Armstrong," he began. "I've come to find out why you don't go to church any more, that's all."

Taken aback by his bluntness, she replied, "I don't have the time."

"Would it be too presumptuous to ask what takes up the time you would otherwise devote to the church?" asked the minister.

"I don't know," she stuttered.

"God still exists," he said, with a slight, supercilious smile. After a pause, he went on: "Michael. . . ."

"Yes?"

"Let me hasten to add that he didn't ask me to come. It's just that he's such a fine young man. I wondered why he comes to church alone."

She looked at him, but made no answer. His impertinence, his arrival at the wrong time, irked her. Above all she was ashamed that she had not been attending church.

"He looks bad," continued the minister, speaking of Michael. "If, if I'm . . . perhaps I'm broaching a subject that — that, um. . . ."

"Yes," said Genetha.

"I see."

And silence fell between them, the minister fearing to pursue a thorny subject and Genetha determined to do nothing that would encourage him.

"What shall I say to him then?" he asked in the end, taking out his handkerchief to give his hands something to do.

"There can't be anything between us," Genetha said slowly and deliberately.

"You're a headstrong young woman; but as I said I won't interfere," he declared regretfully.

After another embarrassing pause in the conversation he looked up abruptly, as if something had suddenly occurred to him.

"Do you believe in God, Miss Armstrong?"

"Yes."

"Miss Armstrong, after all I'm only a humble mortal, trying to make something of a new church. I'll be frank with you. You're a young and attractive person. Someone like you draws others to the church. It's only natural. They see you and say, 'Well, if she goes then there must be something in it.' I know this sounds vulgar and — well, you know, but it's true. . . . I mean I'd be surprised if Michael comes much longer now that we've lost you."

"Do you mind if I attend to the rice?" Genetha asked. "I'm sorry, I've got to get things ready for tomorrow."

She went and fetched the bowl, but it was impossible to find the unwanted bits in a light which suddenly seemed too dim. She returned to the kitchen with the bowl and came back once more to join the minister.

"I know what you must think of me," said Genetha, "but I need a few months to consider things. Besides, I'm a member of the Methodist Church, you know. If I start going to church again it won't be —"

"Oh," he said, crestfallen.

Had Genetha treated this humble representative of the A.M.E. Zionist Church so shabbily because he had no big church behind him? This, at least, was what the minister himself thought.

"Do you want something to eat?" enquired Genetha, wishing to make amends.

"Thank you," he said eagerly.

The cocoa and sweet bread he had just had at the Braithwaites' could make way for anything offered here, he thought.

"Fried plantain and rice! My favourite," he said with a broad smile, as he sat down at the table.

Genetha's evening was ruined. She had to put off washing her underclothes until the following day. And as for the midday meal, she would have to eat at a restaurant. But what about Fingers?

While the minister talked she kept turning these things over in her head. Whatever happened she had to get something cooked for Fingers that very night and in that case she might as well cook for both of them, she decided. Anyway it would have been foolish to let the shrimps go bad.

"I'm sorry, Reverend," she interrupted him, "but I've got to push you out. It's just that I've got a lot of things to do before I go to bed."

God's servant had settled in his chair and was looking forward to a long, uninterrupted digestion. Like many people who had never had to raise a finger in a home he could not conceive of work that could not wait, and only left reluctantly.

A few minutes later, Genetha heard someone coming up the front stairs. She went to the window even before the knock came. It was the minister, who must have left something behind.

"Listen, Miss Armstrong," he said to her when she faced him with a puzzled expression. "Is there another young man living here with you? I mean beside your brother — I know he's in the Essequibo and I just wondered. . . . If Michael asks me about his chances of a reconciliation I'd like. . . . I mean, I want to know what to tell him."

"No, Reverend," answered Genetha, incensed by his officiousness. "But he practically does. You can tell Michael that his name is Fingers."

She looked at the man of God unblinkingly and he turned tail and fled, as if he was being pursued by the devil himself. Genetha cleaned the ashtray in which two of Fingers's stubs lay among the grey and white ash. She made up her mind there and then that she would never cross the church door again.

Genetha was convinced that the minister's conduct lay behind her decision. In fact from the moment when she became intimate with Fingers she had begun to feel guilty about taking the Sunday school classes and instructing little children in morality and the Bible.

Now, without the slightest twinge of conscience, she put away her Bible in the bottom drawer of the chest of drawers, beneath the old dresses and worn-out underwear which she tore up and used as old cloth, as her mother used to do. In the middle of the Bible was a sprig of hyacinth which an admirer had given her when she was seventeen and had no thought of entering into a serious liaison. Pressed and faded, it lay between two pages of the Book that had been her father's favourite reading.

An hour or so later Fingers came in. He had lost an important match against a sailor and was in no mood for chit-chat.

"You're not talking?" she asked him.

"No."

"Why not?"

"Cause I in't got nothing to talk about."

"You want something to eat?"

"Well, course I want somet'ing to eat," he replied brutally. "Y'tink I been to a banquet?"

It was the first unpleasantness between them. She made him an omelette and a bowl of boiling chocolate with fat swimming on top and beside the plate and bowl placed four two-cent loaves of bread.

Genetha went and sat by the window, filled with contentment. She remembered that her father used to sit there, mumbling about the rattling street lamp; and her mother sat there when her father was out. Why, she wondered, had no one ever come to visit her mother?

A gentle rain began to fall. It soon became a downpour and wind blew in from the sea, shaking the paling staves of the house in the yard across the road. She could hear the talking of a man and a woman who had run in from the street to shelter

19

under the house. Although she strained her ears the rain prevented her from hearing what they said. Were they happy? Was the man in love with her? Did they fall asleep as soon as they lay down at night? Or were they plagued by sleeplessness? Was she ever sick? Did she dread dying? Did he ever strike her or was he gentle? Was she afraid of letting herself go when she made love or was she. . . . Was she, Genetha Armstrong, the peer of this girl who ran in from the rain to shelter with her sweet man under the house? She, Genetha Armstrong, who called to mind her father whenever she saw a drunkard go by or heard a voice that bore the slightest resemblance to his. Her father, a depraved, good-for-nothing who had lied, cheated and frequented the houses of prostitutes when he was alive. He had taken no interest in his family, except to revile them.

"God forgive me," she reflected. "I've tasted the fruit of depravity and enjoyed it."

Her love was strong and beautiful. If it was sinful then she would embrace this sin and be glad of her happiness. If Fingers left her after a week or a month she would thank God that she had known a week, a month of joy. He had given her flowers of wickedness in handfuls, black orchids that gleamed like pearls. Every morning when she woke up she believed that she had been the victim of some dream; and every night when she said goodbye to her lover she saw him leave, uncertain whether he would ever come back. Were it not for the shadow of her brother she would give him everything she possessed.

When Rohan was a child her mother said to him, "Why don't you be as good as your sister?" Yet no one knew how desperately she, Genetha, wanted to be as bad as her brother. But she dared not face the consequences. She had been good out of fear, as she had worked at school from fear. Whenever a teacher had occasion to speak to her she used to tremble inwardly lest she had made herself conspicuous. For her this silent suffering had become part of the fabric of her behaviour and, in fact, she had ceased to suffer, and moved about in the world of grown-ups like a ghost in a peopled room. Something had exploded in her first experience with Fingers. She had given herself to him because she was in her twenties and could not wait any longer. She had frequently pictured herself in the grip of remorse if ever it happened before she was married but the remorse had been an illusion, like so many fears. Rohan's favourite rhyme flashed through her mind:

> My grandmother was a leper
> My grandmother died
> But never once
> Has my grandmother cried.
>
> Her face was like parchment
> Her hands were like wood
> But no one could sin
> As my grandmother could.

Genetha began to laugh softly. Then her happiness was marred by a sudden uncertainty, an unexpected doubt. Did people not say that lust had killed her father? And was it not she herself who accused Rohan of lusting after that woman in Vreed-en-Hoop? Would people not say that her lust had driven her to take up with Fingers? What she was doing was a thousand times worse than what Rohan had done. Besides, she was a woman. She closed her eyes and listened to the rain drumming on the roof. Voices started whispering incoherently and as they became louder the sound of the rain grew softer. In the end the voices were thundering at her: "Lust! Slut! Lust! Slut!" Bright lights began to appear on all sides while the voices kept up their thundering, and as they came nearer and she could see the faces behind them they turned out to be all women with bared teeth and hateful faces. She searched them diligently for someone she might recognize, but they were all strangers. She opened her eyes. The rain continued to thunder on the roof and the voices, a moment ago so clear, had gone. The faces had disappeared, like chalk from a slate over which a damp cloth had been passed.

When Fingers came and put his hand on her shoulder she shuddered and resisted his embraces, complaining of a headache.

## 4. A Knock on the Door

Genetha woke up from a dream of Esther, sweating. All her family had, at one time or another, dreamed of the servant, filled with guilt at her out-of-hand dismissal. She looked around, expecting to find Esther in the room with her. But there was only the furniture in the bedroom lit by an unusually bright moon. The dressing-table, the foot of the bed and the chair

21

were covered with that wan sheen whose paleness had given rise to the prohibition against allowing moonlight to shine on one while sleeping. She threw the blanket over the lower part of her body and tried to fall asleep again.

The next morning Genetha tried to recall her dream, but remembered only the anxious awakening. All day at work she was dogged by the image of Esther's face, so much so that her closest associates noticed how preoccupied she was. At the time of the servant's dismissal she did not understand why she was leaving, for her parents pretended that it was Esther's decision. But later, after her father lost his job as a result of widespread retrenchment in the government service, he became less discreet and reproached his wife openly for choosing to send away the more loyal of the two maids. Side by side with the fond memories of Esther grew a fear of her because she had been wronged. And after that night when she heard her father thundering at her mother on the same theme and accusing her of "throwing the servant into the cauldron of Georgetown" although she was from the country and knew no one in town, she found herself spontaneously calling to mind Esther's dilemma.

It was a few weeks later that Esther came to see her. Her face was grey and gaunt, as if she were ill. Genetha did not recognize her at first, but when she spoke her soft deep voice was the same as in the days of Agricola. The dress she wore fitted badly, as if it had been made for someone else, while the lipstick did not follow the curves of her lips accurately and gave her the bizarre appearance of an actor's mask. Her eyes, set in hollow sockets, seemed more gentle than ever.

"This is for Master Boyie," said Esther, who always called her brother by his fond name.

She handed Genetha a small tin of Milo, Rohan's favourite beverage.

"He's in the Essequibo," Genetha told her. "It's been a few months now."

Esther looked surprised. "You keep it then."

"Esther, what's happened to you?" Genetha enquired of the servant.

"I've been sick."

"You've been to see the doctor?"

"I know what's wrong with me," replied Esther. "Look . . . I came to borrow some money."

22

"How much?" asked Genetha, eager to be of service to her.

"Ten dollars."

"Is that all?"

"Some people've got so much and others so little," Esther said bitterly.

"I'm glad to see you," Genetha said.

"Miss Genetha, the women in your family never liked me. And I can see from your eyes. . . . You don't need to pretend, you know."

Genetha felt the same disturbance. If she gave her the money at once she might take it as a hint to go. If she waited she would have to endure her reproaches.

"I'll make you a cup of Milo and some bread and butter," offered Genetha.

"Yes," she said hurriedly, "thank you."

Genetha was also afraid that Esther might have some terrible infectious disease. Maybe she came to give it to her on purpose. There were people like that, she reflected. She must remember to smash the cup when she went, or throw it away.

Instead of inviting her to the table Genetha brought the things on a tray which Esther placed on her lap.

After the snack Esther seemed to be in a better mood, smiling whenever she caught Genetha's eye.

"You'll feel alone in this house, Miss Genetha. You need a man with you. But be careful not to give him anything. He'll only hate you for it." She paused for breath before she continued eating.

Genetha was certain she could not conceal her feeling of oppression. She got up, went inside, and came back out with three five-dollar bills in her hand.

"It's a gift, for all you did for me and Boyie . . . and the rest of the family."

Esther took it and looked at her with what seemed to Genetha like hatred.

"You think that fifteen dollars can pay me for all I did for your family? After I worked myself to the bone for you, your mother put me out on the street. Your Christian mother. You don't know how I lived these last few years. But I prayed for your mother and God answered my prayer. She died before me."

Genetha hung her head and pretended not to see how the

former servant was gasping for breath.

"I can't answer for what my mother did, Esther. She suffered too."

"We all suffer, Miss. If I was healthy I would come back and do for you. But the doctor said I'll be all right in two months or so. I have to take care of myself until then. Any exertion makes me break out in a cold sweat. The doctor said months ago he couldn't do anything for me. But I knew he was talking nonsense. Now he's changed his mind and told me it's because I've got a strong constitution."

She paused again for breath.

"The only thing I regret," she continued, "is that I didn't have any children."

Genetha put out her hand to touch the servant, but she had vanished. She jumped up from the chair by the window. Had she been sleeping? She rushed outside and once on the road looked back at the house. Fingers was not home and she was obliged to go back and wait under the house until he came.

That night she invited him to come and live with her. He was delighted and wanted to get his things at once, but she was unwilling to remain in the house alone.

"Why? Been seeing ghosts?" he asked.

The couple made their nest in Genetha's parents' room. The four-poster bed that had been in the family since her parents' marriage had not been slept in since her father's death, but a few weeks later they felt as if they had been sleeping there all their lives.

She did not install Fingers in the family house with impunity, for she often heard the whispering of her dead parents about her, even in broad daylight, and their squabbling at night-time just as when they had been alive and believed that she and Rohan were asleep. The intrusion could not have failed to offend them, as it had offended her brother. Yet she hoped that the voices would weaken with the coming months; and if they did not she intended to move and take her resolutions elsewhere.

One afternoon when she came home from work Fingers told her that a woman had been to see her.

"Kian' remember she name, but she look as if she jus' come out of the Best," he informed her, evoking the woman's appearance by comparing her with inmates of the dreaded hospital for patients with consumption.

She forgot about what Fingers had said until, in the middle of their meal, he snapped his fingers and declared:

"She name Esther!"

Genetha's cup fell to the table. The coffee spilled over the edge on to the unpolished floor, where it made an ever-widening puddle.

"Is wha' wrong?" asked Fingers, alarmed.

"I don't want to see her," declared Genetha. "Tell her if she comes again I don't want to see her."

"Why? You know she?" he interrupted.

"Yes, she was our servant."

"Oh, but she does talk good, like you."

Fingers went into the kitchen and brought back a cloth with which he wiped up the coffee.

"You want another cup?" he asked solicitously.

"No."

"You feeling cold?"

"No, it's all right."

She was unable to shake off a fit of trembling. Fingers wanted to go out to play billiards, but was reluctant to leave her in the condition she was. He went and made the coffee, although she had declined his offer to make another one, and forced her to drink it before telling her that he was going out.

"No! Don't leave me alone," she pleaded.

He sat down, got up again and then came back to sit down once more.

"Let's go to the pictures," she suggested. "I'll treat you."

Fingers liked the idea. So she cleared the table and began washing the cups and saucers. But when she was on the point of finishing there was a knock on the front door. Genetha grew faint as Fingers opened and exchanged a few words with the stranger. Then he came into the kitchen and said:

"Is the woman."

"I told you not to let her in!" Genetha whispered.

"Come an' get rid of she. I goin' stay by you," Fingers suggested with an encouraging smile.

Esther had the same gaunt face and hollow-set eyes as in her apparition. "Miss Genetha," she said smiling.

"Hello, Esther."

The servant rummaged in her bag for something.

"This is for Master Boyie."

It was a tin of Milo and at the sight of the green container Genetha drew back.

"You know he always did like Milo," Esther reminded her.

"He's in the Essequibo."

"Oh?"

"Yes."

"I won't beat about the bush, Miss. I came because I'm in trouble. Can you lend me some money?"

"How much?" Genetha asked, clenching her fists in agitation.

"How much can you afford?" Esther asked.

"Ten dollars?" Genetha suggested.

"Yes," Esther said hurriedly.

"Wha' wrong?" Fingers asked Genetha, who was staring at her.

"It's just that I feel giddy," she replied, grasping for his arm.

"You're not well, Miss Genetha? She isn't well?" Esther asked, turning to Fingers.

He shrugged his shoulders.

"Get ten dollars from inside and give her quick," Genetha ordered Fingers, who did as he was asked.

"I'll never forget this, Miss."

"That's not what you said the other night!" exclaimed Genetha, more agitated than ever.

"The other night?" asked Esther. "I came in the morning."

"You were here?" Genetha asked urgently.

"Yes. You don't remember? You acted so funny."

"Yes . . . well, I don't know. I'm not well. All right, good-bye," Genetha said, nodding and looking at her askance.

Esther stepped forward.

"No! Go! For God's sake, go."

"All right, Miss, I just wanted to say thank you." She nodded to Fingers and left.

"God's punishing me," wailed Genetha. "But there're people worse than me. Promise you won't leave me."

"What give you the idea I goin' lef' you? If you go on like that I'll slap some sense into you."

"She always liked Boyie . . . and Boyie would do anything for her. That's not right either. She was all smiles tonight, to impress you; but the other night it was different, and when she bared her teeth. . . . She hated me and my mother and my mother got rid of her because she was afraid of her; and my father could never understand. Right up until she died he used

26

to blame my mother for getting rid of her. You see, if you weren't here tonight she'd have dragged up the whole story again."

Fingers slapped her face and she burst into tears and was soon in the grip of an uncontrollable sobbing. Impatiently he started pacing up and down the room, more perplexed than annoyed.

Later Genetha confided in Fingers about Esther's relations with her household. On no account would her brother have done so, she reflected; but she did not possess his iron will. Fingers, bearing a latent hostility to Genetha's class deep within him, listened without comment. Taking his silence for sympathy with her and the family, Genetha stretched her confession back to the time of Agricola when the servant girl was still uneducated. She repeated everything she had heard her mother say, even the remark that Esther did not have drawers when she first came to the house in Third Street. And Fingers stored up all these remarks as if they were directed against him, for one of his sisters was also a servant and spoke ill of the household in which she worked.

But the longer they lived together the more her confidence grew. And she began to tyrannize him in little ways: through his food, to which was added colallo, something he did not care for; through his clothes, since he was made to wear flannelette vests to avoid catching a chill after his billiard matches in the stuffy dockside halls; and in countless little rules she inflicted on him in order to foster the illusion of her mastery over the household. Fingers yielded with a docility that was not in his character.

## 5. Sweet Cakes

Genetha sat at table, alone after a day's work. Fingers had given up coming home to have his dinner with her. She had not been feeling well lately and had seen the doctor on a number of occasions. He had advised her to eat a lot of cheese and join the YWCA and above all to take the muddy-looking liquid he was fond of prescribing.

Apart from the advice to join the YWCA Genetha followed his instructions carefully, but felt no relief from the headaches that plagued her at night. The best hours of her day were at work, when the colourless routine which others found irksome acted like a balm on her. The dark half-moon depressions under her eyes, more prominent to others than to herself, prompted Fingers to tell her that she was getting ugly. He suggested that she take a holiday abroad; and to please him she went to Barbados.

On her return her cheeks were full and her headaches were gone. Yet, a few weeks later, she was as ill as before her trip, her cheeks were as sunken, while a faint line appeared between her nose and the corner of her mouth; and she ceased complaining of her headaches, which had returned.

Occasionally Fingers was his old charming self. One afternoon when she returned from work he offered to take her to the pictures. He made her put her feet up and rest while he made coffee and an omelette, beamed at her across the table and talked incessantly about billiards and snooker.

"I'm in great form," he told her. "I potting bad, bad! I tell you. I just got to look at a ball and it going down. Last night I was playing a chap from the Guild Club. 'You got cramp, Guild Club man?' I say to him. He had four shots in the whole game. I din' miss one free shot, I tell you. One time the white did standing nearly on the cushion and I take it as a free shot out of bravado. The ball sink with a plop. I tell you the Guild Club man look at me as if I was a jumbee. He couldn't even stand up any more."

Fingers laughed and added, "But the best part of it was, at the end of the game he put down another five dollars and say he did want to play again. He really did think that I fluke all them shots. I wrap he up in fifteen minutes. He leave the club as if he was going to murder somebody."

Genetha understood nothing about snooker, but she shared his satisfaction. They talked for an hour or so, and when she went into the kitchen to wash up he followed her to keep her company until she had finished. They then sat on the stairs and continued talking in the dark until eight o'clock when they locked up and set off to the cinema, arm in arm. Once in their seats he took her hand.

On the way home they went to a new shop called "The Patisserie", a stone's throw from the Metropole, where they drank coffee served in a pot and ate sweet cakes coloured like tinsel on Christmas decorations.

At other times he encouraged her to talk about herself and she did so at length, becoming drunk with the opportunity to let

28

herself go.

"When I went for the interview to get this job I was made to wait in the outside office where a man was typing slowly, picking at the keys. Before I left home my father said, 'Oh, you'll get the job, don't bother.' These words kept drumming in my ears and my head and with every clak clak of the typewriter I said a word to myself, 'Clak . . . O . . . clak . . . you'll . . . clak . . . get . . . clak . . . the . . . clak . . . job . . . clak . . . don't . . . clak . . . bother.' And you could hear the voices of the interviewer and the other applicant through the closed door whenever there was a pause in the typing. It was my first interview for my first job and I could hardly bear the waiting and the clak-clak of the typewriter and the sound of the voices from inside. I crossed my legs and started pressing. I don't know what made me do it because it had never entered my mind before to do anything like that before. I pressed, pressed, until. . . ."

And then, for no apparent reason she stopped, ashamed of her confession. Fingers, who had only been half listening, asked, "What happened? You did get the job or not?"

"Yes, I got the job," she said.

She never again came so near to discussing such private matters with him again.

But the occasional access of kindness did not make up for Fingers's temperamental behaviour and his interminable silences. Genetha began to fear his outbursts, especially when he was drunk.

One night she screwed up her courage and told him that she did not want him to live with her any more.

"I coming home early tonight," he said, disarmingly.

"Don't come back in the house, please," she repeated. "I don't know whether I'm coming or going with you, that's all. One day you're considerate and the next you behave as if you don't even know me. In the mornings I wake up wondering what you'll be like and at night I go to bed racking my brains to find out what I did you. You've got something against me. I can tell."

"I in' got nothing 'gainst you," he protested.

"It looks so to me. Anyway, I can't stand your moods."

"Listen," he said in a conciliatory voice.

"No!" she cut him short. "Apart from my mother's death I've suffered. . . everything I've suffered was through men. And in any case you don't intend to work. I can't keep a man: it's not in

29

my nature."

"I'll get a job, Genetha. Look, by year end I'll be working —".

"Don't lie! Even if you get a job you'll look out for the first opportunity to give it up. Why can't you face up to what you're like?"

Fingers was not accustomed to seeing her in this mood and did not know what to say next.

"You always talking 'bout the past," he said, hoping to make an impression. "If you not going on 'bout tram cars that use to run as late as the thirties you telling me 'bout some blue dress you did wear when you was a little girl. That's why I does get fed up with you. That's the only reason for my moods."

Genetha, though she realized how transparent this excuse was, hated him for belittling these memories of her girlhood. For her, the recollection of that single trip, the return in the creaking, grinding tram, the image of the conductor going from one carriage to the other along the running-board, the descent at Agricola in the company of her mother and Boyie and the whining of the tram as it gathered speed and disappeared round the bend on its way to the terminus at Bagotstown, was sacrosanct. Believing that their intimacy had made him sensitive she had disclosed her most secret preoccupations to him only to hear them treated with scorn. Thank God she had held back in time before telling him about what happened at the interview!

Revolted by his insensitivity Genetha fell silent.

"Is what I do you?" he asked, fearing her silence.

"You didn't do anything. My mother and father wouldn't have wanted anybody else to live here, that's all."

"Your mother and father? Your father used to —"

"That's enough!" she jumped up angrily. "You've insulted me over and over, but leave my parents out of it."

"Don't come looking for me, understand?" he said, stifling his rage, " 'cause I in' crossing the door-mouth of this house again. You understand?"

He then went inside to collect his belongings, apparently master of himself.

That night Genetha went to look up her grandparents, whom she had not visited since she took up with Fingers. But as before she hesitated and turned back in front of the gate. On returning home she switched on the radio and listened to a concert on the short wave. Twenty minutes later when it was

30

over she began to rack her brains to recall whom she might visit, but no one suitable came to mind. She got up and closed the jalousies and windows out front, secured the door and turned in, after dosing herself with bush tea. She could hear the animated whirring of the night insects and the sound of talking from next door and see the lights of the occasional passing car reflected on her bedroom wall in muted illuminations. She wished she had a dog to sleep at the foot of the bed. Her aunts once kept two dogs, ugly, ingratiating animals. At that point her thoughts wandered to the work she did and her colleagues, but then she fell into a deep, remote sleep.

A few days later, unable to bear her loneliness, Genetha went round to Fingers's place. She had to go back the next day, as he was on the coast.

Fingers packed his things and accompanied her home as naturally as if they had agreed that he should return on that day and in that manner.

But no sooner had he moved back in with her than she regretted having exposed herself to his ridicule; and for a few days afterwards she remained guarded in her dealings with him, answering only after a pause whenever he asked the most innocent question. If he came home after she had eaten she did not rise promptly to warm up his meal. On waking at night she would draw away from him lest he mistook her proximity for an attempt to worm herself into his favour.

Incessantly she asked herself, "What would other women do? What *do* other women do? How is it that some manage to hold their men with such ease?" Before, she had been content to let him serve her, as hired bulls mounted their cows, for a season, while now she thought of holding him forever, until they grew old together in that unhappy house. Yet she foresaw the outcome: she would relax her vigilance, inevitably, and he, predator that he was, would be soon digging his claws into her, reducing her to a proper state of subservience.

For Fingers's part, he was as anxious as Genetha to promote harmony between them. The brusque manner of his dismissal had impressed him, for what she did once she was capable of doing again. He understood when she rejected his invitation to go to the cinema; but he would wait, he told himself, having gauged the strength of her will.

31

When Genetha was herself again, displaying the same weaknesses, the same over-concern for his welfare, he went along with her, resisting the temptation to take without asking.

She remembered the time she first met him, when he was in steady employment and the mainstay of his sisters, grandmother and father. If only he went to work every morning like all *decent* men, he would add dignity to their relationship and she would disregard the fact that his family were the only beneficiaries of his labour. What did it matter?

She would have liked to stroke his head, to smother him with her indulgence, for she knew no other way. And was that not the very essence of love? At times she sat watching him, unabashed, while he muttered over a newspaper, reading aloud as many half-literate people do. She followed the curving line of his biceps until she came to his hands. Her mother had been incapable of describing a person without referring to his or her hands: "long fingers", "affectionate hands", "knuckles like a workman's", "untended nails" were expressions she had fashioned out of the curious preoccupation. Fingers's hands were of a piece with his body, neither arresting nor insignificant, no open book that gave him away. And if she loved him it was not because of his hands. She was certain she had chosen him because she believed she would know how to keep him and to change him to her liking; unlike Michael, who had taken charge of her as if she were an employee, who saw courtship as the long, sterile season before marriage.

It mattered not what Fingers looked like. Indeed, the very mediocrity of that physical appearance – a matter of great concern to her on contemplating her own reflection in the mirror when she first became aware of her body – was his most powerful attraction. Her own disabilities were the infallible indicators of a woman's unsuccessful journey through life; and the absurd exaggeration of every such lack fed upon itself to the point where she made unflattering comparisons between her behaviour and that of other women in the most trivial matters. The typists at work chose their brassières by the size on the label. She, on the other hand, astonished shop assistants – so she believed – by insisting that she tried on hers before paying for them. What better proof was there that she was odd, she asked herself.

When the period of caution inevitably came to an end Fingers's behaviour improved beyond all expectation. His undoubted kindness was no longer cancelled out by the wilful insistence on doing as he pleased, on going out simply because his spirit gave him to do so. And after several weeks in which Genetha was able to judge the consistency of Fingers's conduct she settled down to enjoying the most satisfying period of her life since she emerged from girlhood and learned to assume responsibility for her actions.

It was just then that an unusual occurrence took place, which was to reinforce her hold on Fingers, as if Fate had been watching closely and had decided to reward her. Ulric, the feck-less neighbour who had been distrained upon because of his unpaid debts, called over the paling fence one Saturday after-noon. Fingers was repairing Genetha's bicycle, which was lying on its saddle with its wheels in the air.

"Give me a hand here, man," Ulric asked, waving a saw in his right hand.

Fingers dropped his spanner and went over to the neighbour's assistance.

And so began their association. Fingers would not have dreamed of addressing Ulric first, for the latter spoke to no one except his mother and appeared impervious to all overtures of friendship. He never attended any of the functions to which neighbours were usually invited, like christenings or funerals, and emphasized his contempt for those living in the vicinity by burning rubbish when a strong wind was blowing.

Ulric's mother was "getting on" and had all but lost the power in her right arm. Needing assistance in the construction of a crabwood wardrobe to replace the one taken away by the bailiffs he had called on Fingers, who was brought up to believe that it was not for him to question a neighbour's appeal for assistance. All he expected in return was a schnapp-glass of rum and a couple of grunts by way of conversation.

Fingers did not come back until the street lights went on. He spoke with enthusiasm about Ulric, who knew everything there was to know about wood. Genetha asked the question that her parents and all Ulric's neighbours had asked themselves at one time or another: "How does he earn his living?"

"He does do jobs for people. He can do anything."

Fingers reported that the house was bare, except for the beds

33

and Ulric's tools, which the bailiffs had left.

"He say he goin' learn me how to polish furniture with bee wax, and other things too."

"Is he going to pay you?" Genetha asked.

"I suppose so."

"So you're going to work for him, then?" she asked, at once glad at the opportunity thrown Fingers's way and sceptical about his enthusiasm for working with Ulric.

But Fingers went over the following day, a Sunday, to continue work on the wardrobe; and when Genetha called out to inform him that the midday meal was ready he shouted back, "Gi'e me ten minutes."

She went downstairs and saw the two men under Ulric's house. Fingers was sweating over a half-finished wardrobe, his shirt cast aside and dressed in his short pants and singlet.

"You're coming?"

"I comin'. Gi'e me a couple of minutes."

The twinge of jealousy she felt on seeing him so devoted to what he was doing, standing in the sawdust, while Ulric's fowls pecked the ground around him for the remains of a snack his mother had brought down, was tempered by her satisfaction at seeing him sweat to some purpose.

Genetha stood at the paling fence, staring at the two men, who exchanged a few words from time to time without looking up at each other. And when at last Fingers, unable to ignore her any longer, shook off the sawdust and put on his shirt she went to the gate to meet him.

"You'd think I been gone miles away," he reproached her.

"You should be glad," she told him, "you've got a woman who comes to meet you at the gate."

Fingers took a shower before sitting down at table, where Genetha was told in detail what he had learnt.

"I can do a dovetail, now," he declared. It was all very easy, and was really nothing but common sense. "You know what you look for in furniture wood?" he went on.

"No."

"It got to be nice lookin', like a woman. An' easy to work, just like a woman. And it got to be stable; like a woman."

"What you mean by stable?" Genetha asked.

"It mustn't twist up or crack."

"Ah," said Genetha, "how do you know?"

"Some woods naturally like that, like huberballi and crab-wood. All you got to do is cure it."

She wondered if Ulric was responsible for his satisfaction or whether it was the work. What did it matter? she told herself. She would keep him as long as he was happy.

She rejected from her reflections everything that might embarrass her. Whenever she sat watching Fingers her eyes never descended further than his hands, so that she could truthfully say that no forbidden reflections had crossed her mind. And even now she had banished the fleeting thought that she would wish to see him maimed so that she might have every reason to care for him, while he would have none for straying beyond the boundaries of her yard.

Yet at certain times she never spared herself an indulgence and threw herself into love-making with an almost morbid exuberance. And at such times she felt she belonged to the earth and understood the despair of those girls who discover a passionate belief in Christ that transcends the adherence to a religion, and those women on the threshold of middle age who rant and rave about Christ's coming, knowing full well that their bodies no longer respond to their husband's embrace. Yes, those were moments of oneness with every single living thing and with every human experience, when her skin blew hot and cold, panting for some eternal affection.

Fingers became apprenticed to Ulric, who undertook to teach him everything he knew. They went around to old customers whose furniture they varnished, for it was only a couple of weeks before Christmas time and people were busy stripping and varnishing the chairs and tables in their drawing-rooms and galleries. After Christmas they took to painting partitions, never the outside of houses, which were left to professional painters. Then, when the searing hot days of February came, Ulric and Fingers remained under the house, doing any work that was offered them, provided it was connected with wood. They made cupboards, wardrobes, chests-of-drawers, bookcases and all manner of wooden contraptions Ulric could make at home now that he had Fingers's assistance. And only the turned work in very hard wood, like lidded purple-heart jars, was undertaken by Ulric alone. Nothing seemed to be beyond him, once he had committed the client's specifications to a drawing. The wonder,

35

according to Genetha, was that such virtuosity was allied to a complete lack of ambition and the need to borrow money he could not repay within the specified period. He had already relieved Fingers of his first weekly wages and, unabashed by his apprentice's presence as a constant reminder of his indebtedness, he boldly approached Genetha to ask for ten dollars, which he would pay unfailingly the next weekend. Genetha lent him the money, believing that Fingers's apprenticeship might be endangered if she refused. And Ulric, without so much as a blink of embarrassment, paid off his apprentice with the money he borrowed from the latter's lady friend.

But as things turned out the matter was not serious, for Ulric appeared never to borrow from the same person twice, unless he was a shopkeeper. Having exhausted his credit with the South Georgetown merchants he was well into Kingston and the area north of Murray Street, where his sincere manner and deadpan expression encouraged all but the most cautious to trust him.

As for Fingers, his enthusiasm for joining and polishing was equal to his passion for billiards. He played only on specified evenings, so that Genetha could arrange meal times with some certainty. She occasionally accompanied him on his outings when he was playing in a decent hall, like the Guild Club or the Tower Hotel. Then she was wont to keep her eye on the green baize cloth as though she enjoyed the game. Sometimes they arrived when the barman was brushing the table with his long soft brush, a useless precaution, she thought, since it never looked less than immaculate to her. On these occasions she sipped her soft drink slowly and to such good purpose that the straw through which she drank disintegrated, so that she had to take the rest from the bottle itself.

At times, infected by the excitement around the large table when a match was close, she would look at Fingers proudly, encouraging him with a glance he never answered. Just her presence was bad luck, which he dared not compound by catching her eye.

After these matches they would walk along the Main Street avenue, under trees with grey, knobbled trunks, where the road surface, transformed by the sodium street lamps, shone like water beneath a spectral moon. He would not allow her to put her arm through his, for fear that one of his friends might see them. But she walked close to him and took side-streets

36

oppressed in daytime by heat that rose from the burning asphalt, coming out again into the broader thoroughfares of young trees protected by rings of flattened iron staves. They had learned to be together without the benefit of conversation, and fell into listening to their footsteps on the gravel, while slipping deftly between the baluster-shaped bollards that marked the end of each stretch of road. Many of the trees were adorned with metal strips bearing the names of their species and genera in Latin, just as a number of mansions off the road carried enamel plaques no less mysteriously inscribed.

Genetha dared not measure the extent of her happiness lest it evaporate like those translucent bubbles of pale blue foam that vanish at the approach of warm fingers. How strange that her contentment had been mediated by a neighbour who had spoken no more than a few words to her in all the years she had lived in Albertown.

Genetha took down the large photograph of her dead father from the partition where it had hung as long as she remembered. While she felt uneasy about those eyes that followed her all the way from the dining area to the gallery and from the gallery to the back of the house, she could not bring herself to touch the framed portrait. Thinking it proper that he should look down on her comings and goings while she harboured a stranger in the family house she kept the glass over his face polished to a shine. But as satisfaction with her treatment at Fingers's hands grew and her guilt concerning her morality diminished, she ceased to be aware of the vigilant eyes; and that day when, during her routine dusting, she climbed on to a chair in order to pass the buff cloth over the frame and glass she hesitated, then with a sudden resolution she raised the picture from the nail. Curiously, it was as light as the lightest thing she had ever lifted, like the most insubstantial cloth or a handful of fluff from a silk-cotton pod. She recalled his wantonness, his palpable anxiety at being challenged by Rohan, her brother, his shameless lying to secure his ends, all of which had not prevented her from accepting the moral strictures and the judgments he passed and, deep down, even his infallibility.

Fingers enquired of the photograph, which he found lying on the dressing-table: "Is what you take it down for?"

"Do you want me to leave it up?"

37

"It don't matter to me," he declared.

He was unable to understand why Genetha was perplexed at his indifference and she was just as surprised that he had never resented the photograph.

At times Genetha, on turning the corner from Albert Street, would hear the humming of Ulric's new lathe above the sound of traffic. The almost sensuous undertones of that voice imbued her with a kind of strength, a powerful, almost sinister conviction that nothing was beyond her, provided Fingers was happy. He was her rock, and she, his mainstay. After putting away her bicycle under the house she would stand at the window for a few minutes listening for a snatch of conversation between the two men.

One afternoon, when she took them tea on a tray, Fingers was put out at the intrusion and from then on she left them alone, having finally understood that theirs was a man's world and that her lover set great store by his manliness as it appeared to the eyes of other men.

She had taught him to respect time and he came over promptly at sundown when the shadows lengthened and the whirring of six o'clock bees filled the brief twilight. But even she did not need the clock, which she nevertheless kept wound up, only because her father had acquired an obsession for clocks and keys from his post office. He believed that it was a sign of good breeding to display a working clock prominently in his home and to fit even his back door with a lock, although he hardly ever used it, the bolts being sufficient for locking up at night.

So time gave rise to an accumulation of new gestures, repeated over and over again like hammer-blows on hot metal, out of which emerged shapes at first tentative and ever changing until the final pattern was revealed, recognizable in form, but distinct as one flower resembles no other. Genetha could now claim to be married: she was the "reputed wife" of her brother's friend and their life together was particular to them.

## 6. Ulric

Ulric resisted all efforts to persuade him to cross Genetha's bridge and converse with Fingers in the same way as he did under his house. He did not go visiting, he declared. He had his principles and would not depart from them. He did not go visiting and did not lend money. At his age he had no intention of compromising himself. And so, one warm evening, when all was peace and, as it seemed, all wickedness was suspended in deference to the awesome beauty of an equatorial night, Fingers got to talking with his friend at the open window. From his own window opposite, Ulric grunted in his usual incoherent manner, as placid as the night itself, even while discussing the political issues of the day, which never failed to reduce stout men to a state of helpless excitement.

Genetha was wondering what to cook the next day, while sewing two buttons on to one of Fingers's shirts.

"You coming?" Fingers asked her, suspending his conversation with Ulric.

"Where?"

"To Morawhanna."

"Who's going to Morawhanna?" Genetha asked.

"Me and Ulric. You coming?"

"When?"

"Saturday."

"But I don't have anything to wear," she protested, more because she was taken by surprise than because she had nothing suitable to put on.

"Is not Georgetown, y'know," Fingers said.

"Come, Miss Armstrong," she heard Ulric call out in an uncharacteristically resonant voice.

"All right," she agreed, thinking that if Ulric was capable of making himself heard across the space between their houses it must be worthwhile to go to Morawhanna.

"Ulric say is no use goin' to Morawhanna," Fingers said, "if you don' stay for two weeks." He made this declaration after a brief consultation with his friend.

"I can't stay away from work," Genetha told him.

"She say she don' want stay away from work," Fingers relayed the message across the gap.

Then a few seconds later he looked round once more and said that it was settled. They would make the trip during her annual fortnightly holiday. Ulric was able to go at any time.

And so their intended visit to the North-West, of which she had only heard stories, and Fingers knew next to nothing, was settled in a few brief exchanges. Her holiday, starting shortly, and which she counted on using to scour the house and run up a few things on the sewing-machine, was to be frittered away in the North-West.

Had she been offered the opportunity of going away with Fingers alone she would have seized it with both hands. But she knew what to expect: the two men would engage in interminable rounds of conversation or play interminable games of Chinese checkers while she languished just within earshot. Why did she say yes? Whatever got into Fingers's head to ask her anyway?

She had no idea how much Fingers had changed. What was at the start an intolerable constraint for him, the time-keeping, the renunciation of three billiard evenings and the innumerable restrictions she had imposed on him, proved to be bearable, even pleasant, provided he could spend all day with Ulric. Whenever she called out to him over the fence, Fingers, believing Ulric to be envious of his good fortune, used to pretend not to hear, while telling himself that he was the most fortunate of men. When he came back to Genetha he was thirsting for revenge because of his injured manhood. Although the males in his home were ruled with an iron hand by his grandmother, who often struck her son – Fingers's father – in front of his own children, his humiliation at having suffered at the hands of a woman was no less great for that. His grandmother was *blood* and two generations removed from him, and had acquired the status of a revered ascendant. He had planned to rob Genetha in some way and then leave her, after a period, during which he would play a false role, so that she would come to rely heavily on him. Things had not turned out that way. The first weeks of uncertainty and caution were followed not by any deliberate attempt to cultivate her confidence but by the slow realization that his independence was like that strange sweet fruit which women in Mara are reputed to use to dispatch their unfaithful men. It was in his interests to resist its temptations. Not only must he put aside thoughts of vengeance, but he would make every effort to accept Genetha's constraints. Should she go too far he need only rear up and snarl at her.

At times her talk of servants and her past was so irksome that he was taken by the desire to injure her in some way. But as the months went by she spoke less and less of these things, and the day she took down her father's photograph was like the end of one way of life, a kind of death, to which he affected indifference, but which in reality had soothed him much.

Fingers was not certain whether he loved Genetha or not, but he liked being with her. Even if he were to fall in love with another woman he did not intend to abandon the charted course of a fertile association in order to embark on a voyage into the unknown and perhaps dangerous waters of self-indulgence. "Better cornmeal pap dat don't got taste dan pepperpot dat in' cook yet."

Genetha was sick on the boat. She began to throw up soon after the *Tarpon* left the muddy waters of the Demerara estuary and started to rock violently. Fingers took her astern, where a wide tarpaulin awning provided shelter from the morning sun and there was space to lie down.

The *Tarpon* had spent most of its life on the ferry from Georgetown to Vreed-en-Hoop, but was pressed into service on the fortnightly North-West run when the old steamer started to break down regularly and travellers claimed that she was no longer suited for the open sea and would rock on a lake.

When Genetha had brought up everything there was to bring up from her inside an ageing man with luxuriant grey hair presented himself to the couple.

"Quashie Uba. I come to help the distressed lady."

He took two phials from his jacket pocket.

"Dis one it has aromatic vinegar and dis one it contains spirits of ammonia. If the lady put one to the right nostril and the other a little way from the left I guarantee she will be better in ten minutes. If I come back and she not up and *laughing* I going to throw my body overboard."

When Mr Uba came back as he promised, Genetha was sitting up and managed to smile at him.

"Thank you," she told him. "I'm feeling a lot better."

Fingers gave him back his phials.

Mr Uba told them that he was a New Brethren preacher and was on his way from Kwakwani to Morawhanna "in haste", because his reputed wife had published their banns of marriage without his consent. She was a practised forger – her father was a calligrapher and her brother a clerk, and writing was in the blood. She must have written out a consent and forged his signature on it.

"She is a very enterprising woman," he added.

The preacher then launched into a sermon on the merits of the New Brethren doctrine and urged Fingers to join the sect.

"The first man was black, I tell you," declared Mr Uba.

When Fingers expressed surprise at the confident assertion the preacher used arguments in justification of his view as curious as those used by others to prove their fancied superiority.

"Is like dis," said Mr Uba, sitting down next to Genetha. "You hear 'bout Cain? Right! Is he did kill Abel. Well, Cain fader and moder and broder was black people. Cain was jealous of Abel 'cause Abel had rich clay soil land and he only had pegasse. So one afternoon Cain he hide behind a moka-moka bush and swipe Abel 'pon he head when he was coming from his clay-soil land. Den he bury the body quick and trample down the earth flat flat. Eh-eh! Who tell he to do a t'ing like dat? A took-ah, a took-ah, a took-ah, he walk walk a few yards when he hear a voice, 'Cain! Cain! Is why you sneaking away like dat? Cain, is where your broder Abel dere?' 'Broder? I in' got no broder!' Cain say, lying like horse trotting. 'I say is where you broder Abel dere?' God he ask again. 'I in' got no broder,' we black ancestor say, getting more and more vex all the while. 'You getting ignorant like policeman. The power we give you going to you head!' 'Den is who lying in dat grave?' God ask. And Cain turn *pale*! And all Cain children he had after he get married was born pale. Dat's how white people come into this world."

Mr Uba went on to relate the history of his sect and took out a newspaper clipping from his pocket.

"Read it," he said, handing Fingers the soiled paper.

"Sect's numbers growing", said the caption in heavier print than the rest of the article.

"I believe you," said Fingers, anxious about Genetha's condition and wishing to be left alone with her.

Mr Uba sat down and began telling Fingers about his travels up and down the rivers in an effort to convert people, and about the failure of other established Christian denominations whose only hold on their members was that they were backed by the colonial administration.

But in the end, perhaps despairing of Fingers's lack of enthusiasm for his infant church, the preacher said, "I would give you more proof, but I can see you not a church-thinking man. But if ever you change you mind remember my name, 'Quashie

Uba, in care of Brother Ebenezer who does sell late beef 'pon the front road at No 2 Canal'. Any time, brother, any time."

With a flourish of his hand he bowed deeply to Genetha, but gave Fingers a look of the utmost contempt.

"Goodbye, mistress. Sit up straight and don't watch the water."

Around midday the steamer arrived at the mouth of the Waini river. Stilt-rooted mangrove trees gave way to the uniform green of riverside vegetation and the silt-laden water from the Orinoco met the ocean surge in shifting unequal lines that stretched across the river mouth. Those who were making the journey for the first time stood up to watch the shore, believing that Morawhanna was not far away. But they were soon back in their places, tired of waiting for their destination to come into view.

Ulric and Fingers were playing checkers, while Genetha leaned against the rail staring at the moving water. The sight of the river and the steamer's smooth passage had encouraged her to get up. Like everyone else she was praying for the journey to come to an end, but having already asked Fingers to enquire of the purser how much further they had to travel she kept her questions to herself, preferring to stare blankly at the narrow strip of foam that stretched behind the boat.

Now that she was away from her home she realized how much she depended on Fingers and how much she cared for him. Deep down he had not changed, she believed. Not having mixed a great deal, her view of men had been conditioned by what she knew of Rohan and her father and the terrible suffering inflicted on her mother by the latter's conduct. If her grandfather did not conform to her view of men as the embodiment of selfishness he was exceptional. Besides, there was something unusually pure about her grandparents' love for each other. Genetha's need for a certain degree of independence precluded that kind of relationship. The stablility of the family had always been bought at the expense of women, her mother had once remarked to her paternal aunt. Yet her mother, having acted as a doormat all her married life, had not attained any worthwhile stability, either for herself or for the rest of the family. And indeed, Fingers had only become tolerable when she showed she could be firm.

Not all the thinking in the world could lay her mistrust for Fingers. She needed him desperately, but was convinced that one day he would leave her. Of that she was as certain as that the river had a source and that it gained in breadth in its search for the vast mausoleum of the sea.

"Look at it!" someone shouted.

There was a general stir, but this time fewer passengers got up to witness the approach of Morawhanna. People were lining the river bank in the distance and further on the houses, which were drawing closer together, seemed to be coming down to the riverside as the people were.

Ulric and Fingers joined her, one on each side, to see the ropes being thrown and caught by two Transport and Harbour employees.

Ulric led them off the boat. He was wearing short pants and his long, hairless legs seemed to say, "I know exactly where I'm going." Fingers was carrying the suitcase, in which were his and Genetha's clothes, soap and other toilet goods.

Genetha had completely recovered and as she followed the men opened her large handbag to check that she had brought her make-up.

It was the two men who were thinking of resting for a while. Genetha, like a girl on her first outing, was determined to drag Fingers out after the sun went down. In the distance the hills rose behind Mabaruma, the new township established ostensibly to attract the inhabitants of Morawhanna away from their malarial swamp-land.

In less than five minutes they were standing on the bridge of a tiny cottage, no larger than the drawing-room in Genetha's house.

"Quickey!" Ulric shouted, then waited without the slightest trace of impatience.

A good minute went by, but no one came.

"Call the man again," Fingers suggested.

"Give him time," Ulric said quietly without turning round.

The sunlight, broken up by the fan-like ite palms behind the house, made patterns on the low, rusted corrugated-iron roof. From a pen under the house came the grunts of an unseen family of pigs, an unhurried snorting, as if the languid afternoon had done to them what it had done to Quickey.

"Is you?" a voice questioned from a head that eased itself through the window.

"Quickey, man," said Ulric, "is how long it does take for you

44

to get up?"

"Come up, ne? You write you was comin' tomorrow and you come today."

"I wrote *today*," protested Ulric. "You in' change a bit."

Genetha marvelled at the ease with which Ulric slipped into Creolese.

"This is Genetha," Ulric introduced her. "And this worthless man is Fingers."

"All you come up," Quickey said, stretching out his hands in order to open the door.

Fingers sat down in a Berbice chair while Ulric, disregarding Genetha's presence, lay down full length on the floor.

"All you mus'e thirsty. I goin' get some coconut. You comin'?"

"No, man," said Ulric. "After that journey?"

Quickey eased himself up with the help of his hands and went through the back door.

"How old d'you think he is?" Ulric asked.

"Late fifties?" Fingers suggested.

"That man is seventy-two."

"What?" Genetha exclaimed with surprise.

"Seventy-two," continued Ulric. "And he still goes hunting in the bush. In fact he's the best hunter round here, except for the aboriginees. And don't think he's slow because he's old. He's always been like that. The only time he hurries is to get out of the rain. He hates getting his head wet."

It had not escaped the notice of Genetha and Fingers that Ulric's tongue was loosened, as if he had been drinking. The way he had thrown himself on to the floor and had begun to speak Creolese told them that he knew Quickey well; but the quickened tempo of his speech was an indication of a stronger connection with the North-West than he had led them to believe he possessed.

Quickey came back with a cutlass and half a dozen coconuts strung together. One by one he cut off their heads with a single stroke and gave them to each of his guests in turn, beginning with Genetha. Then he split each spent fruit into two to allow them to get at the jelly, which they ate with a slice of husk left dangling from the coconut after another deft stroke of the cutlass.

"The lady better take the bedroom, eh?" Quickey said. "Right? I goin' carry the grip inside, then."

He took hold of the grip and hoisted it into the adjoining

room, which could hardly have been wider than the suitcase itself, judging from the amount of space taken up by the drawing-room.

"You in' got ambition?" Ulric said to Quickey. "You still living in this fowl-coop?"

"Is me own," answered Ulric. "If I get a bigger house is more cleanin' and repairin', and I'd only end up with me relations moving in and tellin' me what to do. I in' right? Eh? An' what about you? You in' even married yet. You in' shame?"

"That's a long story, man," answered Ulric.

Fingers felt certain that Genetha's presence prevented him from disclosing the reasons for his single state.

"I better cook now," Quickey said, "seein' as how all you come so far. If you want eat before the food ready I got banana and cashew and t'ing at the back. The trees them full o'fruit."

He left them to finish their coconuts.

"What you want us to do with the shell?" Ulric called out.

"Throw them in the front yard," he said from the back. "A man does come to collect them."

When the three had finished scraping their coconuts they took them out and laid them in a heap at the foot of the front stairs. Ulric then went out on to the road.

"You like it here?" Fingers asked Genetha.

"I like it, yes. You?"

"How you mean? Is mag-ni-fi-cent!"

"How much will we have to give them, you think?" Genetha asked.

"I don' know."

"I brought thirty dollars."

"You hold on to your money, girl," Fingers advised. "Country people generous. Ulric say Quickey would sell the shirt off his back to entertain him."

"Anyway, I can't leave without giving him something."

Ulric came back and joined them on the stairs, where they talked of country people's generosity, of the inhabitants of Morawhanna, many of whom were half aboriginal Indian, of the tiring journey up from Georgetown and of anything that came into their heads. They talked until the sun began to set and flocks of birds came flying up-river. Then the terns appeared as if from nowhere, wheeling like gulls and shrieking like children in a school playground. The noise of the pigs under the house had given way to the humming of mosquitoes, a slow persistent whine that filled the cool night air and reminded the visitors that they were in the country.

When the stars came out and voices from the riverside fell silent, Quickey joined them. He had spent hours preparing their meal, now almost ready but for the rice, which was boiling.

"You got a nice life here, Mister," said Fingers enviously.

"An' we in Morawhanna," answered Quickey, "think all you got a nice life in Georgetown. Is we who does leave here to go there. Is only government people does come down, 'cause they got to do as they're told. Else nobody would come."

"What about your sister?" Ulric asked.

"You in' hear? No, how you going hear? She take in sudden and dead. She was younger than me, only sixty-seven. That woman never had a day sickness. You know she used to go creek-side to bleed she own balata? Yes. She uses to make cricket balls with it and sell them to people from Georgetown who did come up here on holiday and did want a lil game o' bat and ball. Well, one afternoon she come home and say, 'Is who you think I see?' 'I in' know,' I say. 'I see Charlene.' Charlene was she best friend from school days, but she did go an' get drowned years ago during a storm. 'Bout twenty years ago. Well, she say she see Charlene collecting firewood across the creek. She says, 'Is you, Charlene?' Charlene turned round, and was she in truth. She din' say a word, but just stretch out she hand and make as if to call she. My sister was so frighten she say, 'Le' me go home and take this balata, then I going come back.' Of course she din' go back! But that same night she dead in she sleep. Is a nice way to go, though, you in' think so?"

Quickey smiled. He then went on to speak of his family, nieces, nephews, cousins up to the seventh degree, and of frequent reunions when one of them earned enough money.

"They does all come here, though the house is small," he said with satisfaction. "And my second great-granddaughter start to talk a'ready. She does try to ride the pigs them. And I don' like that 'cause you can't trust pigs."

The barking of a dog came from the riverside.

"Is the men setting out to put down they cadell," Quickey told them. "Le' we go and eat."

While the men washed their hands in a basin of water Genetha stood at the window watching the fishermen laying out

47

their calabash floats on the water. Cadell fishing was still widely practised in the North-West, despite the heavy losses caused by sharks. Very often the largest fish on the hooks were eaten up to their heads. The fishermen refused to change their methods, despite attractive inducements by way of loans to pay for nets.

"They put out their hooks every night?" Genetha asked.

"Yes, Mistress," Quickey answered. "They uses to sell they fish in Venezuela, but they not allowed to no more. I in' know what they going do 'cause by the time the fish get down to Georgetown it all stink up and nobody want buy it."

Genetha washed her hands and sat down with the men at table, which was so laden with food that it might have been laid for six rather than four. And through the open window nothing was visible save the stars and the ceaselessly shifting lights of the fishermen's boats.

## 7. A Season in Morawhanna

There began for Genetha a season of ineffable contentment. She could not believe that she had, at first, regretted accepting the invitation, being uncertain of the role Ulric would play and just as uncertain of the strength of her tenuous relationship with Fingers.

The morning after their late meal she awoke last of all and found a note on the dining-table saying that the three men had gone to see some friends of Quickey's and would be back before midday. There were eggs and bread in the box under her bed and the coffee was in a tin on the kitchen table.

After tea, the morning meal, she put on her white frock and went down to the riverside. Little boats were scattered on the water, in which children, some as young as eight years, were making their way to the school house on the opposite bank. Hardly anything was as in Georgetown. Here the absence of cars, the numerous boats, the generous build of the people, the willingness to talk of death, the candid pleasure the men took in going off alone persuaded her that she was at the start of an experience that could not fail to leave a permanent impression on her.

When the last boat tied up in front of the school and the glare of the sun on the ebbing water became intolerable Genetha set off for a walk on what appeared to be the main east-west road, running parallel with the river. She bought a soft drink at a roadside shop with a display of half a dozen bottles and a tray of sweet cakes. A hand's breadth away was the pharmacy on the front of which was painted "Jesus is coming". Some anarchist who must have travelled had written beneath it "Jesus gone".

There were no other shops in the vicinity and Genetha, after slaking her thirst with a second drink – a purchase that seemed to alarm the lady behind the counter – went back to the house to await the men's arrival. She promptly dozed off and slept until she was awakened by the squealing of the pigs, which were being tortured by Ulric.

"You in' die of loneliness?" Fingers mocked her.

"Where did you go?" she asked.

"To see a man who going hunt with Quickey and us. You coming? He say you can come as long as you know how to walk quiet."

"I'll see."

Ulric asked if she had slept well and actually looked her straight in the eye.

Genetha helped Quickey to prepare the main meal, breakfast, which was not ready before two in the afternoon.

And for the first time everyone spoke freely. After the meal Genetha, emboldened by the new sense of well-being, followed Fingers's suggestion to take off her dress and walk around in her petticoat, as so many of the women of Morawhanna did, he said. She lay on the floor, her head on his lap, and listened to him talk and felt the vibration of his voice through his thighs.

"This is the main street, Quickey?" she asked.

"No. Is two streets away," he replied.

She told him of her trip to the shop.

"The woman does own the pharmacy next door, too," he said eagerly. "If you go to buy cascara she does got to run over and leave she customers in the cake shop to sell you in the pharmacy. On Saturday night when people come from up river to sport she does sweat like pig, runnin' from one shop to the other."

Ulric spoke of one of the periods he was in steady employment during the war. He was then a member of the militia and often had to do guard duty on one of the cargo ships in harbour. Once when he had been relieved and was descending the rope ladder to the launch which was to take him back to land he dropped his rifle in the space between the launch and the ship. To his surprise the incident caused such consternation among his superiors that he began to tremble for his life. He was made to write several reports, fill out forms specially printed for the occasion and finally recite and sign an oath of loyalty to people and institutions he had only read about in the papers. As if that were not enough he was brought to trial before a specially constituted court which, after lengthy deliberations, decided that as he had not thrown away his rifle, and as it was unlikely to fall into the hands of the crew of a German submarine, he would be absolved of blame. But since such negligence could not go unpunished he was to be discharged from the militia in disgrace. Ulric hung his head in a suitable display of grief and disappointment.

Quickey spoke of Sibyl, his spirit-child, who came to visit him every Friday. She was one of the two teachers who worked in the school across the river. The first Friday after arriving to take up her post she came and sat on his doorstep as if she had known him all her life.

"She come an' go, just like that," said Quickey. "Always on Friday afternoon. Then one Friday she come through the door and sit in that very chair Ulric sitting 'pon. And is so I get to know she."

"How you mean she's a spirit-child?" Fingers asked.

"Oh, you can tell," Quickey answered. "First you suspect, then things happen that make you know. They don't get malaria like we. And they does hear the faintest noise. She going come this afternoon."

Quickey went on to tell them that before Sibyl started working at the school the aboriginal Indian children used to go off in their boats during recreation. No one had succeeded in pinning them down to a pattern of behaviour alien to their way of life. But Sibyl had no difficulty whatsoever in keeping them within the school precincts. People began talking about her; and when she increased the practical side of the curriculum at the expense of Arithmetic and English she was dismissed. But even more children began treating recreation as the end of the school day, so that at mid-morning the river stretching away on both sides of the school was dotted with boats heading in every direction, as if the children were fleeing some kind of pest. In the end the authorities were obliged to climb down and Sibyl was reinstated.

"People don't talk 'bout she no more," Quickey said. "They

50

just accept she."

"And where your family live?" enquired Fingers.

"All over the place. They in balata bleeding mostly, so they spend a lot o' time in the bush."

Quickey fell asleep during one of Ulric's stories. Genetha went inside and was followed by Fingers, who lay down beside her and began fondling her breasts lazily. Hanging from the window ledge above their heads was a line of pupae strung out like dried fruit. Genetha was thinking of the swarming insect life in Morawhanna as her lover stretched out his strong fingers over her breast, of the covered walks through which termites marched to attack the woodwork of houses, of the protection afforded them by Morawhanna's inhabitants, as though they were bringers of good fortune rather than destruction. When Fingers mounted her he found her weeping from contentment and rode her gently, understanding at last the extent of her dependence, that she was wearing her petticoat as a bridal gown and her impenetrable expression like the veil behind which teemed a hundred gestures of welcome and despair.

As they lay beside each other they heard Ulric's snoring and the half-hearted chattering of squabbling birds. Then Fingers fell asleep and was awakened briefly by the monkeys of the monkey-woman who sold her captives at exorbitant prices to people from town. And in the wake of their screaming and hissing Genetha herself dropped off, her body moist with sweat.

Genetha, who awoke with the scent of herbs in her nostrils, heard muffled voices coming from the adjoining room. When she put out her hand she found that Fingers was no longer on the bed.

From the tone of the men's voices and the quality of their laughter she knew that there was someone else in the house. She knelt down on the bed, through the mattress of which she could feel the bed-boards. Cupping her chin in her hands she looked down into the yard, where the only cock was treading the hens. They ran in a frenzy along the narrow space between the house and fence, releasing feathers in a vain flight from persecution, then submitting to the cock's attentions with tails spread out like fans.

"There'll be more eggs," she thought, lazily trying to work out at the back of her mind whether the visitor was a man or woman and how she would manage to go down to the yard and get washed without being seen. Craning her neck she only managed to see a patch of the river reflecting the sun on its surface sheen. The latrine and bath-house in the back yard stood side by side like companions, unpainted structures under a coconut tree that went curving away over the neighbour's yard. The sun was sinking on a horizon of rainbows where God the mist-maker sat and judged men's deeds, according to a Macusi hymn. One fatal day he would decide that the accumulation of wickedness had overwhelmed his compassion and then he would hold back the wheel on which the sun climbed to its ascendancy in the east.

Genetha decided to leave by the window. She put on her frock and panties and eased herself down into the yard. With a calabash standing on the rainwater barrel and a bucket she washed herself from head to foot in the bath-house before going back into the house through the front door.

"Mistress," said Quickey, standing out of respect for Genetha. "This is Sibyl."

Genetha shook the young woman's hand and could not conceal her surprise that it was this frail, ethereal creature who had such influence on the children she taught.

"If you hungry it got food on the table," Quickey offered.

"No, I'm not hungry, thanks."

So well had Genetha settled into her new way of life that she had forgotten to put on her shoes. She went and sat down on the floor next to Fingers who, she saw right away, was embarrassed in Sibyl's presence.

"Sibyl was just starting to tell we 'bout school," Quickey said, pointing with considerable pride at the young woman.

When Sibyl rested her eyes on her Genetha felt that she had come under a powerful scrutiny, and even after Sibyl turned away and began to talk, Genetha believed that she was being gazed at.

Speaking softly Sibyl said, "No, Uncle. They told me old stories, some of which were false because they know I like listening to old stories."

"And what 'bout you?" asked Quickey. "All your stories true?"

"No. I mean false because they made them up just for me. The Warraus can tell stories all night about the Carib-Warrau wars."

"Are there any Caribs left?" Ulric enquired in a carefully enunciated English.

"They got some up this very river," Quickey informed the company. "And I hear they got a lot in Surinam. Long, long ago they was much more than the Arawaks. This river self got a Carib name: Waini. It was up this river and the Orinoco that they come into South America. To this day the Arawaks and Warraus frighten of them even though only a handful left."

They talked until Quickey said that he, Ulric and Fingers were going to drink rum.

"When you going, niece?" Quickey asked Sibyl.

She looked at Genetha then answered that she would be leaving soon, but would come the next morning.

"Saturday!" exclaimed Quickey. "Good. Careful how you go cross the river. They in' got moon tonight."

The men left the two women alone. Only the crickets and tree-frogs could be heard and the murderous humming of the mosquitoes.

"I wonder how the Indians can go about naked with all the mosquitoes," remarked Genetha, put out by Sibyl's presence.

"In the bush where they go about naked the same dye they use to paint themselves with keeps away insects. And the wood from which they get the dye is like cocoa wood: they make fire with it. They plant whole fields with it."

"Truly?" asked Genetha, her embarrassment growing with every word the young woman spoke.

When the men were there her presence was bearable, but alone there was something curiously oppressive about her frail body. Was it because of what Quickey had told them? Or would she have felt the same otherwise? Genetha was certain that there was little between them in their education.

"Why you don't like me?" Genetha asked, preferring to make a fool of herself rather than to endure a long silence.

"You only ask that because you don't know what to say."

And this retort only increased her malaise.

"Look how I'm trembling," Genetha said. "A half-hour ago I was sleeping and now I'm trembling like a leaf."

"You're sure you're well?" Sibyl asked.

"Of course I'm well! I've got more weight than you."

Sibyl got up. "I'll go then," she offered.

"Right!"

"Look," Sibyl said, hesitating by her chair. "This only happened once before. I can't help it. Come with me across the river, ne?"

Genetha recoiled at the suggestion that she should hazard her life on the river with Sibyl in a frail craft when she could not even swim and had no confidence in her.

"All right. I'm gone," Sibyl said softly.

She went through the back door, down to the riverside where her boat was moored. Genetha followed, realizing that the stranger was hurt. Standing in front of the bath-house she waited until Sibyl was in her corial then she called out.

"I don't know how to sit in that thing."

"Try it."

Genetha went down to the bark canoe and sat down as carefully as she could, but as she had anticipated, the craft nearly capsized.

"I'll come tomorrow and you can practise sitting in it," said Sibyl, when Genetha was standing once more on the bank.

"All right."

Sibyl headed for the open river and was soon lost in the gloom on the water.

Genetha went back to the house, ashamed at her loss of control. She reflected on the opinion others had of her, of an unruffled character, which she herself had come to believe, in her habitual way of looking in other people's mirrors.

"I like this mirror," her mother used to say about the looking-glass on the dressing-table, "because it fills me out."

She had come to believe in a serene presence that dwelt in her, now exposed as a figment by a school teacher Quickey and the other two men treated as a sage.

The next morning Sibyl came when the sun was hardly over the horizon and the men were preparing to go hunting. The actual hunt was to take place the coming night, but they had to paddle some distance up-river.

Sibyl sat down on the back stairs without announcing her arrival and it was Ulric who first saw her.

"Howdye," he said.

"Howdye."

"You always use that small boat?"

"It's easy to handle," Sibyl explained. "How far are you

going?"

"A few miles up the creek."

Quickey came out on hearing them talk.

"Howdye, niece. You want to come?"

"No. If it was cooler," she declined.

"Miss Genetha don't want come either. She think she going get snake bite."

"So she's staying?" asked Sibyl.

"Yes. First she say she coming," said Quickey, affecting exasperation, "then she say she staying. Take she round to Miss Gordyck, ne."

"I'll see."

Genetha had heard every word. She was sitting at the dining-table, watching Fingers unravel a length of knotted string. The talk of hunting, the day before, had posed one problem for her: should she or should she not go? Now, however, as she witnessed the actual preparations for the trip, she began to imagine that Fingers might be exposed to all kinds of perils. He might be bitten by a labaria, a snake quite common in the surrounding bush. Quickey had talked the night before of the ineptitude of townspeople during a hunt, yet denied the possibility of her lover being in any danger. She sat following him with her eyes, but on hearing Sibyl's voice she rejected the idea of asking him to stay behind with her. Although he did not stop what he was doing when Sibyl came he nevertheless kept looking towards the back door.

A good half-hour later the men left amid much laughter and ribaldry. Genetha kissed Fingers in front of everyone. The latter, acutely embarrassed, wiped his lips in jest, so that Ulric and Quickey laughed out loud. She went down to the gate while Sibyl stood at the window watching, waving once in answer to Quickey's rapid gesture of farewell.

Genetha, on returning to the house, was overcome with the same hostility towards the visitor as she felt yesterday until the moment she said she was going home. The desire to meet her again that Genetha had felt, watching her boat move away towards the opposite shore, had vanished some time that morning, perhaps when she heard her voice.

Sibyl spoke first: "I was to teach you to sit in the corial. You're coming?"

"Teach?" asked Genetha. "I'm not one of your pupils." No

sooner had the words escaped than she was ashamed.

"You're coming or not?" Sibyl persisted.

"What have you got that makes men run after you?" Genetha demanded, knowing that she would be unable to keep up the pretence of being friendly.

Sibyl did not answer.

"I mean, you're not even good-looking," Genetha continued. "And you're small. Men don't like small women."

Genetha listened to herself talking, and as in a dream could not help behaving in a way contrary to her real nature.

"I got up early," said Sibyl, "just to come and see you, and you're chasing me away again, like yesterday."

Genetha did not reply at once. She stood in the centre of the room, helpless in face of the young woman's calm.

"You want some ginger tea?" she said at length, without turning to the visitor.

"Yes, thanks."

When she came back again from the cubicle at the foot of the stairs — in which there was a clay stove and the most rudimentary kitchen furnishings — she was carrying two large enamel mugs, both of which were badly chipped around the rim.

Genetha sat down at the dining-table, where Sibyl joined her.

Then, partly to atone for her rudeness, partly on account of a desperate need to share her secrets with someone, Genetha began to talk of her past, of her parents and brother, of her Queenstown aunts and her paternal aunt and of her grandparents. She spoke of the former servants of the family, Marion and Esther, who had left a legacy of guilt to them all, like lead embedded in the flesh, that caused pain when all seemed well.

"I want my freedom from Fingers, yet I can't do without him. I've never been so happy in my life as since I've been here in Morawhanna. But I know it can't last."

"What if it doesn't last?" Sibyl asked.

"You don't think it matters," said Genetha. "For me it is of the utmost importance . . . the utmost importance."

"Why?"

"Why does Quickey call you a spirit-child?" Genetha asked.

It was the first time that Sibyl appeared to be less than mistress of herself.

"The aboriginal Indians are all spirit-children. Because I'm not an Indian people think it odd that I can do certain things,

56

that's all."

"Like what?"

Sibyl turned to look her in the eye, and once more she was afflicted with that feeling of oppression.

"What people can't do always looks extraordinary. The Indians can see fish under water when you couldn't see them. They can call birds towards them and make monkeys come down from the trees. They can harm people in strange ways. And they know the bush: they know that jaguars never move about during a full moon, and that vampire bats avoid places with dogs."

"Can you do all the things they can do?" Genetha asked.

"Not all."

"I see."

"You talk about your family," Sibyl said. "The Caribs are all but extinct. I can show you a group of Caribs without children. Their women are terrified of conceiving because they feel they're doomed. They're afraid of the bush, of darkness, of strangers, even of their own dogs."

"So I shouldn't complain," Genetha remarked.

"When you don't *want* to complain, that's freedom," said Sibyl.

"Resignation," retorted Genetha quietly.

"People who struggle don't complain."

"Neither do people who're resigned," Genetha returned hotly, thinking of her martyred mother.

Then, after a long pause, Genetha said, "You make me feel ashamed. . . ."

"Why not stay here? Your friend could buy a piece of land and farm it."

"Fingers wouldn't stay, because Ulric wouldn't."

"You can still ask him. He looks as if he's having a good time."

"I'll ask," Genetha agreed, knowing full well that *she* could not stay away from Georgetown.

Once more she had talked too much, Genetha thought. One day she had confided in Fingers, with the result that he began taking advantage of her. Heaven knows what Sibyl must think, for *she* had confided nothing in return and had even failed to answer directly when asked what those powers were that had earned her the reputation of being a spirit-child.

"I'll take a swim while you learn to sit in the corial," Sibyl suggested with a smile so warm that once more Genetha experienced the extraordinary effect of her personality.

The guest went down to the river, Genetha remaining behind to change her dress and put on a pair of sandals.

From the top of the back stairs she could see Sibyl's corial, its stern moving from side to side on the water, and, beyond, the flight of marsh birds straying from the reed banks. Then, just as she decided to fetch a hat against the sun, she saw Sibyl come out of the bath-hut and run down to the river, stark naked. Genetha knew that outside Georgetown nude swimming was commonly practised, yet the sight of a woman unclothed in the open was the witnessing of something unforgivably immoral. She took down Fingers's panama hat from the nail, telling herself that her astonishment was yet another proof of her ignorance of the world around her.

"When you can balance," Sibyl called out, "try and paddle a bit. It's shallow for about ten feet out. Don't be afraid."

Balancing was far easier than it had been the previous day and almost at once Genetha tried her hand at paddling.

"Don't scrape the paddle against the boat," advised Sibyl. "Hold it a little away from the boat. That's it. . . . Now paddle on the other side, softly . . . like that. When you want to come back, keep paddling on the left side and the corial will turn gradually."

A feeling of elation overcame Genetha, who forgot that her companion was swimming naked, that she herself could not swim and that her jealousy had burgeoned like a mysterious cloud. She paddled, propelling the corial now in one direction now in the other, like a child discovering a new world of sensations through walking. Sibyl, who was treading water as expertly as the aboriginal Indian children she taught, now swam away from the shallows, certain that Genetha knew what she was about.

Beneath the morning sun the two women moved in the solitude of a derelict civilization which, hundreds of years ago, pushed up the great rivers into the hinterland of a continent of profoundly disturbing echoes, a solitude of buried potsherds, of once ruthless conflicts and bleached bones, of cowering remnants of a proud nation that had lost the instinct to bear children.

The marsh birds shrieked over the mud-banks, and far above in an endless circling, a pair of vultures scanned the islands of a

58

waterlogged landscape.

Genetha paddled towards the open river, towards the place where the sun dazzled and the deep water was still in slack tide, and the births and deaths of a million small creatures were neither celebrated nor mourned.

## 8. The Spirit-Child

Night fell and with it a plague of hard-backed beetles and yellow moths with diaphanous wings. The beetles were everywhere, on the table, the floor, crawling up the walls and occasionally penetrating the women's hair. Quickey, Ulric and Fingers were playing cards in the corner, huddled under a pale kerosene lamp, from time to time interrupting their game to curse a beetle that crawled up an exposed leg or into an ear.

The guests were leaving the following day and the grip stood on the floor by the door with a leper-wood bow lying next to it.

Twice the men had gone hunting without success and on each occasion Sibyl kept Genetha company, the second time staying overnight at her request. Genetha came to consider her a close friend, though she would have admitted that to no one. Sibyl's influence on her was undeniable and after her initial resistance to the young woman's criticism of her tendency to brood she set about systematically putting into practice some of her advice. Her first aim was to overcome the senseless jealousy of Sibyl herself, and now that she was all but successful it was time to go back to Georgetown.

While the men played cards the women could only talk, Genetha reflected. Men talked, went hunting and played games. Only for little girls was it seemly to play games. When the family moved to Georgetown she remembered well how difficult it was to join a group in her new primary school. Her mother had asked, "Did you make a friend, Gen?" And not, "Did you manage to get in with a group?" Boyie simply took up a fielding position in the playground cricket match, while she stood by the girls with their skipping rope, waiting to be *called*. Now, she had no recollection of how she managed to get in with the girls; it just happened, just as, after a painful start, her friendship with Sibyl just happened. Sibyl had shown her that she need not be at the mercy of the past or of other people's actions, a lesson so momentous to her that she was disposed to tell Fingers about it, and even Quickey, who was goodness itself.

The rains had come, hence the plague of beetles, which would vanish by morning, as if they never existed.

"How do the fishermen manage in the rain?" she asked Quickey.

Everyone laughed, and Genetha was at a loss to know why.

No one except her was thinking of the following day, it seemed. The rain clouds would burst then, according to Quickey, and all the passengers would huddle under the awnings and throng the saloon, so that the purser would give up trying to sort out the first-class ones from the second-class, who belonged downstairs.

Genetha and Sibyl were unable to make conversation, their talk being unsuitable for men's ears, so they watched the candle flies that kept invading the window spaces at the front of the house, their lights vanishing and reappearing a few feet away.

"The hard backs going put out the light," Quickey warned when two beetles fell down the kerosene lamp chimney at the same time.

"Good," said Fingers. "Is more nice in the dark when the ladies around."

"Hunting in the dark didn't do you much good," Genetha teased him, recalling the men's elaborate preparations for two fruitless expeditions.

"You right, girl," he said, shaking his head.

"I know a man who caught deer on the sea wall," Ulric joked.

No sooner had he spoken the last word than the lamp went out as Quickey said it would.

"All you hold on," he told the company. "I got to clean out the hard backs. They worse than last year, I in' telling lie."

In a few minutes light was restored and the men went on with their game while Genetha and Sibyl discussed the forthcoming trip back to Georgetown. The last time they were alone they had spoken at length about marriage and Sibyl's man friend, who was a dispenser on the island of Wakenaam.

"You falling asleep again," Fingers complained.

"Me falling asleep?" Quickey protested. And with that he chose a card at random and played it confidently.

"They could play forever," Genetha told Sibyl, to whom clung the scent of vanilla from the cake she had baked that afternoon for the departing guests.

When Sibyl got up to go, everyone rose with her.

"Careful with the cassava near the bottom step," Quickey warned.

They picked their way through the newly harvested cassava piled in two heaps by the foot of the stairs.

"You gone then," Fingers said to Sibyl as she took the paddle, ready to dig it into the mud and shove towards the open river, now shadowy under a starless night.

"Next time you come this side," she told them, "stop off at Wakenaam. Ask for the dispenser. The young dispenser. And you all can stay as long as you like."

Quickey and the guests stood watching Sibyl and the boat and her paddle dripping whenever it was raised out of the water.

"She forget to take the fat-pork," Quickey said. "I going give her next Friday."

With that the men went back to their card game, leaving Genetha standing by the river's edge.

Her thoughts wandered from her travelling friend to the street with two shops and she deemed it strange that in the past fortnight she had gone nowhere yet had been happier than ever before, that she had stored up memories in the way her mother used to keep her girl's hair and other momentoes of her life in Queenstown, in little carved boxes scented with naphthalene balls. She had also learned to guard against the tortures of jealousy, for when Fingers said, "You gone then," she had schooled herself to pay no heed. If she had not understood why her friend was regarded as a spirit-child she nevertheless discovered what in the past she had missed by way of friendship, and that her exaggerated regard for Sibyl was perhaps the shadow of a childhood lack.

The next morning Quickey would not come with them to the boat. Goodbyes were for women. He tied up the bag of vegetables and fruit and strung it from a cord, so that Genetha, who was carrying little else, could hang it over her shoulder.

"Ulric, man," he said, "I know you in' going come back 'cause I cut you ass at cards."

"I goin' come back," Ulric replied, "if you promise not to chase away all the animals in the bush with your ugly face."

Their laughter attracted the attention of an old man sitting on the porch of the house opposite.

"Neighbour," he called out to Quickey, "you goin' away?"

"No! Is where I goin' go at my age? Is me friends from Georgetown. They goin' home."

"From where?" the neighbour enquired.

"Georgetown!"

"Yes, well," he grumbled.

"I goin' come with you to the corner," Quickey declared.

And he ended up on the stelling where the gangway rose steeply to the boat, which was riding on a high tide.

Ulric, Genetha and Fingers toiled up the gangplank, over-burdened with their luggage and presents from Quickey, only to find that all the good seats in the saloon had been taken.

Placing their things together in a corner they went out to wave to Quickey who, meanwhile, had got into conversation with another old man; and it was only when the shouting of the Transport and Harbour employees took his attention that he turned and waved as the boat drifted away from the stelling and the mooring ropes were hauled aboard.

Back in Georgetown they took a hired car home. The streets were teeming with people as though some fête were being celebrated.

"Political meeting," Ulric said knowingly.

Since the Enmore sugar-estate riots when several people were killed or hurt by police bullets political meetings had become a commonplace.

Now the hired car slowed down almost to a halt in order to negotiate a passage through a crowd, many of whom bent down to look into the vehicle, whose occupants were too tired to take an interest in the reason for the gathering.

Finally they arrived and Fingers jumped out in order to pay before Ulric could do so. Not having been asked to contribute to the cost of the stay in Morawhanna he was determined to show that he, too, could be generous.

Having said goodbye to Ulric the two lovers laboured up the stairs, Fingers carrying the grip while Genetha struggled with Quickey's presents.

Fingers picked up a piece of folded paper lying on the floor just beyond the doorway.

"My grandmother want see me," he said, after reading it.

"Go tomorrow, ne," Genetha told him.

"Suppose so. If it urgent she'll come sheself."

Genetha sat down in an easy chair, but Fingers got undressed and went straight to bed. She picked the paper out of the kitchen bin when she knew he was asleep, but learned nothing more from it than she had been told. Until then she had never enquired as to his relations with his grandmother, his father and sisters, and he had told her nothing. After the holidays when she had him to herself the sudden realization that he was bound to others came as a jolt. Instead of retiring as Ulric had done, she remained in the gallery turning the matter over in her mind.

Already Morawhanna was a dream, a garden where flowers were memories, deep-hued or yellow, blood-red roses and lady-of-the-night. That table where they ate together, the base of its legs wrapped in silver paper and standing in old tobacco tins half-filled with disinfectant as a protection against marauding ants, always laden with fruit on those glittering mornings, was as vivid in her imagination as the children paddling to school or Sibyl running down naked to the river's edge. She and Quickey were of Morawhanna as Ulric and Fingers were of Georgetown, all shadows of a particular place. Was not Ulric *levied* upon by the bailiffs? Not many people in Morawhanna knew the meaning of the word; of that she was certain.

## 9. Strangers in the Kitchen

Fingers went to see his grandmother the next afternoon and the following day as well. Then he assured Genetha that when he went out the night after that he was going to play billiards and not to visit his people. He became secretive and resented Genetha's ceaseless questioning as if he were a child. In the end he was obliged to admit that his grandmother was demanding that he continue to support the family; for his father, in his late forties, was unable to find work.

"Support them!" said Genetha angrily, failing to understand why he was making such a song and dance of a simple matter.

"If you don' mind."

"Of course I don't mind," Genetha said, peering into that gulf between them which she always knew had never been bridged.

They began quarrelling frequently. Fingers had changed and she could not bear the uncertainty of her position.

One afternoon she came home to find Fingers's father, his

three sisters and grandmother in the kitchen. The oldest girl, in her late teens, had taken off her shoes and was sitting with her legs sprawled and her plate on one knee for the world as if she were mistress in the kitchen. The two other girls, about eight and nine years old, were eating with spoons rice heaped on their plate, while Fingers's father and grandmother kept an eye on them.

"He gone downstairs," the father told Genetha, who had as yet said nothing.

She went into the bedroom, placed her handbag on the bed, then left in search of her lover, who came to Ulric's front window when she called out for him.

"Is you?" he asked sheepishly. "Wha' you doin' home so early?"

"Please come over. I want to talk to you."

He took his time and even when on her bridge he found it necessary to strike up a conversation with a passer-by. She met him at the foot of the stairs.

"Can you tell me what your family are doing in my kitchen?" Genetha asked him, filled with rage at his apparent indifference to the urgency of her summons.

"Is my food," he lied. "Truly."

"So that's why —"

"Look, Gen. Is this once. The ol' man not working. It not goin' happen again."

Genetha pressed her thumb deep into the back of her hand, determined not to lose her temper with him.

"You will never change," she said, "and I can't go on like this."

"Listen, Gen. Listen! I goin' get rid of them now!"

"No. . . ."

But he did not wait for her to finish. Genetha heard the clamour of raised voices and stamping in the kitchen; and soon afterwards someone's legs appeared on the back stairs, only to disappear promptly. Then Fingers's grandmother began descending the steps with great dignity, followed by the girls and her fifty-year-old son. And none of the group addressed Genetha as they filed by.

Fingers did not come down and Genetha on going upstairs found him in a dejected pose by the kitchen sink.

She was the one who was wronged, Genetha told herself, resisting the urge to climb down. Besides, she did not know how long Fingers had been entertaining his family behind her back, perhaps as long as the time they came back from Morawhanna, when he claimed that his appetite had grown. His eldest sister could not have looked more relaxed in her own house; and his father's unsolicited advice to seek his son downstairs confirmed the impression that the family had had some practice in making themselves at home.

Through all the contradictory thoughts that raced through her mind flowed the strong, persistent current of a single emotion, her anger at being used.

"I know how you feel," Fingers said. "But is my family. I can't see them starve."

"You'll have to choose between me and them," Genetha said.

If only she was certain of him she could bring herself to stomach this invasion of her home. How solid and healthy the girls looked, in spite of the family's privations. And this observation only served to fire her resentment all the more. If Fingers's grandmother had got up deferentially, as Esther and Marion had been trained to do, the impertinence might have been softened and she might have dismissed her lover's boldness as a lack of breeding.

Fingers, at a loss for words, and terrified lest he had gone too far, came and put his arms round her waist.

"I care for you a lot, Gen," he declared, in that honeyed tone that might denote either sincerity or hypocrisy.

"Do you?" she said with a flat voice.

"You don't know that? Look how much you do for me."

She felt his arm round her and recalled that his hands had brought her a measure of peace, that she took pride in watching them grip the tools of his new trade, which, after all, promised to earn them years of tranquillity. It was through her that he had learned to love and respect work.

Genetha turned and looked at him.

"The trouble is," she said, "you know you can twist me round your finger. But if you want us to go on living together don't bring your family to eat here."

"You make me forget," said Fingers. "I had something to show you. Wait, I goin' bring it."

He went inside and came out again with her father's framed photograph in one hand and a small sepia print in the other.

"This one drop out of the back of you father photo," he said, while handing her the two.

The small photograph was that of Esther, Boyie and herself. On the back of it was written: "Rohan, Genetha and servant."

"You an' you brother small, eh?" Fingers nudged Genetha, delighted that he had found an excuse to take her mind off his family's intrusion.

Genetha waited until he had gone back over to Ulric's before picking up the old print again. Boyie was standing on a wicker chair, one hand clasped in hers, while Esther stared at the camera with that proprietary expression that so irritated her mother. What, indeed, was family? Marion, with her flamboyant dress, her men friends, her independence, had been, as a servant, as much a part of the family as Esther. But no one would have described her as *family*. Esther, never as close to her mother, had an essential place in that web of relationships that bind groups together, and if her parents would never have included her in the term "family" Genetha and Boyie had had no doubt as to her position. Ah, those days of long ago, those gentle hours, the things one loved, the strange, absurd attachments! Genetha had never come to terms with the knowledge that her father did not perform miracles, with the altered landscape of adulthood. So passionate were its embraces, yet how much would she not give for her mother's gentler touch, or Esther's, before she was shown the door.

Fingers began complaining that his own conduct was due to his feeling of insecurity, for he had nothing while she had a steady job and the ability to find another if she lost her present one. She even had a house. He harped on this theme so consistently and sulked so often that she agreed to see a lawyer with a view to transferring her share in the property to him. When everything seemed settled she changed her mind at the last moment. Fingers packed his things and said that he was going abroad to get away from her.

Genetha, although she had changed her mind, went to see a lawyer nevertheless, who explained that to deal with the property she would have to secure Letters of Administration from the Deeds Registry. She would not be granted them unless Rohan gave his consent.

Glad at the opportunity to contact her brother she wrote that she wanted to raise a mortgage on the property but was unable to do so without Letters of Administration. Rohan answered in an affectionate letter granting her what she sought.

"That he can hold it against me for so long," she thought, dismayed that he did not invite her up to Suddie.

Fingers left her once more, saying that the length of time the business was taking showed how insincere she was; and when, once again, she went to fetch him back, he showed her his passport. He had definitely made up his mind to go away. Genetha pleaded with him, promising to be his slave; for all the conversations with Sibyl had come to nothing, and the resolution to be independent at all costs. He demanded that she make over to him the property, without including in the transport that a half share belonged to Rohan. It was as if the spirit had departed from her body, leaving it powerless to resist her lover's demands. She agreed and Fingers went back with her. When finally the court proceedings were over, transport was passed and the property was in his name, Fingers jokingly threatened her with eviction if she did not behave.

He disappeared for a fortnight and on returning disclosed to her his plans for the house. He intended to have all the outstanding repairs done. In addition he would paint it blue, the colour of the dress she was always recalling.

He and Genetha talked about his plans for a long time and agreed that she would have to find temporary accommodation until the work was over. She put a brave face on things when she read the carpenter's report: crumbling pillars, rusted guttering, ant-infested wood and a host of other defects that brought home to her the necessity of urgent action. It was surprising that the house was still standing. The gate was hardly doing that at all.

Genetha went to stay with her father's sister, who upbraided her for not having visited her. And, as if out of revenge, she dragged out Genetha's father's misdeeds every day of her stay, and the arrogance of her Queenstown aunts. Obliged to put up with this implacable hatred Genetha learned not to be offended; but this was not enough for her aunt, who took to seeking her approval for the opinions she expressed.

In the end Genetha, exasperated by her insistence, declared, "Can't you see how you're offending me, Aunt?"

"So I'm offending you! And what did your father do to me? The whole world knows what he did me. But it didn't stop him ending up a pauper, the pauper he made me."

"I know, Aunt," Genetha replied. "But can't you forget?"

"Never!" came the reply, like the recoil of a weapon. "I had gold and tables made of mahogany. People used to come to my house to admire my furniture, and the brass was cleaned every week by a girl from the village. Every Sunday she used to sit in the middle of the brass pots and the lamps and bed-knobs and she left the drawing-room and gallery glistening. Go to Anandale and ask them about Miss Armstrong. Even now they remember my house. But your father respected nothing! I went to him for advice and he robbed me as if I was a stranger. That day he treated me like a dog while your mother tried to console me. Then suddenly he was all smiles. He took my hand, saying that he would help me because we were brother and sister and we should stick together. And in a few weeks I was destitute and was glad to take a room under his house later when he offered it. It was like that, God is my witness. It was like that."

Her voice fell to a whisper.

"That man used to pass me on the stairs," she continued in a whisper, "even after he robbed me. Yes . . . and he had friends, believe it or not. He had friends who did stick to him through thick and thin as if he was a good man. . . ."

Genetha, for the first time, felt sorry for her, until the hysteria came back into her voice and she began to behave as if she was at war.

"But the sins of the father will be visited on the children. You and your no-good brother will come to a bad end. I'll pray for you and you will go under wishing you were never born! Look round you and see what I'm left with. I use enamel plates, like a range-yard woman, and have to empty my own po! And I was once respected in Anandale. Who respects me now? Who can respect a woman who does empty her own po? God is my witness that I've never had a moment's peace since he stripped me of everything I had."

Then, losing her temper completely, she stamped violently on the ground like a small child in a rage, so that a piece of furniture in which she kept a few glasses shook alarmingly. And Genetha sat opposite her, her head hanging as if she had been the cause of the disasters that had befallen her aunt all those years ago.

For weeks afterwards she never saw Fingers who, according to his sisters, was in the islands on business. The workmen who were painting the house knew nothing of his whereabouts. One night when she knocked on the door, from the front of which all the debris had been cleared, it was opened by a young girl of about ten.

"Ma! Is a lady!"

The girl's mother came out and asked what Genetha wanted.

"This is my house. I live here," Genetha said helplessly.

"Stanley! Come, ne?" the woman called out to someone in the back of the house.

"Is what?" came the answer in a booming voice.

"A lady say she live here. Come, ne?"

"Is what you talking 'bout? Live where?"

"I say come!" his wife called back, raising her voice in a show of irritation.

The booming voice appeared, followed by two younger children, a boy of about seven and a girl a year younger, both of whose faces were smeared in what they had been eating.

"Is what wrong?" the man enquired, evidently angry at being called away from his meal.

"I live here," declared Genetha. "I live in this house. It was under repair. . . ." She was lost for words. A wild look came into her eyes at the sight of the strange furniture.

"You must be mad, lady. We rent this house from Mr Bellamy."

She looked beyond the man's stocky figure towards the dining-room. Little was recognizable and the painted walls gleamed, and the place where the hatstand used to be was empty. She would write Boyie and ask him to come and settle things for her. He would evict these strangers, who were eating and sleeping in their home.

Genetha went away, but on turning the corner it occurred to her that Ulric's mother could help her. She could convince the strangers that she was not lying.

Ulric's mother was glad to see her and agreed readily to support her story.

"You should see how their children does climb over the paling! Of course I'll come, child. Of course."

She shuffled round the house in search of her hat.

It was Ulric's mother who knocked on Genetha's door with

her walking-stick. A child came to the window and shouted out:

"Is same lady! She come back with another lady, Ma. And a stick!"

Following the sound of hurried steps the door opened and the man of the house stood before them, hands akimbo and a terrible expression on his face.

"Is what you come back for?" he demanded. "You think I can spend the whole day opening and closing my door? This in' a hotel."

"This young lady lives here," said Genetha's neighbour. "I've been her neighbour for years."

"I don' doubt you, lady. But I living here now," the man retorted indignantly.

"You want me to call the police?" asked the widow, brandishing her stick.

"An' you want me to throw you off my stairs? Eh, eh! Some people wrong and strong!"

"Right! Come, girl," the widow said to Genetha.

The two women retreated down the stairs, accompanied by a torrent of obscenities from the man.

"That's what the district is coming to now," said the widow, when they reached her gate. "You go straight to the police! This minute!"

Genetha lost no time in going to the nearest station, the large Albertown Police Station.

"From what you tell me it's got nothing to do with us. See a lawyer. He'll tell you how to recover possession."

"But the neighbours can tell you I lived there," protested Genetha.

"People're always moving out and in, lady. According to what you tell me yourself you did make over your house to the Fingers chap of your own free will. Didn't you? Isn't that what you did say?"

She left the station and went back to the house. As she stood in the street looking at her former home the lights went out. Genetha could not resist the impulse any longer. She opened the street gate and went up the stairs. Timidly, she knocked at the door. There was no answer. She knocked again, more loudly this time, but no one came to the door. She knocked again and again, no longer fearing what the man might do. At last she abandoned her efforts and went to the back door which apparently was only bolted, for it rattled under Genetha's fist and threatened to yield at any moment.

In the end she gave up and sat on the back stairs, still unable to comprehend her misfortune.

"He thief he own sister house," somebody had remarked at her father's funeral, referring to her dead father.

She was now sitting on a staircase her family had gone up and down all these years, the approach to a door now bolted against her. And all was silent now under a forest of stars.

## 10. My Father Stole a House

A doctor was holding Genetha's wrist with his left hand. She was lying on a hospital bed and had been talking intermittently, sometimes with a feverish urgency and at other times in monosyllables, as if she could only speak with difficulty.

"The candles are wet," she said decisively, and tried to wipe her hands on the sheet on which she was lying.

"I have it here in my bag. Here . . . I told you, you're like a little boy."

The nurse wiped her forehead.

"I've always got to bring something home for you," Genetha continued in her delirium, "but when you. . . . Why're you looking at me like that? The trouble is you're too sure of me. I can't pretend. My eyes give me away. I wish I could pretend; it makes things so much easier. . . Can't you love me? Can't you try? When I was a girl in Agricola a man who played the 'cello used to live opposite us. You look like him, but what's in your hand is uglier. You've caused me more pain than my mother and father; and the 'cello screamed one night because it was alone. . . . With you everything is pain. My brother said you were always laughing and joking. But with me you hardly laugh at all. As soon as you come into my house, my house. . . . My father stole a house. . . . No! No! Father! It isn't true!" she screamed the last words, sobbing.

"Why did you wear rags?" Genetha continued. "If you only didn't wear rags! Father, why don't we go back to Agricola? All you've got to do is follow the pitch road and turn off by the rum shop."

She fell silent for a few minutes.

"Once," she began again, "Boyie pulled a hair from the police

71

horse's tail. I promised not to tell, but it doesn't matter now . . .
I used to stay awake until you came home and then when I
heard you cross the bridge my heart used to beat as if a hammer
was in my chest. There was always pain, pain . . . and then this
man, all because Boyie went away. If I had a daughter I'd teach
her to. . . . Snuff out the candles, please . . . then I'll say all the
unsaid things. . . ."

"Nurse," the doctor called, "pull the blinds, please."

The nurse complied and then returned to the bedside.

"She'll have to go to New Amsterdam."

The nurse stared at him.

"We need the bed for patients, nurse," he said irritably.

Genetha was transferred to the Berbice Hospital for the
mentally ill, where she spent six weeks before she was then discharged. Her condition had been diagnosed as a form of
hysteria, occasioned by acute distress, which did not amount to
a mental illness.

Many years later, the hateful stay in the mental home was
erased from her memory, except for a certain incident. Once
she and a score of patients were taken on a bus trip to East
Canje where they got out and were allowed to roam about at
will. She went a couple of hundred yards up the drainage canal
with a young woman and they both sat on the koker, the only
place that provided shade from the fierce morning sun. The air
was filled with a terrible stench they were obliged to endure
because they were not permitted to go back to the bus. In the
end her companion discovered the source of the smell, a dead,
bloated alligator which lay upturned in the canal at the base of
the koker.

Genetha's only memory of New Amsterdam was an abiding
stench and the slack water of the canal.

## 11. Tiger Bay

Genetha rented a room in Albouystown while she looked for a
job and tried, through her lawyer, to regain possession of her
house. Her former employers made her an ex-gratia payment of
sixty dollars, but declined to re-employ her. In the end she had
to take a job selling sweets and cigarettes at the Empire Cinema,
where she earned just enough to pay the rent and buy a little
food. Her one concern was to spend as little as possible until she

found satisfactory work before her savings gave out.

Rohan had remained ignorant of Genetha's stay in the mental hospital; but, convinced that he wanted nothing more to do with her, she did not get in touch with him.

She sold her bicycle and a few weeks later pawned her gold ring. But, inevitably, she began to draw money from the bank in order to pay for food, shoe repairs and a hundred and one other expenses. In the end she was forced to give up her efforts to re-occupy her house, for lack of money to pay her lawyer.

Some weeks later, despairing of ever finding work, she was taken on as a cashier at a Chinese wholesale grocer shop in a side street off Water Street. The twenty-five dollars she earned a month barely saw her through, provided she cut down on food and clothing; and when her umbrella was damaged she could not afford to repair it. But after facing the fierce midday sun for a week, she could bear it no longer and drew on her dwindling savings to have it mended. And so it went with the passing months until there was no more money left in the bank.

One morning she found she could not get out of bed. The sun was streaming through a chink in the wall and she heard the voices of children on their way to school. Her shivering was so bad that she plucked up the courage to hammer on the wall in order to attract the attention of her neighbour, whom she hardly knew. Moments later there was a knocking on her door and only then she realized that her neighbour could not get in. Summoning up all her strength she eased herself on to the floor and crawled over to the door, which she managed to open.

"Is wha' wrong, chile?" her neighbour muttered when she pushed the door and found her, face down on the floor.

She dragged Genetha to the bed and hoisted her bodily on to it, and on feeling her burning forehead covered her with the blanket. Later in the morning she brought her soup and bandaged her head with cochineal.

At midday Genetha heard the neighbour talking with her husband, but was unable to make out what he was saying. Later that afternoon when she came back to bring Genetha more soup she told her that her husband had been annoyed on account of the soup which, he claimed, they could not afford.

"Don't worry," she assured her, "he heart so soft he stupid sometimes. I tell you he'd give you he shirt if he take to you."

Genetha could only try to keep her teeth from chattering. She drank her soup greedily, but the dryness in her mouth remained and she asked her neighbour to leave a cup of water on the table beside her.

The afternoon stillness was broken by the school children returning home. The neighbour came back to open the door and window, in order to air the room, and the wind brought the scents from the streets with it and the cool air; and Genetha felt that the fever had fallen.

When her neighbour's husband appeared at the door she wished she could muster a smile. He placed an orange on the table and left without a word; only afterwards did it occur to Genetha that he could have let the owner of the grocery know why she was away.

Towards midnight, after she had given up all hope of her neighbour coming, there was a knock on her door. The good woman had gone to the pictures with her husband and was dropping in for the last time that day to see if she needed anything. Genetha asked if her husband might tell her employer why she was away and was assured that he would go early in the morning before he went to work.

"You're sure he'll do it?" Genetha asked.

"Oh, he like you. He say you look so thin and weak."

The next morning she came back unexpectedly, before the street had become noisy. Somebody, a woman in her thirties, was enquiring after Genetha.

"Tall?" Genetha asked.

"Yes."

Genetha knew at once that it was Esther and nearly wept with relief.

"Y'know she?" asked the neighbour.

"Yes. Her name's Esther."

Esther was already standing in the doorway. She was well dressed and had an attractive wicker basket in her hand, while on her left wrist she wore a gold bangle and a watch.

"I go'n see you," the neighbour said as she left Genetha, nodding a silent goodbye to Esther.

"You see?" Esther said, spreading out her hands. "I didn't forget."

She opened her handbag and took out a wad of notes from which she pulled the amount Genetha had lent her.

Genetha had never before seen Esther smile so readily. There was a certain verve in her bearing, a certain confidence in her speech. Her even white teeth gleamed and her arms, plump and dimpled, gestured while she spoke. Yet there was a shrillness in her manner that was equally puzzling.

"How you knew where I was living?" Genetha asked.

"I live near where you working and I've seen you a lot of times."

"They told you I was living here?"

"Yes."

"So you live near there?" Genetha asked, for want of something to say.

"Yes. Well, you can't pick and choose, can you?" She sat down on the bed, beside Genetha.

"You know . . . they've got a new girl," Esther told her, hesitating a little to soften the blow.

"Where?"

"In the grocery."

She fumbled in her handbag and brought out a packet.

"They asked me to give you this," she said, handing her the sealed, lined envelope.

Genetha looked up at Esther.

"Don't bother," the older woman reassured her, "they know me in the area. He trusts me."

Genetha opened the packet and found a week's money with a dismissal notice. She said nothing, but sank back on to her pillow.

"What happened to your house?" Esther asked her, after allowing her time to recover.

Genetha, whose face was turned to the wall, did not answer. The noise of bicycle bells stood out among the assorted sounds of Albouystown.

"That's life, isn't it?" Esther observed. "I asked him if he had to do it, but he said he couldn't afford to have you off sick. He said you're sickly in any case and he didn't think you could last." She took out a cigarette and lit it, then got up, went to the window and leaned out.

Genetha could not believe that Esther's presence had terrified her when they last met.

"You didn't seem surprised to find me sick," Genetha remarked.

"I knew. I came yesterday and your neighbour told me. She's nice."

Then, after a long pause, Esther said, "The same thing happened the last time. I came twice before I could see you."

"Why didn't you come in, then?" asked Genetha.

"I don't know."

"You should've come in. The lady next door's been helping me, but I'm not sure if her husband likes me. He doesn't talk much."

"Probably he hasn't got anything to say," observed Esther flippantly.

For the first time Genetha looked Esther up and down.

"You look well."

"You notice," she said, with an expression of feigned indifference.

"I went back to Diamond, you know," Esther began again, as if she were confiding something she wanted to get off her chest. "A few years ago I couldn't stand it in Georgetown any more. Ha!" she laughed dryly. "I was soon back. I missed the noise and the pictures . . . and everything, you see."

She put out her cigarette and began tidying the place up, and when she had finished she asked Genetha if she wanted her to make the midday meal.

"Yes. You'll have to get ground provisions from the market, though."

"You know you look bad. I suppose you know," Esther said.

"Very bad?"

"Terrible. . . . You still like cook-up rice?"

Genetha nodded.

As Esther was getting ready to go Genetha said to her, "Go and tell the lady next door you're doing the shopping. Probably she intends to bring something for me. And, listen . . . say thanks for what she's been doing."

Esther slipped out of the door without saying goodbye.

Genetha was overcome with a wave of bitterness. The firm in which she had worked for years dismissed her because she had been in the mental asylum, even though she had not been mentally ill; and now a short illness was sufficient to cause her dismissal from the grocer shop where, she thought, she was liked and appreciated by the owners.

She had gone so far as to work late in order to help with the backlog of work. Besides, she had been ill only once in all that time. She pulled the blanket more closely round her and turned over on her side to face the wall. The old wood had been recently given a single, inadequate coat of white paint which made it look even shabbier and the damp, musty smell that came from beneath the bed caused her to long for the soup the neighbour had been feeding her.

Genetha was incapable of fixing her thoughts on any single thing. Above all, if she attempted to dwell on Esther and the significance of her visit, some other less important train of thought interrupted the main theme of her reflections. She remembered that she had not given Esther any money for the shopping and almost at the same time she became aware of the extent of the change in her.

As soon as she returned, Esther asked:

"You want to come and live with me?"

Genetha propped herself up on her elbows and said:

"If you really want me to."

"I can get a taxi," declared Esther, "and the driver and I'll lift you out. I can't very well walk over here every day." Her last words were uttered as if she needed the utmost self-control in order to speak patiently.

"All right," Genetha said, trying not to show relief.

"Good. I'll cook and then order the taxi. We'll move this afternoon."

Esther unpacked the provisions and set to work picking the rice, while Genetha soon fell into a deep sleep, during which she perspired profusely.

That afternoon the two women got ready to make the journey by taxi to Esther's place.

Genetha had never recovered her clothes and furniture from Fingers. She had gone to his house several times, but in the end his sisters became so hostile she decided to keep away. When Esther asked where her belongings were Genetha told her that the man whom she had paid to move them had stolen everything.

"You don't have to lie to me. I know all about you and that Fingers that thief you out. Anyway, you must be a fool to give a man your house! Starting with property like that I would've owned a whole block in Georgetown by now," said Esther with as much feeling as if she had been Fingers's victim as well.

"You know where I live," said Genetha reproachfully, "and you know about me and Fingers."

"But everybody knows how you lost your house and that

77

you've been up to spend time in New Amsterdam."

"Oh," was all Genetha could reply.

"You should be accustomed to it. People've been talking about your family ever since the Agricola days."

"Why?" asked Genetha, out of annoyance rather than curiosity.

"Don't ask me. Some families attract attention. Besides, a lot of things happened when you were young that you don't know about."

"Well, tell me."

"You won't like me for it," warned Esther.

"Why did you mention it then?"

Esther was vexed by the younger woman's attitude and, partly out of spite, partly out of the need to communicate a secret that fascinated her, told of an incident at her father's funeral which at the time caused a considerable stir in the neighbourhood.

"At your father's funeral they had to stop a woman from coming upstairs. They had to turn her away by force. And you know what she did? She got a crowd of people outside the gate and told them that she had a child by your father. If they had let her in she would've caused confusion, she said. She came to make it a funeral people would never forget. When your grandfather went out and asked her to go away she went to the car that was waiting for her and came back with a little boy. He was the spitting image of your father."

Genetha bowed her head.

"You said you wanted to know, didn't you?" taunted Esther. "You're a big girl now. . . . You know that your father was at home in Tiger Bay? He knew every house, every rum shop. It's true. Your family wasn't ordinary. They were never happy if they weren't suffering. Admit that you like hearing about your parents, ne? You like it, don't you? Go on, admit it. You're no different from them. If you're not torturing yourself you fall sick and only get well again when you're sure that there's confusion. I've never seen people like you. To God I've never seen people like you. Your mother —"

"Don't talk about my mother, please," Genetha pleaded, afraid of any further revelations.

Esther lit another cigarette on the one she had just finished smoking and, satisfied with the revenge she had sought, fell silent.

"What did Father do around there?" enquired Genetha in an

almost inaudible voice.

"The same as all the other men," replied Esther, "the men from 'good homes', as your mother liked reminding me."

"You don't hear from Boyie?" Esther asked after a while, yielding to a feeling of pity for her erstwhile mistress's daughter.

"From time to time," Genetha lied.

"Boyie isn't like any of you."

"How do you mean?" Genetha asked, suspicious at the sudden shift in the conversation.

"He's just different, that's all . . . I bet women like him. But he won't make a woman happy. He's got the Armstrong cross. It's marked all over him. When he was a boy if anybody touched him I used to suffer, but I never showed it, because your mother didn't approve of the way I used to pet him and fondle him. She used to watch me whenever I took him on my lap and began kissing him on his neck and face. 'Put him down, Esther,' she used to say quietly; but I did know that inwardly she was boiling and wanted to scream at me."

Esther got up and went to the door.

"When's this man coming?" she said, with an irritable expression. "Did I tell you why I went back to Diamond? Yes, I told you; didn't I? I wanted to get married. I couldn't take the life here any more. . . . But there the smell of the sugar factory was the same and people were as poor as ever. My brother didn't get the dray-cart he wanted and my father still complains of his drinking. So I came back, back, back. Why do people always want to go somewhere and do something? And do this and do that? As if just living isn't enough."

As she spoke there was the blast of a horn outside. Esther took a battered suitcase filled with Genetha's few belongings out to the waiting chauffeur, then came back to fetch Genetha, who winced in the sunshine and gathered all her strength to descend the few stairs. The chauffeur glanced at them, then at his watch and no sooner were the two woman installed than the hired car shot away up the street.

Genetha closed her eyes and fought back the tears. She did not know why she wanted to cry; the sun, her weakness and the sensation of abandonment were all too much for her. Esther was about to speak, but shrugged her shoulders and said nothing when she saw her closed eyes and trembling lips. As the taxi swerved into High Street Genetha's shoulders were forced against Esther's body.

"These damned chauffeurs!" exclaimed Esther, making a grimace.

The sun streamed mercilessly into the vehicle, where Genetha leaned back on the worn leather seat. The whole street seemed to be on fire. There were a few pedestrians on the tree-lined walk between the two arms of Main Street, where flowers shuddered amid the foliage of the hundred-year flamboyant trees. The two-storeyed houses with their flying staircases slept behind closed shutters, indolent and aloof.

On opening her eyes Genetha noticed that the car was driving more slowly in the Tiger Bay area. It came to a halt in front of a low cottage, typical of those houses behind which festered a range of rooms for the desperately poor.

Esther got out, paid the chauffeur and then helped Genetha to come down. This time the man hoisted the grip on his shoulder and followed the women. He placed his burden on the lowest stair, smiled and waited to be paid. He then went off without a word.

Once in the room Esther helped Genetha off with her dress and made her lie on a bed with a thick mattress. From a chest of drawers she took out a blanket with which she covered her sick companion.

Through the single window the steely, implacable sky stared and Genetha closed her eyes to shut out the fear of the sky and the strange dim room. A few minutes later she heard Esther calling her, but pretended to be asleep.

When she awoke it was dark, and for a long while she was unable to tell where she was. The fact that the window was on the opposite wall instead of on the wall beside the bed confused her.

Suddenly she heard a man's voice; a moment later Esther appeared in the doorway and then a man, much taller than she.

"Don't make any noise. Shhh! I say. You not in a rum-shop, you know," Esther said sharply.

The bed on the other side of the room began to creak noisily.

"Well, tek it off, ne?" came the man's voice.

"God! You want everything."

"You t'ink I pay me money to —"

"Shut your mouth and get on with it," came Esther's angry voice.

80

Then there was heavy breathing, followed a few minutes later by a long drawn-out groan and then silence.

"Christ be praised!" Esther said mockingly.

After some shuffling and bumping Esther said with intense irritation, "Is what you waiting for, Christmas?"

"Well, gi' me a chance; le' me get me breath back," said the man.

Genetha saw Esther get up and pull her skirt on, while her client stood by, surveying the room.

"Is who that?" he suddenly asked, pointing at Genetha when he noticed her for the first time.

"Is my grandmother!" Esther exclaimed, beside herself with exasperation.

"You grandmoder? I din' know you was living wit' you grandmoder."

Esther sucked her teeth for a reply.

"She don' mind you carryin' on?" he ventured once more.

"Put your two dollars down and get out! I'll tell you about her another time."

"All right, all right," he said, slipping on his trousers and looking at Genetha from time to time as if he were afraid of what she might do.

When he had gone Esther lit a candle so as not to wake Genetha, and placed it on the dressing-table, where she adjusted her hair and put on fresh lipstick. Before she left she went over to see if Genetha was sleeping, then returned to the dressing-table, blew out the candle and went out again.

Genetha got up and hurried to the window, through which she could see Esther pass under the feeble lamplight and stop some distance beyond to light a cigarette. Her unusual gait gave the impression that she was walking on inordinately high shoes.

Once she had disappeared into the darkness Genetha looked more closely at what she could see of the street from the window. Opposite was a dingy little eating place, lit by bright bulbs, where two men could be seen just inside the doorway. They were engaged in an animated conversation and one of them was gesticulating violently. Next to the shop was another range-yard, wrapped in gloom. Next to that was a cottage, the porch of which was faintly lit by the street lamp. Although the area was as poor as Albouystown the latter was noisy and alive; the scene Genetha was looking at was like the section of a street leading up to a cemetery, sharing nothing with the bustling part of Tiger Bay where she had worked. It seemed to her strange that, though the men in the shop were obviously talking in a loud voice, she could hear nothing. Someone who must have been the proprietor appeared beside their table and said something to them. After that the man who had been gesticulating appeared more calm.

Genetha began to feel tired and went back to bed where she soon fell asleep.

## 12. Anandale

When Genetha was well again she began talking about looking for a job.

"Where?" Esther asked her. "When you been up to New Amsterdam people don't forget. Try getting a job without a reference; you won't get far, unless you want to sell in a cake-shop and get next to nothing."

"I can't go on living off you," Genetha protested.

"Anyway," said Esther, ignoring the younger woman's objection, "tonight we'll go out and eat somewhere nice, somewhere you'll like."

"You've got your work."

"You needn't say it like that. I've got a bank balance to show for it."

Esther jumped up, stung by what she fancied to be the derogatory tone in Genetha's voice. She drew out the lower drawer of her dressing-table, pulled a post office pass book from under a pile of clothes and opened it at the last entry, where Genetha could see the total of four hundred and fifty dollars.

"You think I'll end up like those rats at Mamus?" she asked heatedly. She was prompted to curse Genetha and her family, but restrained herself, fearing that she might only end up by driving her away.

"Anyway," she continued, "it's nothing to crow about. I could've had more if it wasn't for some money I lent a friend. I could kick myself. Men! They suck your blood. It's like an instinct with them. If I ever see him hanging round here I'll put the police on his tail before he knows what hit him."

Genetha was curious about Esther's acquaintances, but dared not ask.

Esther tried to find a way of proposing to Genetha that they should dine out with two of her men friends, but felt almost certain that she would not approve of the company she kept. If only she knew that Genetha had witnessed the love-making between her and her client the night when Genetha arrived, and the effect it had produced! Her body, drained of its energy by the bout of sickness had caught fire like a parched stubble field. The vicarious experience had left her exhausted. She had wanted to put out her hand at the departing client and ask him to lift up her petticoat and molest her and brutalize her as Fingers used to. She had wanted to drag him down on to the bed on top of her and partake in the act. When the torrent had subsided she felt ashamed and said a prayer, just as a child who, replete after a forbidden meal, allows itself the luxury of a short and silent penance.

"A friend'll be waiting for us tonight," said Esther, trying to be casual. "He might be bringing someone. You don't mind?"

"No," answered Genetha.

"He's decent. You won't mind him. A Trinidadian. They're nice, Trinidadians. Talk well. He's been to the States and all. A bit crazy, but he's got good manners. He's a gentleman. The first thing he said to me was that I'm the best spoken – well, you know what I mean – he's ever been out with. And he liked my teeth. Sometimes he says, 'Let me see your teeth,' as if I was a horse or something. I got your mother to thank for the way I talk."

"When you were with us you never talked much," observed Genetha.

"I didn't have anybody to talk with, except your mother. And you couldn't say the things you really wanted to say when you were talking to her."

"You were telling me about this Trinidadian," Genetha reminded her.

"Oh, Daley. He's a character. He always likes to see my teeth. . . . Oh, I've told you that. Let me see. Oh, yes. He says he likes ugly women. He says a lot of men like ugly women. No! It's true."

Esther burst out laughing and slapped her legs.

"He likes ugly women. So I said to him, 'You mean I'm ugly?' 'No,' he said, but I was an exception. We killed ourselves laughing. He said that ugly women drive him mad in bed. Once

83

in Trinidad – this is what he says – he had a girl friend. She was good-looking, because he couldn't *marry* an ugly girl, you see. It's just for screwing, you see. Anyway, this girl wore glasses. So one day they were climbing a hill near Port-of-Spain and he threw her down in the grass and began kissing her. Eh, eh! This girl took off her glasses and put them down in the grass. So he told her to put them on again because she drove him wild with her glasses on. And she said she hated them, so she told him. She hated them and wasn't going to put them on. But he insisted. Anyway she was stubborn about them and told him to make up his mind if he wanted to or not."

"And what happened?" Genetha asked.

"I suppose they made love in the grass with her glasses on. But I don't see how she could've enjoyed it if she hated wearing them," Esther said thoughtfully. "When you hear him talk you'll break your sides laughing, 'cause he's like that."

"What's his name?" Genetha asked.

"Daley. I told you. . . . Oh, yes. I said to him . . . what was it I said? Oh, yes, I said, 'What you really need is an ugly woman with glasses.' We killed ourselves laughing. He said he couldn't stand it, going out with an ugly woman who wore glasses."

Esther was in high spirits. She lit a cigarette and prepared to continue her monologue. Genetha's father used to say, "People don't change," but in her eyes Esther had changed. The only thing that was left of the old Esther was the capable way she organized her life and the lives of others.

"Go on, try one," she said, tending Genetha a cigarette, but the younger woman declined.

"This business is hard work," continued Esther. "But you meet some characters. Now Daley, he said I'm useless in bed . . . I was really lying when I said that he never made a pass at me. Anyway, he said I'm useless in bed. Now, if anybody else said that to me I'd be up the wall! But we laughed at it, just as we laugh at everything else. And it must be true, because all he wants to do when he's with me is talk. One day I told him that instead of talking to him I could be making money, so he pulled out a five-dollar note and gave it to me. Just like that. Well, I felt so . . . so . . . well, embarrassed! I gave it back to him; and it was the first time I was ever vexed with him. He looked at me in a funny way. . . . Another time a German sailor came back with me to my place. I wasn't living here, was I? No, it's true. I wasn't living here at the time. He had a stick with him. I mean he wasn't lame or anything. Anyway. . . ."

Esther talked on and Genetha felt that she was expected to take her into her confidence by disclosing some secret about her private life. But she was unable to make any confessions, restrained by that feeling of superiority that lingers even after a person ceases to occupy the position that, in the beginning, gave rise to it.

She looked up at Esther, who smiled; and for a moment that warmth and repose she once knew so well while still a little girl appeared in the older woman's eyes.

That night Esther and Genetha went to meet Daley in front of a club in Water Street. He was waiting with another man, whom he introduced as Cecil. Daley suggested that they should walk to the restaurant, as it was such a warm night.

At first an embarrassed silence fell on the company, but Daley then launched into an exaggerated account of his friend's prowess on the saxophone, which he played in a local band. His gestures and manner of talking soon had the two women laughing.

Cecil was just as retiring as Genetha, who found herself walking next to him. Daley had promised his friend that she would be beautiful. Her sunken cheeks revealed the unprepossessing bone-structure of her face; and the lack-lustre eyes gazed wanly beyond the company as if she were looking for someone.

Indeed, a marked change had overtaken Genetha's features. Like many people whose attractiveness appears to depend in no small degree upon how gaunt or well-covered their faces are, she had progressively lost her good looks as she grew thinner.

The eating house into which they went stood opposite the one where Rohan and Fingers had taken their first meal together. The proprietor brought the pepperpot in a deep bowl, which he placed on the table. He then went back to the kitchen and returned with four enamel plates, spoons and a bottle of cheap rum. Daley poured an excessive amount of pepper sauce on his food, partly to impress the company. Everyone agreed that the food was excellent.

Genetha declined the rum Daley had poured for her; but,

pressed by the others, she took a sip and made such a painful face that they laughed.

The sound of conversation, the reek of curry, the muted jazz from the radio and the dim lights created an atmosphere at once intimate and public. People kept coming through the open door and leaving, without attracting any attention, and occasionally a light breeze blew in a piece of paper from the pavement.

The meal and the surroundings had the effect of a heady wine on Genetha, who immersed herself in it like a swimmer in a warm sea. Even those who were sitting alone seemed to belong there, to be part of the fabric of the life of the district. Some came to be alone, others came to meet an acquaintance, while others came simply to be surrounded by people.

Esther watched Genetha obliquely. She noticed that the younger woman was sweating and kept wiping the palms of her hands. As a girl she often came to have her small hands wiped and Esther, jealous of the child's awareness of her needs, felt slighted if she went to her mother instead. She resisted the impulse to offer her a handkerchief.

During the meal Genetha felt Cecil's leg against her own, but the sense of well-being induced by the meal prevented her from doing anything. If she took her leg away she might offend him.

Towards the end of the meal a beggar came in from outside and started making the round of the tables. When the proprietor caught sight of him he shouted, "Get out!" waving a cloth after the beggar, who fled with little dignity. But a few minutes later, the proprietor having gone into the back-shop, the beggar re-appeared to complete his round. On arriving at Genetha's table, instead of putting his cap out he stood staring at her, and as she looked up at him his eyes widened.

Esther delved into her purse for a coin.

"I know you. . . . You in't shame?" he said to Genetha, his face twisted into a grimace.

He looked at Esther and at the two men in turn and crossed himself slowly, almost theatrically. Then he turned round and left without accepting Esther's money, which she was holding in her outstretched hand.

A gloom seemed to fall on the table and Esther, impatient at the silence, testily put out a half-smoked cigarette.

"I hate beggars," she said.

Daley was annoyed with the beggar for having spoiled their

meal, while Cecil, uncomfortable because he was unable to contribute much to the table conversation, felt even more ill at ease, now that everyone else at the table was.

Genetha racked her brains to remember who the stranger was. There was something familiar in his appearance, though the appalling condition of his clothes seemed to exclude all possibility of a previous acquaintance.

"Do you know him?" Cecil asked.

"Mind your own business!" Esther snapped with unusual vehemence, and both Genetha and Daley turned to look at her.

"Come on, let's go," Daley suggested.

The company got up and Daley went to the counter to pay the bill.

Outside, grey clouds had massed over the sky. The air was close and humid and the hoardings on an adjoining building site were damp.

"Rain going fall," Daley said as he joined them outside and stopped to look up at the sky.

"Le' we take a taxi," Cecil said, in an effort to placate Esther. "I going to pay."

They waited on the pavement until a taxi came into sight.

On the way to Esther's place it began to rain heavily and all along the way people were sheltering under the awnings and the overhanging sections of shop fronts. Cars flashed by without dipping their headlights, while the four stared outside at the driving rain, preoccupied with their own thoughts.

Daley and Esther began a whispered conversation in the back of the car.

Then Esther announced, "I'm going dancing with Daley. You coming?"

"No," Genetha answered.

Esther guessed that Genetha did not dance well. "You can take her home, Cecil," she urged.

"Sure," Cecil said hesitantly.

Shortly afterwards it stopped raining, though the clouds remained thick and dark. Esther leaned forward and spoke to the chauffeur. A few minutes later the car stopped somewhere in Water Street and Esther and Daley both got out by the door on the left.

"I'll see you later, Gen," Esther said.

It was the first time she had addressed her by her fond name since they had begun living together.

Cecil got out of the front seat and joined Genetha in the back.

"All the bounce gone out of Daley," he said, trying to stifle his excitement.

Genetha smiled.

"I've just been thinking," she said, "I've not been to church for weeks."

"Me neither; but I should."

"Aren't you ever afraid of the consequences?" Genetha asked earnestly.

"How d'you mean?"

"I mean what would happen to you if you didn't go?" Genetha retorted, curious as to why he had not understood her.

"Could anything happen?"

Genetha turned and watched him in the darkness. Suddenly she felt a tugging sensation in her belly. Just as she closed her eyes the car stopped in front of Esther's room.

Cecil got out and paid the driver, then went round to open the door for Genetha, who hesitated a moment before stepping from the car, which drove off, leaving the couple standing in front of the range yard.

"Good night," she said, giving Cecil her hand.

"I goin' see you in," he declared. "You never know; booboo man might get you."

He laughed and followed her, then when they were inside, said, "I don' want to give you the wrong idea, so I goin' go."

"You can stay if you want," Genetha said.

Cecil, taking her offer as an invitation to intimacy, was emboldened to take hold of her arm; but Genetha shook herself free. Cecil grabbed her and tried to kiss her forcibly, but she insisted, "No!" and freed herself once more.

"I thought . . ." he began.

"I'm sorry. I can't give myself to somebody I don't love."

"You make me look like a fool, then. I mean you ask me to stay."

She did not answer right away.

"Tch! I don't know what I want. Couldn't you just keep me company?" she asked.

"You must take me for a damn fool or something," Cecil said.

The long months of abstinence had stored in her a fiery hunger for a man's embrace, but when it came to it there was no desire to give in to this man.

"I gone," Cecil said finally, taking a step towards the door, but hoping that Genetha would change her mind.

"You're not coming back?"

"No. Unless. . . ."

"Can't you wait?" she asked. "I hardly even know you, and. . . ."

"I gone," he said, and left, closing the door behind him.

Genetha could not bear to be left alone. She put on an extra blouse and went out into the chilly night.

She found herself walking in the direction of the sea wall, past the dingy shop-fronts of Upper Water Street. Her life was in a haze, she reflected. Before, there were landmarks by which her thoughts could pause: mother, father, a steady job, Boyie, even Fingers, who had treated her like dirt. Esther was only a shadow from the past, matching in no way the memories she had of her while still a small girl. The uncertainty of the future gnawed at her inside. If her mother had been alive she might have pulled the "strings" she and her father always talked about as being indispensable in securing a job. Alone, and dogged by her confinement at the mental hospital, she felt helpless and frightened. The area she now lived in was as alien as the people she was now forced to associate with. Late at night and in the early hours of the morning there was often shouting and hammering on doors, and sometimes there was fighting among customers of the rum shops, who left at closing time, besotted with rum. It was the quarter of the damned, silent in the day-time and rowdy late at night.

Genetha approached the sea wall, which was deserted although it was no later than ten o'clock. She sat down on the wall and watched the flamboyant trees that rose from the edge of the road. The lights of Georgetown were hard and cold and the houses roused in her a fierce jealousy of those who lived in them. Couples were entertaining in their drawing-rooms or looking out of the window, and in the morning husbands would go off to work while their wives would send their children off to school and laze around or go back to bed, relying on servants to cook and do the housework. The shutters and painted wood of the palings embracing the yards spoke of security and ease.

Boyie must be living like that in the Essequibo. Why should she not write him and tell him everything? The thought came to her that he must have heard about her being put away. In a small area like the Guyana coastlands no one went to New Amsterdam without the news being bruited about even in the remote Essequibo. Boyie was unable to forgive her for her friendship with Fingers, to the point of pretending not to know of her confinement in the mental asylum. She must write and ask him if he knew. No! If he had cut her off she would not be the first to ask him to forgive her. What was Boyie's attitude to her in truth? But why was she afraid to write him or go to him? After all, he was the only person she had in the world, so that once and for all she wanted to know where she stood with him. Had she disapproved of one of his associations it would never have come to this. Her parents had always expected her to observe a higher standard of behaviour than he, to be careful about what she did and said, about the way she sat and the way she walked.

All this thinking gave her a headache. Sometimes she wanted to make love all night and perform all the depraved acts that had so often beset her erotic fantasies.

"You alone, lady?"

She looked up into the face of a young, handsome youth. Deliberately she stood up and walked away without answering.

When she arrived back at Esther's place the latter was in. Sitting on the bed in her slip she was putting varnish on her toenails.

"Thought you were with Cecil," Esther said to her.

"No, I went out alone."

"Where?"

"On the sea wall."

"Alone?"

"Why not?"

"Anything happened?"

"What?" asked Genetha, irritated at the suggestion that she might have picked up someone.

"Don't bother. There's bread on the dresser and some peas in the pot. Eat as much as you like, because I'm not hungry."

"Where're you going?" Genetha asked.

"To work."

"Can I come?"

Esther looked up at her. "No, you're not better yet. There're some American magazines on the bed."

When Esther left, Genetha lay on the bed, an open magazine by her side. Music could be heard coming from another street, the potent music of Tiger Bay where sailors, prostitutes and drifters make a festive season of every Saturday night.

Genetha lay on her bed, her hands serving as a pillow. She called to mind the asylum and the new doctor who took up his post the week after she arrived. He asked to see all the patients and soon afterwards there was a rumour that he considered many of them were perfectly sane and ought to go home. Indeed, some began leaving at the end of the month, while others, encouraged to believe that they would be sent home, waited in vain for the word.

She remembered the day she left vividly. On the ferry from New Amsterdam to Rossignol a man was performing magic. She recalled his good-naturedness and the wonder of his audience; she had felt so lonely in the midst of it all that she went aft to be on her own.

The journey from Rossignol to Georgetown she had made by bus. It was the first time she had seen the coast at close quarters, so to speak, and the swampy land and the lonely houses appealed to her. If she could raise the money she would buy a house in one of those villages: Mahaicony, perhaps, or Union or Anandale. Places with such names must be harbours, with stellings for the tired souls. Anandale, Anandale, Anannnnnn-dale. On the steps of one house, which was leaning heavily to one side, about a dozen persons were sitting, ranging in age from about two or three to about seventy; and the harmony of the group had had such a profound effect on her that she looked back and watched the house until it went out of sight behind a clump of trees.

Two women, bent double in a large field, were collecting cow dung in baskets, while a herd of cows grazed placidly on the sparse grass. Then came the coconut plantation, an endless succession of palms along the border of which ran a trench overgrown with weeds and water hyacinth. Occasionally the road came close to the sea defence wall, so that the expanse of mud and sand could be seen, broken here and there by shimmering puddles or long stretches of courida bushes. Every now and then a koker rose from the flat, featureless landscape, its sluice gate raised to let out the drainage water. This was her country, this sprawling, sea-beleagered land; the roar of the sea by night, the heat of the sun by day would follow her wherever she went, as would the trenches, the wild eddoes, the dark folk and the tamarind.

For the rest of the journey everything seemed unclear. It was only at La Bonne Intention that she was awakened from her half-dream, for there had been an accident on the Public Road. Two men were trying to right an overturned car, but Genetha looked away and stared in the direction of the sea wall. She wished that the driver of the bus, who had stopped to give the two men a hand, would get back in and drive them home. Were there not enough people to help? And was the business of the people in the bus not as urgent?

"Anandale," she thought. "I love night and the silence of night time, and the cocks flapping their wings long before dawn . . . . One day I'll go to Anandale and build a house. I'll find someone who would teach me to dance and treat me like a woman."

## 13. Veil and Gloves

Genetha felt that she was on the threshold of a new life that would overwhelm her. Too weak to struggle she saw the only possibility of escape in a confession of her plight to her maternal aunts, who would without doubt invite her to move in and share their house at Irving and Laluni Streets. But the thought of disclosing her association with Fingers, in order to explain how she lost possession of her house, and the certainty of humiliation at their hands, was intolerable.

She decided to go and see them at least once before it was too late; so one Saturday afternoon when Esther had gone out on her business – "picking fair" as she bluntly described it – Genetha put on her best frock, took care to use as little make-up as possible and walked all the way to Queenstown.

Her elder aunt, Deborah, on catching sight of her, promptly gave her a piece of her mind.

"You're anaemic. Go and see Doctor Bailey. Every Tom, Dick and Harry can eat well nowadays and you have to be anaemic. Aren't you ashamed? What're you doing? Saving money?"

Genetha had to endure a lecture on the dangers of anaemia and constipation, conditions that should never be tolerated in a decent family.

"Do you know that your grandmother went to St Rose's school? In those days you had to be somebody to go there, I can tell you. Money alone couldn't get you in. Your parents had to be somebody. She had to wear ribbed black stockings to school and gloves and a panamá hat with a veil to hide her face from men's eyes. And every week she and the other girls had to submit their boxes — with veil and gloves — for inspection by the nuns. And look at her," she declared, nodding towards the back of the house where her parents were, "she'll outlive us all. Discipline doesn't kill. When discipline goes everything else goes. . . . You'd better sit further back in the gallery, so that Mama doesn't see you in this condition when she comes out."

Genetha listened without interrupting, near the window where her mother used to sit for hours as a girl, watching the drifting clouds.

"You favour your mother so!" her younger aunt, Alice, once said, and was at once chided by her elder sister for using the word "favour" instead of "resemble", as the common people did.

No, Genetha thought, she could never come back to this house after she set off on the same road as Esther had been travelling.

They were joined by their father, Genetha's grandfather.

"Genetha! How well you look!" exclaimed the old man.

She got up and embraced him before he sat down to take part in the conversation.

"You must come more often," he said. "Things're changing so fast! You know the picture-house opposite has got a new name; and they've begun showing Indian films. East Indians used to have to go to the country to see films in Hindi. And now, just on the edge of Queenstown, you see them thronging to see a film in a language they no longer speak. Change, change, nothing but change. The other day I saw a funeral procession passing and there wasn't a carriage in sight! Even the hearse was motorized. What're things coming to when you're driven to your long home by an internal combustion engine? But some things remain the same," he added with a sigh, at the same time glancing meaningfully at his two unmarried daughters.

The older aunt, out of respect for her father, did not venture an observation, although she had strong opinions on the subject.

The old man sighed, tried to cross his legs, but failed, then

93

sighed again.

"Since I was fifty I began preparing for death," he declared. "But here I am, dragging along, witnessing all these changes round me." He sighed again and went off in a reverie. Then, without warning, without taking leave of Genetha, he got up and left the women, seemingly irritated.

"His chocolate," Deborah, whispered urgently, whereupon the younger aunt got up to prepare her father's afternoon drink.

"Have you heard from Boyie? Is he yet married?" came the inevitable question.

"He hasn't written yet, Aunt, but I don't think so. He would have written if he had – or so I imagine."

"And your job? How's your job? Are you climbing ladders?" Deborah pursued.

Genetha stammered, unable to find a ready answer. "No ladders, Aunt. I'm managing."

"No disgrace in working, especially in your circumstances. I myself started giving piano lessons. Your grandfather's pension doesn't go up, although the cost of living does . . . . But my heart's not in it. If you do intend to work you must start young."

"Nowadays most women work, Aunt," Genetha declared, as tactfully as she could.

The younger aunt came back and joined them and Genetha got the impression that she would have made some remark had she not been there.

Deborah went inside for a while, leaving her alone with Alice who, no sooner was her sister out of sight, put her hand on Genetha's arm without a word. And Genetha, touched by the gesture, had difficulty in restraining herself from confessing everything she sought to keep from them at all costs. She started groping in her handbag for a handkerchief, only to look up and see her older aunt standing before her.

"Now what's this?" Deborah asked severely. "Tears? From a working girl?"

"I'm so tired, Aunt," Genetha said.

"Go and lie down then."

"No, I have to leave now. I just dropped in for a minute," Genetha said decisively.

"As you please, child," Deborah retorted, with a slight gesture of the hand.

"Stay, Genetha, like a good girl," urged her aunt Alice.

Genetha stayed, and saw evening fall. She clung to the silence in the house and the repose of her two aunts, who were content to do nothing but sit and exchange at intervals brief remarks that might just as well have been left unsaid, but which in the gathering dusk seemed apt, like the bands of embroidery adorning their window blinds.

The potted cochineal cactus on the Demerara window ledge melted into the shadows made by the fading light, until Alice, the younger aunt, put on the gallery bulb which brought it to life again.

"He was only fifty-one," said the younger aunt.

"Heavens," came her sister's retort, "in the 'thirties many people died in their forties and fifties. People're spoiled now. Everybody wants to live on into their seventies."

Silence fell again, broken only by the noise of a moth vainly charging against a window pane.

They were in their late fifties, Genetha's two aunts, and dressed in the fashion of the early 1930s, as if time had been suspended and the clothes other women wore were the result of some collective aberration. Deborah was dressed in a bodice that gripped her neck in a vice, while Alice wore a pleated skirt of great length.

"Do you know," said the older aunt, "that there used to be a pomegranate tree in the garden before you were born?"

"And red flowers no one could identify," added Aunt Alice eagerly.

"They were blue," Deborah corrected.

"No, I'm sure they were red."

"Then there were blue ones and red ones. In the end a very knowledgeable young man came to visit your grandfather. He identified them."

"Did he?" asked the younger aunt incredulously.

Their exchange was followed by an even longer silence. In the hours she had visited, in the weeks of her stay in this house, Genetha had never once heard a quarrel. There had been a pact to banish dissent and confusion; and any threat to harmony was quashed before it could grow. Genetha recalled the violent scenes in her parents' home, all caused by her father, as she remembered. How her mother must have suffered!

Yet, she reflected, there must have been some purpose in this turbulence, for in the end the thought of living the sterile life of her aunts revolted her. Thinking of the way Fingers had revealed her own body to her always sent a warm sensation coursing through her. She recalled the slow hardening of her breasts under his palms, the heat generated by his embrace. When she became a practised lover he needed only to leave his manliness at the door of her body and her vulva engulfed it in a series of rapid contractions, so that Fingers never stopped wondering at her prowess.

"You don't know where we can find a carpenter, do you, Genetha?" asked Alice, breaking in on her reflections of a sudden.

"We can't get hold of one for love or money," added Deborah.

Genetha knew no one she could recommend and in any case the thought of a carpenter brought back distressing memories about the home of which she was robbed.

"Do you, Genetha?" asked her aunt Alice once more.

"No, Aunt, I don't."

"Never mind," she reassured her.

One of the new big buses passed by, its yellow erased by the gloom. Above New Town the first stars sprinkled the sky to the rim of the horizon.

Genetha now knew that if her older aunt had been like the younger she would have confessed that she had no decent place to live in and could not, at least for the moment, find a job; that a haven for a few months would be sufficient for her to find her feet again. But she was never certain where she was with Aunt Deborah; whether she was pleased or displeased, whether she looked down on her on account of her father, or accepted her wholeheartedly because she was the daughter of her mother. Genetha could never cut through the undergrowth of dissembling that surrounded the things this aunt said and the things she did. She now knew that it was her younger aunt who brought her back to the house with her few words and youthful smiles.

Genetha was suddenly overwhelmed with grief, as though someone close to her had died. And this readiness to weep took hold of her and fought with her until she could bear it no longer.

"I don't know," she apologized. "It's so foolish. There's no reason for it. It's so these last few days. I must be anaemic, as you say, Aunt."

She wiped her eyes, now more put out by the scrutiny of her

aunts than by her pain. From the look in their eyes they must be imagining the worst.

"You're not . . . expecting?" Deborah enquired, with panic in her eye.

"Certainly not, Aunt," Genetha said, thinking that that would be infinitely preferable.

And her aunts' eyes were unashamedly examining Genetha's belly for evidence of the disaster.

"There's no retching?" Aunt Deborah pursued, evidently unconvinced by Genetha's denial.

"Aunt, I'm not pregnant! In any case it's not possible," Genetha protested, looking her senior aunt straight in the eye.

Deborah raised her head in a non-committal gesture, but said nothing, while her sister, pained by the turn the conversation had taken, was looking at her niece sympathetically.

Genetha got up and went inside to say goodbye to her grandparents.

That night she struggled with sleep as if her life depended on it; for it seemed that the last chance of maintaining her status as a decent person lay in keeping awake. But in the end she fell asleep and dreamed of raindrops scattered in the dust, of dripping candles and soiled hands. And she stared in the candle flame as if it were impossible to look away, as if in it lay all the memories of childhood and the antidote to the condition that kept draining her will. Then she relived the night when she went out with Esther and her two friends and met the beggar with his peremptory manner and wagging finger. The paper that blew in from the pavement alighted on her table, a paper smeared with filth which the others did not seem to mind. She turned away to avoid looking at it, but Genetha's companion picked up the paper and deliberately thrust it in her face, to the amusement of everyone in the restaurant. Then her younger aunt, Alice, appeared and led her out of the eating place, away from her companions.

Occasionally Genetha awoke, but kept still so as not to embarrass Esther's clients who came and went like shadows, leaving Esther to tidy herself up and prepare for the next.

# BOOK 2

## 14. Reflection from a Hand-Mirror

Genetha lay on the floor, drunk and half-naked. The customer outside was clamouring for a Portuguese girl.

"I want a Putagee, I tell you. I gwine pay too! I gwine pay. Me pockets full of money. I got money an' money does talk, although it only whisperin' now. . . . Is who does run this place at all? Come on, I ask is who does run this place?"

Esther came out, dressed in a silk dressing-gown.

"Why're you keeping all this noise? You don't have what you want?" she asked the drunk.

"I want a Potagee an' dat in't no Potagee there," he said, pointing to Genetha on the floor.

Esther closed the door and shouted out, "Vera!"

The girl appeared almost immediately at the top of the stairs.

"Where's Irene?"

"She's got someone with her."

"You hear that?" Esther said to the drunk. "You can wait or come back another time. But whatever you do, don't come in here keeping that noise, you understand? Or we'll have to bar you from the house."

"Hey, hey, who . . .?" the drunk began.

"Bigfoot!" Esther shouted.

A few moments later a strapping man in his middle twenties came out of the room opposite the one in which Genetha was.

"Well, you don't got to get rough wit' me," the client protested. "I know me place wit' a customer like dat," he continued, nodding in Bigfoot's direction, "I can tell you."

He measured the giant from head to foot, showing his teeth in a wide grin as he did so.

"Allow me to feel them spectacular muscles, mister."

He put both hands around Bigfoot's biceps, then went towards the street door. Without warning, he shouted, "Kiss me ass!", turned tail and ran down the stairs, leaving Bigfoot and Esther staring at the door.

"Genetha's drunk again," Esther said to Bigfoot, "Since her brother died I can't get any work from her."

"But that's four months ago. You goin' keep she?" Bigfoot asked.

"Course; but I can't allow her to work. Go and take her to my room."

Bigfoot went to Genetha's room and emerged soon afterwards with her over his shoulder. He took her bodily up the stairs to Esther's room, where he placed her flat on the bed. It was a job he enjoyed doing. He had conceived an extraordinary respect for her and might even have fallen in love with her if he were not convinced that she was above his station in life. The fact that she was a prostitute now seemed to make little difference to him.

Bigfoot was undemonstrative, but Genetha sensed his interest and treated him with deference.

There were five girls in the establishment. Besides Vera and Irene there were Salome, Shola and Netta, the last two being new arrivals from the country. Both Shola, who came from a village on the East Bank, Berbice, and Netta, who was from Wismar, were much sought after by the clients for their fresh, innocent appearance.

From the very beginning Esther was firm with the girls and they respected her for it. Should one of them infringe the rules of the house she was to be warned once, while the second occasion meant the door. But the condition of service that attracted the girls was the one which provided them with a bonus of two hundred dollars if they decided to leave Esther's employment, provided they had worked with her for at least two years. She was the first to admit that at the end of two years she would have made a good deal of money out of them. The condition guaranteed the girls' loyalty and clients liked to know that if they went away and came back again they were likely to find the same girls working for her. Esther gave them seventy-five cents for every client they entertained, keeping four dollars and twenty-five cents for herself. She made a handsome profit on each girl after paying rent for the house, feeding them, putting aside a cut for the police and defraying other expenses. She herself did the cooking and ran up dresses for the girls on her Pfaff foot-machine.

In fact, only half of the profit belonged to Esther, for she had been set up in business by a man who lived abroad and had established a number of such houses in other parts of the world. This one had been going for two years. Esther had bought the house in her name, as a nominee of the stranger, who had been impressed by her the night they met at a party in Tiger Bay. When he found out that she had seventeen hundred dollars of her own he did not hesitate to put the proposition to her. She saw it as a chance of a lifetime and set to work to make the concern a profitable one.

She was now worried by Genetha's inability to work, for any reduction in the profits would make a bad impression on her employer. Boyie's death had come at the worst possible moment, when Genetha was at last finding her feet in the profession. After a bad beginning, when her unco-operative attitude had led to violent quarrels between them, Genetha gradually became accustomed to the company Esther was keeping. But it was Esther's disinclination to threaten her that finally brought Genetha round. However badly they quarrelled Esther fed her as before and gave her money.

At first Genetha chose one young man to sleep with, and thereby prompted Esther's taunts about making a fortune with one client. When, eventually, she tried a second, she complained that it was physically impossible for her to satisfy two men on the same day.

"Then thousands of women throughout the world are performing the physically impossible every day, eh?" Esther rejoined.

Esther taught her how to manipulate the men and showed her the tricks of the profession and, in time, she was able to work as the other women did.

Just before Rohan's death Esther had come home to hear her singing a song to the accompaniment of music from the radio. The next day, the news of his death was published in the newspapers and since then she spent most of the day listening to the radio and drinking cheap wine. Esther had left her alone, in the hope that she would snap out of her condition and begin working again.

"You know you costing me over twenty-five dollars a day," Esther told her.

"You're lying," Genetha retorted. "You're lying, Esther. There you go, lying again."

"I'm not lying, you little idiot. If it wasn't for me you'd really be on the road, picking up men at the corner for fifty cents."

"Leave me alone. You've changed. You're coarse and you think of nothing but money all the time."

"I was always coarse —" said Esther.

"When we were in Agricola you weren't coarse," Genetha interrupted her.

"I was coarse in Agricola when your mother wasn't looking, I can tell you. And your father was coarse when your mother wasn't looking, too. And I bet your mother was coarse when no one was looking. Huh!"

"You see how coarse you are, Esther. I've just been telling you so and you go and prove it to me."

Esther stalked off in a rage, leaving Genetha with her wine and her radio.

She decided to take on another girl and give Genetha a couple of weeks to leave. When, however, two days later, an applicant presented herself, Esther found all sorts of objections to hiring the girl. She was sickly; she lacked experience; she looked like the type who would attract trouble from clients. Bigfoot thought that the girl was attractive and men would like her, but Esther told him to mind his own business. In fact, he had no idea that the girl was to replace Genetha.

Esther sent her away and at the same time gave orders that Genetha was to have no food or drink. At midday, when everyone sat down at the big table to eat, no one called Genetha, who was sleeping. In the middle of the meal she appeared at the door of the dining-room and there was a sudden hush as the others became aware of her presence. Esther, who hesitated momentarily, continued eating, pretending not to notice Genetha, until finally, unable to contain her anger any longer, she exploded.

"What's happened at all? You all gone dumb?" Then, turning towards Genetha she asked: "Who the hell invited you anyway?"

Genetha turned away and went back to her room.

The girls, resentful of Genetha's independence, were glad that Esther was standing no more nonsense from her, though their silence was interpreted by Esther as support for Genetha.

After a while the company began talking and laughing again and Esther made a show of enjoying herself, determined not to give in on this occasion. Rohan's death had shaken her as well, but the last years had drained her of all sentimentality. Life had to go on. Genetha could have begun to work, if only out of gratitude.

That evening Genetha went to Esther and asked her if she

was to have anything to eat.

"If you work, yes. If you don't work you can go to hell," came Esther's reply.

There were deep, indelible rings around Genetha's eyes, and the furrows in her face appeared more pronounced than ever.

"I'm not begging, you know," said Genetha, "I'm just asking."

"I don't care what you're doing. You're not eating unless you work."

"Can I have a bottle of wine?"

"No."

"I won't beg you. I won't lower myself to beg you!" exclaimed Genetha.

Esther looked up from the table in the drawing-room, pretending to be amused. Genetha went to the chair by the window, which overlooked South Road and Croal Street, divided by a wide trench. As it was getting dark Esther turned on the light and then went back to sit at her table.

"Money is everything to you, isn't it?" Genetha suddenly asked Esther.

"You'll soon find out if it's not everything," declared Esther, maintaining her show of indifference.

"No, but it's everything to you, isn't it?"

"Yes, you —" replied Esther losing her composure. "And if your sweet man didn't rob you, would you be waiting now for me to put bread in your mouth?"

"You're right, you know. Money is everything," said Genetha.

"You needn't be sarcastic. It's your parents that taught me that first. I worked my fingers to the bone for your mother and she kicked me out. Then I realized how important money was. More important than loyalty and trust and such . . . . When people like your mother talk about loyalty and trust they meant my loyalty and my trust, not theirs. It's she, when all is said and done, who taught me to sell my body for sixpence on the race course. You remember how people used to say what a good Christian woman your mother was and how your father didn't deserve her? And she did give you the same education she got herself, that makes you hate housework. I mean, did you learn from anybody how to satisfy a man in bed? You just lie down like a piece of wood . . . ."

"You know," said Genetha, "when you talk like that it goes

through one ear and comes out of the other. I've heard it so often before."

Esther went inside and came back with a hand mirror, which she held under Genetha's nose.

"I don't want to look," declared Genetha, turning away abruptly, "I don't care. In any case I'm too ugly to be vain."

These last words touched Esther, who put the mirror down on the table.

"You're going to work?" she asked Genetha.

"No!" she exclaimed with violence. "I'm going to join the Catholic Church so that I can confess to someone. These Methodists don't do anything except sing and pray. I don't like singing anymore. Things die, just like people."

Esther took up her newspaper and continued to read, for she had already relented, but did not want to appear soft in the younger woman's eyes.

"You know," she said, without looking up from her paper, "if you worked we could have good times together."

There was no answer for a while and then, as if giving expression to an afterthought, Genetha declared:

"I notice that you don't work since you got this place."

How exasperating she could be, this blasted woman, Esther thought. When she recalled the years of hard work, the foul men she had to put up with, the back streets and alleyways she frequented, the encounters with the police, the constant fear of disease or being assaulted by a client. The ignorant fool!

"No, I'm the boss now, you see," Esther answered in a measured voice.

From one of the rooms came the voice of a man singing the tune "Trees" with improvised words:

"And when I'm feeling very dry
I point my cock up to the skyyyyyyyyyy;
And if it then begins to rain
I put it ba-a-ack againnnnnnnnnnnn,
Poeeeeeems are maaaade by fools like me,
But only Gooooood can make a tree."

When he emerged, followed by Netta, Esther could not conceal her irritation. She had secretly hankered after an establishment of a higher tone and was disappointed that the clientele was similar to the one she had while she was still practising. The well-maintained exterior of the house, the painted jalousies and

103

chintz blinds had failed to attract the select types who would pay more, speak quietly and occasionally come to play dominoes or bridge in the back room. The refuge away from their wives turned out to be a convenient drop-in, like a dog's favourite tree.

"You sing loud like that and the police'll close the place, you understand! Just keep your voice down in future," she said peremptorily.

When he reached the foot of the stairs Netta burst out:

"He smell o' fish! Next time tell him I out."

She then handed over her money and Esther opened a canister with a key she kept round her neck. Having placed the notes inside and locked it she put the canister back into the desk drawer.

A few minutes later Shola saw off her client, a well-groomed middle-aged man, who kept his lips pursed so as to conceal his embarrassment. She, too, handed over her money to Esther, who secreted it in the canister as before, leaving the change on the table.

Bigfoot, who had been sitting on the veranda, came in and whispered something in Esther's ear. She got up and disappeared with him through the front door.

"You in' working today, Genetha?" Shola asked, taking advantage of Esther's absence to pick a row.

"No."

"Why? You too great?"

"Yes," replied Genetha.

Shola said something to Netta and the two girls burst out laughing.

Genetha got up and went over to Shola, asking her: "You've got any wine?"

Shola placed her right hand on her chest and said:

"I don' drink, I don' smoke an' I don' talk to strange men."

Shola and Netta exploded in fits of laughter, at the same time hugging each other for support.

"You in' a lil old for this work?" Netta ventured. She herself was only seventeen.

Genetha went back to her seat.

"You're young, with soft skin and dimples," said Genetha, "but it'll all go, and then you'll find yourself alone, just when you need someone more than ever."

"Is what she talking 'bout?" Shola asked, turning to Netta,

who shrugged her shoulders.

"I had my first experience with a man . . ." Genetha began.

"That must a been twenty years ago," Netta interrupted her, in an attempt to make Shola laugh.

But Esther came back into the room and all laughter was stifled.

"Go and warm something up for her," she ordered, nodding towards Netta.

"She goin' eat?" the girl asked naively.

"Yes, 'she goin' eat'," Esther mimicked her.

Netta went inside, wearing a surly expression.

"You'd better come over," Esther beckoned to Genetha, who got up, went over to the table and sat down opposite Esther.

"Bring the Correia wine," Esther ordered Shola, who went off unwillingly and came back a few moments later with the bottle of cheap wine. The girl was still in her slip and her full breasts danced about, threatening to burst out of their confinement with every step she made.

"The trial's beginning tomorrow," Esther told Genetha.

"Which trial?"

"The Ali chap . . . about Boyie's death."

"Oh."

Genetha took a mouthful of the wine Esther had poured out for her and when Netta brought in the food she fell on it like a dog fed only on rice for months.

Vera came downstairs and looked in disapprovingly. She was dressed to kill. Pulling up her dress slightly she sat down at the head of the table.

"Look who coming! Is Teeth!" Vera warned the girls, as she saw Teeth's head bobbing up through the window.

Teeth, a man in his thirties with an array of gold teeth, was the establishment's most mysterious client. He was always impeccably dressed, had excellent manners, but managed to give the impression of the utmost severity behind the façade of concern and attentiveness. The girls were afraid of him and complained that he was brutal in bed, so that there arose a tacit agreement that they should take it in turns to entertain him.

"Is Irene turn," Shola whispered.

"Get her quick," Netta urged, nodding in the direction of the stairs.

Shola came back with Irene, who welcomed Teeth with a

broad smile and shepherded him upstairs to her room.

"At least he don' beat about the bush like some of the rest," Netta said.

Indeed, less than fifteen minutes later, Teeth reappeared at the top of the stairs with that superior manner which might have misled strangers into thinking that he owned the place. As he left he bowed slightly and went out through the front door.

"You got the itch or what?" Esther asked Vera, who sat fidgeting at the head of the table. "Why don't you go for a walk and get it over with?"

Vera had been going to the window at frequent intervals as if she were expecting somebody. At Esther's suggestion she sprang up and went out through the front door. She was going "to take a little air", she said.

And so the girls spent the days and nights, unable to leave the house except with Esther's express permission. The money that came into their hands was just enough to keep them in clothes, make-up and cigarettes.

In proportion as the money came and a regular clientele was built up, so Esther became stricter. She came to discover a severity in herself that was never apparent before. The girls grew to fear her and began whispering among themselves that she needed a man. Salome had already made up her mind to leave with her two hundred dollars when her two years were up.

One morning at about two o'clock the girls were awakened by screaming and the sound of breaking glass. From the top of the staircase they saw Bigfoot belabouring Shola with a strap while Esther stood looking on a few paces away. At a signal from her Bigfoot stopped and Shola was ordered to her room.

The next day Bigfoot told the girls that Shola was caught trying to open Esther's canister, in which the girls' earnings were kept. Then a pall fell on the house. But within a few days the girls had recovered their gaiety and the incident was forgotten. They needed only to be careful, to abide by the rules and to keep in Bigfoot's good books, and all would be well.

In time, too, the girls accepted Genetha's special status as hanger-on. Indeed, she did work from time to time, when the spirit moved her. And despite the state of continual warfare that existed between her and Esther they recognized the peculiar relationship that seemed to bind them together.

# 15. Sunday in the Red House

It was Sunday evening. Some of the girls were sitting at the windows and on the veranda. The street lamps had just gone on and the church bells of St Andrews were ringing to remind the faithful of evening service. From the house could be seen the shadowy figures of people hanging about the Law Courts. The men kept away on Sundays, either as a form of tribute to their conscience or because they were immobilized by the general apathy that infected everyone on the Lord's day. The empty street of day-time had given way to the empty street of night-time where, occasionally, a car rolled past, filled with young people who were bent, no doubt, on defying convention by enjoying themselves. The rum-shop at the corner, a source of loud music on weekdays, was curiously quiet.

The girls sat, enveloped in a complicity of silence, weaving their own thoughts. Shola was recalling the village she came from, while Netta reflected on her neglect of the Bible. Her mother would never forgive her if she knew what she was doing. In her letters home she wrote that she was getting on well with her typing and English.

Vera had caught sight of the young man whom she had once invited in when no one else was there. He was lurking in the shadows of a nearby house.

"He's too young," she thought, "I going have to brush him off."

Irene was not thinking anything, or rather she was incapable of dwelling on any one subject sufficiently long to be certain of what she had been thinking.

Esther was the only one in the house to remain in her room, lying on her bed, mentally revising the accounts she had made up that day. Salome was not well and would not be working for a few days. The doctor had repeatedly warned her against leading the "life", but Esther was leaving the decision to her, with the remark that she was old enough to make up her mind. Esther's partner, in his last letter, had written sarcastically about the profit the establishment was making, reminding her that none of the girls was indispensable. What would he say if he knew about Genetha? she thought.

"To hell with him," she said to herself, but could not dismiss the nagging anxieties. She was looking forward to his next visit to the country and would have it out with him, though there was no doubt that Genetha would have to pull her weight.

One of the clients had offered Bigfoot a job with higher wages than she paid him. She was especially reluctant to let him go for he could turn his hand to nearly every type of repair.

There was a knock on the door.

"It's who?" she asked irritably.

"Me, Vera."

"Come in, ne?"

Vera came in. "I want to go out for ten minutes," she told Esther, avoiding her eyes.

"Where?"

"It's private."

Esther waved her consent and as the girl turned to go she looked at her suspiciously.

Vera went up to the youth who had been hoping she would come out. He seemed less good-looking than she remembered, and very thin.

"Is what you want?" she asked.

On seeing her coming down the stairs he had felt the excitement welling up in him and imagined that they would just walk off to another part of town where they would be able to be alone.

"You coming for a walk?" he asked her.

"No!" she replied.

"Why?"

"What you come hanging 'bout the house for?" she demanded. "You want to get me in trouble? You can't just come an' wait. . . ."

"How else I could see you again?"

"Who said I want to see you again?" she asked him, emphasizing the first word cruelly.

Her irritation puzzled the youth, who could not believe that she had dressed up to tell him that she did not want to see him again.

"Well, if you don' want to —" he began saying, only to be interrupted without ceremony.

"No, I don' want to." Thereupon she turned away brusquely and went back to the house.

"You got typee, girl," Shola teased, as Vera came through the door.

"If looks could kill," Netta said, noticing the way Vera looked at her friend.

Shola and Netta watched the youth disappearing up the road, in the direction of the Law Courts.

The service had begun in St Andrews and the congregation were singing "For those in peril on the sea". Two women in their Sunday best were hurrying down the road towards the church.

When a client pushed the gate open the girls cursed him inwardly and Shola withdrew from the window, while Netta got up and went inside.

"Esther!" Shola called out.

Esther came out to see the man, who was standing by the big table, arms akimbo. After a short conversation with him she pointed to Shola, who looked up to the roof in exasperation, but got up and went to her room, followed by the client.

Esther went out on the porch and asked Genetha to come inside. The two women sat down at the table.

"You got to work like the other girls, starting tonight if we get sufficient people, you understand?"

Genetha did not reply.

The next morning Genetha's grip stood by the front door. She sat with the others, eating her breakfast, and they looked at her furtively. Esther, conspicuously absent from the table, was sewing on her machine, and when there was a knock on the door she knew what it was for.

Esther went to say goodbye to Genetha, who was standing next to Bigfoot. He took up her grip and carried it to the waiting taxi.

"Is where she going?" asked Netta, to which Shola sucked her teeth and said, "Is why you always asking such stupidness? 'Is where she going'! "

"I wonder where she going to go?" Vera asked in turn, to spite Shola for the remark she made the previous evening after she had seen the youth.

"I in' know," replied Netta, "probably to family. I hear she got family."

They all watched the taxi drive off, and Bigfoot standing on the bridge long after the vehicle had left, his gaze fixed in the distance. The girls avoided him for the rest of that day.

Their attention turned to Genetha's replacement. Would she be tall, short, ugly? Anyone would be an improvement on Genetha, one of them observed, a remark with which they all agreed.

Shola wanted her room, and since no one else dared object the matter seemed to be settled. Apart from Esther, Genetha was the only one who had had a room to herself. Shola went at once to see Esther who had no hesitation in agreeing.

Not concealing her delight, Shola set about transferring her things at once. From now on she could furnish her quarters as she wanted, read as late as she liked, choose her own radio programmes without the eternal wrangling with Netta.

Netta kept looking at the door of Shola's new room, and seeing this Vera nudged Irene, who nodded and smiled. The others did not fail to notice Netta's interest either.

"You looking for something?" Salome asked.

"What?" Netta replied absentmindedly.

"You loss something?" the young woman repeated, with a vindictive smile on her lips.

"Oh, lef' me alone!" she burst out. "Mind you own kiss-me-ass business, you whore."

"Who you calling a whore?" Salome asked, jumping up from her seat.

"You!" declared Netta defiantly.

Salome sprang at her and the two women rolled on the ground, scratching and slapping each other. Salome, tall and strapping, had no difficulty in overcoming the younger women, while Netta, hands pinned to the ground, burst into tears and showed no more resistance.

"All right, all right," Salome said, consoling her opponent, "take a cigarette. She got her own room, but that don't mean she going stop being friends with you."

Salome got up, reached for her packet from the window ledge where she had left it, and gave a cigarette to Netta, who took it with an unsteady hand.

The new girl came two days later. She was from Wakenaam, but had been in Georgetown for two years. Her aunt, with whom she had been living, had just died and rather than go back home to Wakenaam she tried working as a waitress in a restaurant. But she was unable to earn enough money to keep herself, so she supplemented her income by going out with

110

customers who bought her things. Esther persuaded her that she could earn more living in her establishment, and would not need to pay for food or lodging. If she did not like it she could always leave.

All the girls watched her from head to foot when she stood in the doorway, holding her ancient grip in her right hand.

"Madame dere?" she asked in her Essequibo lilt.

"Esther!" Shola shouted out, not bothering to greet the girl.

"Girl, you must've been born shouting," Esther said to Shola as she came from the kitchen.

The new girl's face beamed when she caught sight of Esther and she put her grip down on the floor.

"Netta, show her to upstairs, ne?" Then, to the girl she smiled and said, "You can then come out and get to know the girls."

"Is where she come from?" Vera remarked. "Look at them clothes!" She opened her eyes wide in feigned astonishment.

"You just jealous," Salome joked. "Wait till Esther fit she out, she going take all you men away. You hear what I telling you."

"Her name is Clem," Esther told the girls. "Try and be nice; she's from the country."

"You don't say!" Shola mocked. "And we din' even guess!"

Esther tried to get the girls on her side.

"You remind me of my father," she said. "He was always making fun of people. Once when somebody asked him why he painted his house with ordinary paint, but painted the latrine with whitewash he said, 'Well, the latrine's almost as big as the house and so that people would know which is which I paint the house and whitewash the latrine.' "

The girls laughed. She promised chocolates after lunch, but as soon as she went back to the kitchen they began running down the girl again.

Once in the kitchen Esther brooded over Genetha's going away and the emptiness which was bound to follow her absence. She detested Shola, not for her thieving habits, nor for the hold she had over the other girls, nor even for her impudence; she hated her because she had never shown Genetha the deference she deserved. Now that Genetha had finally gone she harboured a deep feeling of vengeance in regard to Shola and on that account decided that she would forbid the girls to call Genetha's name in the house.

# 16. Zara

Genetha once more hired a room in a hovel in Albouystown and immediately looked around for work as a waitress. Her speech made an impression and she was taken on in a dive near the Stabroek Market, but her wages were too low to live on, so she decided to get another job. She was paid a dollar a week more and had to work four hours a day longer. At nights she could only wash and go straight to bed where, exhausted, she fell asleep at once.

One Saturday night she went to the pictures and hardly fifteen minutes of film had gone when she dozed off and slept all through the show. She found a peculiar satisfaction in this lonely existence, for her soul was her own at least.

Another evening when she was passing the Brickdam Church she felt an urge to go in and sit in a pew, and on an impulse she took her place behind a line of women who were waiting to confess to the priest. It was not uncommon for people to change their religion. Indeed some belonged to two faiths, practising one in the day and the other at night.

When her turn came she sat in the cubicle and waited.

"I'm not a Catholic," Genetha began, and waited for the effect of her words.

"Why have you come then, my child?" the priest asked with exaggerated indulgence.

Genetha hesitated. She could not answer, in fact.

"Well, why did you come, my child?"

"I don't know . . . . I don't go to church any more. But I feel that something's gone out of my life."

"Do you then want to become a Catholic?" enquired the priest.

"I don't know, Father."

"Well, go on, my child," said the priest softly.

Genetha started to tell him of the life she had been leading and of her need for forgiveness.

"God is generous, my child. He bears no grudge. What God and the Church are interested in is the kind of life you're leading now. Do you think you have the courage to face your new existence and the character to resist the temptation to return to your old ways?"

"It was not temptation that led me into it, Father," she said, suddenly irritated. "I was sick."

112

"These are excuses, my child. Christ suffered on the cross to redeem our sins. You could not suffer a few weeks of hunger. Besides, you spoke of relations. Couldn't you have seen them and asked them to take you in?"

"It was pride, Father," Genetha declared, suppressing her mounting annoyance.

He uttered an exclamation and said harshly, but quietly, "There is no pride in the true Christian, my child. Look what your pride has done for you! You have sold your body and soiled your soul. Do you think that your pride was worth it?"

Genetha bowed her head.

"What will you do now?" pursued the priest.

"I'm working, Father."

"Come to see me whenever you can, my child," said the priest. "And think of what I said about joining the Catholic Church."

Genetha left the cubicle and went to sit in one of the pews. Throughout the building were scattered figures in various poses of meditation, mostly old women. The fiery candles hypnotized her. They seemed to have a significance that was important to unravel and burned with a steady flame that occasionally swayed like the muslin cloth of a Chinese dancer. From time to time an old woman would take a new candle and light it with the flame of another after depositing a coin in the collection box. People were continually entering and leaving the church, taking care to make their genuflections and signs of the cross. Genetha resolved to come to church whenever she could.

The sense of peace the visit gave her lasted until the following day, when the demands of work cancelled its effect.

Genetha became friendly with a young workmate named Zara, who invited her home. The girl lived beyond the trench and after putting off the visit for a few weeks she finally went.

She worked to support her parents, who lived on her father's meagre pension. The tiny drawing-room was dominated by a large picture of Christ wearing a crown of thorns and exposing his bleeding heart. Zara's brother sat in a corner of the dining-room, eating a plate of rice and salt fish, but Zara did not think it necessary to introduce Genetha to him.

Zara would have invited Genetha long ago, but felt ashamed of her home. However, when Genetha invited her friend in turn

113

to her room, Zara thought rather less of her, and from then on she became more communicative and started to confide in Genetha. Her brother had spent six months in prison. He used to go out at night and come home early in the morning, and when his father demanded to know where he had been he would reply, "Nowhere." Her parents did not bother any more and the young man was allowed to go and come as he wished.

Zara, as she and Genetha drew closer to each other, turned out to be quite different from the person her friend had imagined her to be. On warm nights they used to go walking up the East Bank as far as Meadowbank, exchanging in their long conversations their ambitions and anxieties, and it was on these walks that Genetha discovered that Zara's apparent self-confidence masked a surprising vulnerability. She confided that she was afraid of going out with boys because she did not know what was expected of her. When she was eighteen, a year ago, she went out with a young man with whom she had fallen in love. At night she waited for his knock with an expectancy that was physically oppressive. When, however, he began making demands on her, she took fright and broke off. Genetha found out later that the young man lived in Meadowbank. The mere sight of his house, the blue door, the broken jalousie, the porch and stairs filled her with vague yearnings.

Zara complained that Genetha never told her much about herself, except that her people were dead; but Genetha objected that her past was painful and she hated recalling her family, with whom she had been close.

"Everybody's close to their people," remarked Zara once.

"But mine are dead!"

Zara explained how she and her brother wanted to give their parents a comfortable old age and how difficult it was.

Genetha tried to teach Zara shorthand, but her English was so poor that she gave up. Besides, Zara had no ambition to improve her situation.

Once the two friends went to a fair at the Chinese Cricket Club. Having spent their shillings in the first few minutes they wandered round the ground watching others ride on the merry-go-round or lose their money on the gambling games. When they were tired they sat down on the grass, closed their eyes and listened to the shouting and the music that came from the pavilion, where couples were dancing to a quartet. The coloured lights shook with the flailing bodies and made swiftly changing patterns in the dark. The wooden horses of the round-about rose and sank like porpoises in a calm sea, presenting their expressionless faces with every revolution. It was one of those rich nights that tell the gentle hours beneath a profusion of stars, when humans catch a fleeting glimpse of a redemption beyond their grasp.

Genetha took her young friend's hand and held it while she watched the fair. Soon they began to recognize people they had seen earlier, who had made a tour and, unwilling to leave, were making a second round of the fairground. Snatches of conversation came down to them.

"Every time he throw up and he still going 'pon the round-about." Or "Is what Nancy doing? She hanging 'bout that dance hall and she know she kian' pay to get in."

Two young women sat down near to them and one began talking about her mother whom she never succeeded in pleasing, and then about her husband who spent a large amount on gambling on horse races run abroad.

"Everything is horses, horses, horses. Yesterday I say to he, 'I don' know why you didn' get married to a horse'!"

Both Genetha and Zara listened intently, to save up stories to giggle at when there were together.

Others, tired from the incessant walking and standing around, sat down on the grass as well, couples, groups of boys and individuals. The boys seemed more curious than others as to what was going on around them and spent their time devouring with their eyes every young woman who passed by.

Momentarily, a threatening cloud passed overhead, but it was soon gone and the stars re-emerged, as bright and splendid as ever. A number of people were now gathered round the dance hall and at the end of a piece clapped to show their approval. The vendors and those in charge of the gambling stalls had ceased shouting, while the roundabout was now carrying only half its complement of passengers. Genetha and Zara got up and went over to the dance hall, pushing their way through the four-deep crowd until they stood against the railing.

"Genetha!" someone called.

She looked round and saw a man gesticulating in her direction. It was Daley, the young man to whom Esther had introduced her some time before. He was in the company of

115

another man and was pushing his way towards her.

Genetha took Zara's hand and thrust herself through the crowd in the opposite direction.

"Is what? You know him?" Zara asked.

Genetha, without answering, shoved and nudged her way through the crowd and, once free, she ran across the field with her friend in tow.

"Stop, Gen, I out of breath," Zara pleaded.

But Genetha kept on running and only stopped when they reached the gate. She leaned against it for a few seconds to catch her breath. On looking back she could see no sign of Daley.

"Let's go," she said to Zara.

"He's still coming?"

"I don't know," Genetha replied.

The two set off down the road at a brisk pace, only slowing down on reaching Regent Street.

Zara wanted to stop and buy a mauby to slake her thirst, but Genetha insisted that they should go on, upon which the younger woman became annoyed and stopped in the middle of the pavement. She refused to continue unless Genetha told her what they were running from.

"It's an old friend, if you want to know. My brother used to know him, but I don't like him. You satisfied now?"

"You should've say so," Zara said, content with Genetha's explanation.

They walked on without talking.

"Why you don't talk?" Zara asked.

But Genetha answered nothing.

## 17. White Corners

It was late December and the big stores in Water Street were overflowing with people buying presents or admiring what they could not afford to buy. Everywhere in the town the sound of carol-singing came from houses, creating the mood that justified a name for the time of year. It was now less a religious festival than an excuse to dance, to eat and drink excessively. Bottles of sorrel, fly and ginger-beer ripened in cupboards and under beds, to be opened on Christmas Eve or offered to acquaintances who dropped in during the season. Rich, black Christmas cake, jealously guarded until the festive lunch, appeared on the

116

dining-table in plates with gilded rims, while a leg of York ham spiked with cloves was served at night and strictly rationed until the New Year, to prolong the nostalgia of the succulent fare of Christmas Day.

Genetha looked in the mirror and saw the white corners of her mouth, the unmistakable signs of malnutrition. She and Zara had decided to attend one of the public dances, impelled by a desire to take part in the general merry-making. Zara, thin and haggard-looking, and Genetha, her white corners clearly visible, looked like candidates for a "before" advertisement of a fattening diet. There is an indomitable streak in human nature, which permits vanity to grow in the meanest of soils.

Both girls were working on Christmas Eve until midnight, but they planned to go home to Zara's and ask her parents for permission to go out again. Genetha thought that it was a better idea to ask a few days before, but Zara knew her parents. They would agree and change their minds afterwards. Whenever they had a chance the girls talked of the dance that night, Genetha confessing that she had already laid out her dress on the bed at home. She would wear a flower in her hair and her silver earrings. Zara had bought a new pair of shoes with a decorative buckle at the front.

By midday Genetha was already tired and had to exchange her breakfast hour with Zara, who should have eaten first. When the proprietor was not looking she took a piece of mutton out of the pot and put it on her plate, which was filled with rice and sauce. She ate the meat quickly and then proceeded to consume the rest of the food at a more leisurely pace. Of late, she had experienced difficulty in focusing and objects often appeared blurred.

"Oh, to hell with it," she thought, "tonight I'll dance my legs off."

Zara was primed for any adventure. If only a man knew how to handle her he could have his way with her that night.

At midnight the two women left the restaurant arm in arm. They turned into Princess Street by the timber yards, then right into Russell Street, crossing the Sussex Street trench with its stagnant water. The dances had long begun and no sooner had they left the music of one dance hall behind than the strains of a pick-up came to them from a private party. They quickened their steps until they reached the back streets of Albouystown.

117

The door of Zara's house was unlocked and she pushed it, followed by her friend. She lit the kerosene lamp, placed it on the little table, hesitated for a moment and then went over to her mother, who was lying on a low bed beside her husband. It had slipped her mind that she would have to wake her parents in order to speak to them about the dance.

"Is you, Zara? Is what?" her mother asked, turning over to look at her.

"Is me," her daughter answered. "I want to go to a dance."

"A what?"

"A dance," Zara said, summoning up all her patience.

"You mad?"

Zara's mother, about fifteen years younger than her husband, shook the sleeping form.

"Is your daughter. She want to go to a dance. She crazy."

"She crazy!" he echoed, then turned his back to the wall and began to snore almost immediately.

"You big old fool!" Zara shouted, stamping her feet.

The snoring stopped abruptly.

"Is what she say?" he asked his wife.

"She call you a big old fool," his wife declared, repeating the invective with unconcealed satisfaction.

He got up, climbed over his fat wife and, taking no notice of Genetha, cuffed his daughter on the side of her head. Thereupon he climbed back over his fat wife and lay down again. In a few moments he was snoring more loudly than ever.

Zara's mother turned her head away from her daughter, who stood motionless next to her friend. She was consumed with chagrin and humiliation. Her brother was out, enjoying himself, caring little about anyone's feelings and she, concerned to please them, could not once in a year go out and do what everyone else was doing. When Zara's anger subsided she looked up at Genetha and raised her head apologetically.

"You couldn't help it," Genetha said, in an effort to console her.

"What you going do?"

"Go home."

"At this time?" asked Zara.

"I've got to."

"Sleep here, ne?"

Genetha was tempted to accept the invitation, but was not

118

certain that Zara's parents would have approved.

"No, I gone."

Zara stood in the doorway and saw her walk away into the darkness.

Back in the street alone, Genetha was afraid of every shadow and every rustling, and, turning back incessantly, she kept to the middle of the road. She pushed her own door and, without bothering to take off her clothes, fell on the bed, fatigued and disappointed. Her body was aching so badly she felt like vomiting, and the thought came to her that the disappointment was a deliverance. No one could have danced in that condition.

She got up and went to the mirror to examine the whites at the corners of her mouth, which were more pronounced than ever. Dismayed, she took off her shoes and went back to bed. Here in Albouystown the sound of Christmas seemed to have been banished to less forlorn quarters. An almost irresistible urge to pass by Esther's establishment seized her, for she imagined the girls dancing in fancy dress, wearing masks and coloured paper hats. At least Zara had a home, she thought, where she could talk to someone and even quarrel.

Genetha fell asleep suddenly, like a candle blown out by a gust of wind.

When she was off on the same day as Zara, Genetha was in the habit of going to her home after finishing her washing and other household work. One night Zara's brother came in, swaying unsteadily. His father looked at him suspiciously. The youth, who hardly ever looked Genetha straight in the eye, offered to take her out for a drink.

"Thanks, I don't drink," she said.

He flung his head back and laughed.

"Don't tell me that! That's for them," he said, indicating with a sweeping gesture the others. "I know all 'bout you," he sneered. He then sat down on a chair in the corner of the room and fell into a surly silence.

In the end he got up and demanded of his mother, "Any food?"

She pointed to the enamel plate on the table.

"That's all?" he asked.

"When last you bring money in the house?" his father asked the youth, who did not answer.

He ate his food quickly and left, slamming the door.

Everyone was relieved. Zara's mother, who was in the habit of saying to Genetha, "We's decent people. Is only that we in' got education," went in dread of her son behaving in such as way as to prove that they were not decent people. They were Portuguese, their grandparents having come from Madeira to work on the sugar estates as indentured labourers. They had tried hard to give their children a good education, but both had got into bad company, which ruined their chances at school. Besides, their teachers had had no particular liking for them. All this both parents firmly believed.

Genetha was waiting for an opportunity to leave and when she announced her intention to go Zara's father would have none of it.

"Stay an' eat," he told her.

Zara's parents considered her a good influence on their daughter and hoped that Zara would emulate her "superior talk". Genetha had become fond of the couple, especially of the old man, who spoke little, but had the gift of instilling confidence in others. He spent half of his life at the window, only going out for walks in the burial ground and to collect his pension. He used to be a carpenter and went about shaking his head at the work of the younger generation of carpenters. His ambition was to own a house in Camp Street, where he would really have something to see from his window. If he had his time to live over again he would pay attention to his own "heducation". It would give meaning to his happiness. Although whenever Genetha came he did not return her greeting, nor by his expression show that he was pleased to see her, he felt, in truth, a kind of inward glow and followed her with his eyes, fearing that she had only come to see Zara home or to stay a short while.

Genetha stayed as she was asked and went home at about eleven that night.

The following day she thought she detected a coolness in Zara's manner and feared the worst. When, however, at lunch she laughed louder than ever and put her arm round her, her fears were allayed.

That afternoon, on the way home Genetha said; "I'll go home with you."

"No," her friend answered hastily. Then she stammered,

"Mother sick, you see."

Genetha's feet suddenly felt heavy.

"I gone," she said abruptly to Zara and turned into a street that could not possibly take her home.

"Where you going?" Zara called out.

Genetha just waved her hand and hurried away.

She thought of the priest to whom she had confessed and cursed him. Seized by a kind of elated hatred for the rest of the world, she told herself that there was no one she could trust and was glad of it. All those she loved had died and all those she trusted had spurned her trust. From then on she intended to make her way through life alone and resist anyone's attempt at forming an association with her.

Zara's brother had come back after Genetha's departure the night before. In fact, he had waited at the street corner, watching for her to leave. No sooner had he seen her turn the corner than he left his hiding place and went back home. He immediately picked a quarrel with Zara, reproaching her with bringing her friend home too often. His mother objected that it was none of his business and his father accused him of being jealous. It was this last remark that caused the youth to lose his temper and declare, "She's a whore!"

He was standing in the middle of the room, under the gaze of his family. His father got up and came over to him.

"Genetha's like me own daughter, you understand. She can come when she like an' go when she like. If you got any respect lef' in you, you'll respect she as I does respect she."

"You don't believe me, eh? You know what they does call she in Tiger Bay? They does call she 'Nora lie down'."

"Liar!" Zara exclaimed.

"Why you don't ask she then? Ask she when she come back."

"You in' got nothing to do but make mischief, boy?" his mother asked, already half-believing what her son had said. "Is what you trying to do? Just 'cause you don't like the girl."

"I trying to tell you," pursued the youth, "that some-one eating you foot and in' fit to come in the house. You always saying how I don't bring money home. This woman never bring nothing in this house, but she does sit down and eat we food. . . ."

"We food?" Zara asked mockingly. "Is me bringing in the

money, not you."

"Well," her brother said, "if we couldn't eat fish or beef before she used to come here how we can manage now, eh?"

"You're the only one in the house objecting," his father interjected. The old man sat down again. A cloud had come over his face.

Zara's brother left the house muttering under his breath and no one spoke after he left. Night had fallen but the lamp remained unlit. Zara's father was staring out of the window, while her mother had gone into the kitchen to prepare the evening meal. Zara had picked up a magazine which she was pretending to read in the dark.

The frogs filled the early night with their ghostly concert and the breeze, penetrating the half-open doorway, was moist and cool. Someone in the street was practising on a saxophone, repeating a phrase several times before moving on to a new one.

Zara's father got up to close the door as the breeze was now chilly, then lit a lamp and adjusted the wick to prevent it smoking. Zara closed her book and prepared to go to bed.

If Zara had been asked whether she believed her brother she would have denied that she did. Yet the incident at the fair, offhand remarks vaguely remembered now, implanted in her mind a nagging doubt. Whatever anyone said about Genetha her father would never believe and if he were faced with proof he would still shake his head stubbornly. But her mother was not capable of such faith. Had it not been for her father her mother would have questioned her brother further and would have asked Genetha round to question her about what her son had told them.

When Zara met Genetha the following day she was incapable of formulating the question on the tip of her tongue. If it were a matter of dealing with her father and her brother she could let the matter pass; but Genetha would notice the change in her mother's attitude. The latter would not rest until she had come right out and broached the subject.

It could not be possible, reflected Zara. Tiger Bay? Those painted women! She was determined to find out more on her own account. In the meantime Genetha would have to stay away for a few days, even though her father would miss her and ask after her.

Genetha, offended by her friend's unwillingness to take her home, went looking for another job the next day. She could not face Zara again and decided to forego her three days' pay.

That afternoon while she was sitting on her bed mending a dress there was a knock on the door. It could only be Zara. Genetha's hand shook as she plied the needle. She wanted to open and apologize for her behaviour the night before, but the thought of being hurt again gave her the determination to ignore the rapping, which was loud and insistent. The only other sound was the water simmering on the coal-pot.

## 18. Parade

Weeks after she started working at her new job in the Lombard Street cake shop she recieved a message by hand. Delivered by a small boy it said that S. was coming to see her when she had time. The boy did not know the lady who had given him the message, or her address.

The following Sunday when Genetha was sitting on a stool behind the glass cases, looking out on the pavement, Salome walked in. Genetha was not sure if she was glad to see her or not. They had not been on friendly terms at Esther's and she was the last person Genetha would have expected to pay her a visit. She had sent the note the day she caught sight of her from a taxi as she was driving away from Medici's cloth store. A client had taken her out to buy some cloth.

"But you looking bad!" Salome said, surveying Genetha with staring eyes.

"I know, I don't feel so well."

"That white corner! You going get sick," she continued, not realizing how deeply the observation affected the older woman.

"I feel better now that I can sit down," Genetha said. "In the last job I had to stand up all the time."

"God! Anyway, I going bring Netta to see you soon."

"No," protested Genetha at once. "You must come alone."

Genetha took a pine tart from the glass case and gave it to Salome.

"Thanks. I better don't tell the girls or they'll all come round. You should see Shola! She gone fat. And the new girl name Clem. Clem! Imagine a name like that. Anyway, I got to go now."

She bent forward and kissed Genetha on the cheek and was gone before the latter could say goodbye.

Genetha decided to change her job again. The last thing she wanted was the girls finding out where she was and what she was doing. Her decision was forestalled by an unexpected rise of a dollar a week given her by the proprietor, who came himself to see her. His wife ran the shop and had reported favourably on Genetha. The rise was no great inducement to remain, but it did persuade her to change her mind about leaving. However it did not take her long to notice that the proprietor's wife spent less time in the shop, leaving her to do most of the work.

One morning, while on her way to work, Genetha noticed Zara's brother coming from the opposite direction, but on seeing her he quickly ducked into a doorway. Genetha had to steel herself against looking back. If she had, she would have seen him standing in the middle of the pavement with his hands in his pockets, staring after her. On reflection, she realized that he had never looked her straight in the eyes, and his shifty manner was the lasting impression he had left on her.

After work, instead of going home, Genetha found herself walking up Lombard Street into Water Street. It was eleven o'clock at night. In front of the vast wrought-iron structure of the Starbroek Market the pavement was empty, apart from a few carts strewn with rotten fruit, pieces of paper and vegetable peel. A solitary old woman sat behind a cart on which were a smoking carbide lamp and the remains of her load of nuts. She had nodded off, but looked up at the sound of Genetha's footsteps.

Down Regent Street she walked and back through a side street until she found herself in South Road; and from where she stood she could see the lights of Esther's establishment. She walked towards it and, as if drawn by some magnet, she mounted the stairs.

When she stood in the doorway she heard someone say, "Is Gen!"

It was Salome, who was sitting at the large table with Netta and Vera. The latter looked at her as if she were a ghost.

"You look terrible!" Netta exclaimed. "Is what happen to you at all?"

"Who's it?" a voice came from inside, followed almost immediately by the figure of Esther.

She was wearing heavy golden earrings and on her right arm were several gold bangles, which made a clinking sound whenever she moved her arm. An elaborately embroidered bodice joined a blue skirt at her waist. Her face seemed smoother and her eyes reflected more light, while the rings round her eyes had all but gone and her once lack-lustre hair was tied in a molee above her neck.

Esther could not conceal her astonishment at Genetha's appearance. The greyish white corners on her mouth, the thin, whip-like body and the slightly bent shoulders caused her to hesitate, as when, after an absence of several years, a man sees his mother again, ravaged by age, and draws back momentarily, believing that he is mistaken, but on closer scrutiny discovers the features he knows and loves so well.

"It's you?" she asked.

She was about to embrace her, but put out her hand to shake Genetha's instead. And for a few seconds neither of them spoke.

"Where's Shola?" Genetha asked.

The girls looked at one another.

Then Esther said, after hesitating, "She had to go. She wasn't too good. Besides, she got so uppity, she wanted to run the place."

"Go and get Genetha something, ne?" Esther asked, speaking to no one in particular.

"What?" enquired Netta.

"Black cake and wine. Not the Correia. Get out the French wine." Then, turning to Genetha, she said: "A chap from the boats brings me wine and perfume from Guadeloupe."

Genetha fell on the black cake and consumed it without touching the wine. Esther made Netta fetch some more cake from the kitchen.

"I want a piece, too," Netta pleaded.

"No!" came the firm reply.

The young woman went off and soon came back with another piece of cake.

"Salome told me she saw you in the cake shop," said Esther.

Genetha looked reproachfully at Salome.

"Don't bother with her," declared Esther, understanding what had happened and nodding in Salome's direction. "She's as bad as Netta."

"What've you been doing all this time?" asked Esther, trying

125

her best not to look embarrassed.

Genetha resented her composure and when she caught Esther looking at her shoes she drew her feet in under the bench and took a handkerchief out of her handbag to give herself something to do. She had a pain in her stomach and the room began to spin. Thinking that she had to get away as quickly as possible she made an effort to stand up.

On recovering consciousness Genetha found herself in a room through the window of which the air was making billowing patterns in the blind. The night outside was dark, but a bulb shed its light over the low partition from the adjoining room. She could hear Netta talking to a man. It seemed that he wanted to go back to her room with her again but she refused.

Then there was silence, followed soon afterwards by the sound of a radio being tuned, picking up successively a number of stations in Spanish, and finally a programme of Flamenco music. The sound of the guitar in the late night hour filled the house with, as it were, a wave of reassurance. Occasionally the music died away but came back in greater volume, punctuated by cries of "Alla! Alla!"

Genetha cast her eyes round the room and could tell by the furniture and the upholstery that Esther was doing well. She was overwhelmed by the soft bedding, the night air and the seductive music. She remembered her first night in Tiger Bay in Esther's room, with its unpainted walls and hard bed. The blinds were dirty and tattered and did not yield with the gentleness of this diaphanous cloth.

Then she could hear voices again, and the sound of soft laughter.

"You wicked," a woman's voice said.

"You vex wit' me?" a man asked.

"I kian' vex with you."

"Well, let me feel you bubby, then."

Another fit of softly repressed laughter came over the partition.

"But you feel it already."

"But it so small and hard!"

"All right, but jus' quick."

Then silence fell once more.

Genetha fell asleep again and when she awoke the walls of the room were transfigured by a bright, almost white light, like the screen of the cinema she used to attend after she broke with Michael. The rest of the room was in darkness and Genetha could hardly make out the upholstered chairs. So she was not dreaming!

She closed her eyes, and when she opened them once more the walls were just as bright as before. Far from being afraid Genetha marvelled at the steady phosphorescence that had transformed the wood. She sat up and looked round her as if she were expecting a companion.

Suddenly the wall ahead of her became animated with indistinct shapes which gradually became clearer. And as the forms became more distinct, music could be heard coming as it were out of the wall. The scene might have been taking place on the street under the sunlight of noonday and she might have been watching it through an open window. A brass band was playing a rousing march of such transcendental beauty that the windows of other houses, which could be seen at the top of the wall, were soon filled with people. Louder and louder the music grew until it seemed to fill the whole world.

Her attention was drawn to the wall on the right of her bed, which represented a street, smaller than the one in which the march-past was featured. A group of little children were running towards the main street shouting, "Parade! Parade!" and when they reached the point where the two streets joined they stood to watch the uniformed men in awe, marching in unison to a music that gripped the heart. A few boys, caught up in the occasion, started to accompany the procession down the road, but the fast-growing crowd soon reduced their progress and they were obliged to remain in one place. Then out of the side street emerged the well-dressed figure of a woman who, with dignified gestures, was trying to restrain two young children from breaking away and joining the others. And as the young woman, wearing a maid's cap and long white dress, grew larger on the screen Genetha recognized Esther. The little boy unmistakably resembled Boyie, her dead brother, while the girl, who must have been herself, she could not recognize. On the photograph Fingers had found her face was blurred and she had forgotten what she looked like as a child.

Genetha gazed intently at the little girl on the wall whose face and ancient dress drew her like a magnet. Her wonderfully dark eyelashes looked as if they were covered with layers of mascara.

Genetha studied every pleading look, every wide-eyed expression of the well-fed, smooth-skinned little girl. And finally, like all the children who had come out of the side street, Genetha, Boyie and Esther were lost among the crowds.

Genetha tried to retain the tune the band was playing, feeling certain that it was connected with some forgotten incident from her childhood. But soon the band itself had passed and the wall was now filled with marching, uniformed men with chins raised under severe expressions like those on the faces of the freemasons as they marched down the Public Road at Agricola, their silver-painted wooden swords glistening in the sunlight. And just as the band and their playing had roused her these men turned her blood cold. But they were soon gone and the only sound they left behind was the tramp, tramp of their steps when the music died away. Long after the street was empty, except for its steady phosphorescence, there could be heard that tramp, tramp of absent feet which, like the music a few moments earlier, filled the room with its pervasive sound and, seemingly, the whole world.

Genetha tried desperately to recall the tune that she had heard repeated several times, but could not. She knew that the second note rose from the first, but she was unable to remember the interval and in the end gave up.

But the wall ahead of her was already coming to life once more. On the western corner of it, black clouds intruded, darkening the edge of the screen, along the middle of which ran a thick wall of sugar cane, while at the bottom stood a small cake-shop next to which was a vegetable patch planted with cassava and pumpkin. Genetha knew she was in East Canje, for that one visit with the patients from New Amsterdam had left an indelible impression on her mind. There was no one in sight and the dusty, pot-holed road stretched along the cane field out of the picture. Then the first drops of rain began to fall while the wind whipped the ribbon-like leaves of the tall cane this way and that, so that the tiny cake-shop seemed threatened. The raindrops in the dust became magnified before Genetha's eyes, leaving tiny craters in the road which, however, soon disappeared in the deluge of rain that all but blotted out the landscape. The wooden shop became darker and the cane fields presented the appearance of a mass of growth, waving about like giant seaweed in a translucent stretch of ocean. She had come to East

Canje in bright sunshine and only the cake-shop, the cane fields and the dusty road were recognizable. This forlorn scene, the complete absence of people, made her wonder whether she might be somewhere else. But on turning to the wall on her right she recognized the koker, rising out of the landscape above the drainage canal, and the spot where she had taken shelter from the threatening sun.

A sudden longing for this landscape gripped Genetha, an absurd desire to be in a place whose air, at the time of her visit, was filled with an almost unbearable stench; a sun-drenched, flat landscape, criss-crossed with ribbons of stagnant water, accessible only by means of the infrequent bus or taxi. Perhaps because the rain had obscured it, or perhaps because the air was now clean again, she saw it as the primeval landscape of her childhood, filled out by the curiously large figures of her mother, Esther and her shadowy father.

The rain came down, endlessly, monotonously, with a deep, hollow sound, joining sky and earth with innumerable threads. The dust of the road was gradually changed into slime and mud and ran away into the gutters and low-lying cane fields. Genetha looked for the bus that had brought her there, for a moment enchanted into the belief that she was in that gloomy landscape. With relief she saw that there was no bus in sight, that the only man-made structure was the diminutive shop battered by the downpour.

Increasing in intensity the rain now sounded like the concerted lowing of a herd of cattle; and when, as if from nowhere, the hardly discernible figure of a man materialized in front of the koker, Genetha sat up, afraid. Cutlass in hand, he walked hurriedly along the dam and turned into the shop, out of view, leaving Genetha more astounded by the apparition than by the ferocity of the rain and wind and by the veiled landscape.

And as the landscape faded on the wall, so the sound of the falling rain diminished, until the room was once more silent.

Hardly had Genetha begun wondering about the significance of what she had seen than the wall of a sudden presented another different scene. She immediately recognized the drawing-room of the family home, which appeared so desolate after her father's death. There was the familiar furniture, the familiar door opening on to the porch. But everything was covered in a layer of dust and the roof of the porch, seen

129

through the open front door, was in such a state of disrepair that it was threatened with collapse. The bedroom door was closed and as the scene shifted to the back of the house she saw that the other bedroom doors were closed as well. The kitchen was dark, for the window above the back stairs was closed.

Genetha knew, somehow, that her father had only recently died. There was no evidence of this from what she saw, but she was convinced that it was so.

As the scene shifted back to the drawing-room the conviction grew that, despite the apparently empty house and the dilapidation of the scene, someone was there, either in a locked room or even in the drawing-room which at that moment lay before her on the wall. Back and forth the scene shifted, now to the dining-room then back to the drawing-room with the gallery door open out on to the derelict porch.

Then, as though to dispel any doubts she might still have, the scene narrowed to take in two upholstered chairs which were pressed near to each other and behind which grunting sounds could be heard. The scene then took in the narrow passage between the chairs and the wall and there, in a kind of twilight, two figures were making love on the floor. The woman's face was turned towards the space under the chair while the man was lying down, making imperceptible movements over the woman in his embrace. And the light sought out the two figures, exposing first Genetha's still young features and then, as he collapsed on her at the moment of climax, Boyie.

Genetha shuddered at what she beheld. It was not possible, she told herself. Yet it was indeed her face and her arms clasping Boyie's and urging him to go on. And the features were unmistakably his. Even his shirt and trousers were familiar. Had she not washed the shirt herself, fearing that he might have them washed at that woman's house in Vreed-en-Hoop?

She saw him get up, ponderously, for there was just enough room behind the chairs to accommodate one person. He left her alone behind the chair and went inside, opening and closing the door of the bedroom which adjoined the drawing-room. And she lay on the floor, one leg resting against the wall and the other against the upholstered chair and the black recesses of her legs exposed to the light that spared nothing.

It was not possible, she kept telling herself. And she could not know that it was precisely the fear of incest that had driven

130

her brother away to live in Suddie. She kept denying the possibility of what she saw and the uninhibited way in which he rode her and then walked off. Yet she made no attempt to look away. She had made no attempt to look away.

Then she recalled the two previous scenes that had unfolded before her on the wall and remembered that neither the procession nor the downpour at East Canje were real. This reflection calmed her somewhat, but there still lingered the feeling of having been exposed, that it might be commonly believed that Boyie had seduced her, that whatever she said would not dispel the cloud of guilt which had surrounded her.

What were these visions anyway? she asked herself, looking round the room to ensure that she was alone. She was not asleep, that was certain. It was equally certain, she told herself, that she was not having hallucinations.

Jumping out of bed she left the room in search of one of the girls. She did not wish to meet Esther, but she did not know who slept in the special room. It was almost certain to be one of the girls who had been there from the opening of the establishment. Perhaps Netta or Salome.

Then Genetha changed her mind and decided to leave the house without telling anyone. She opened the door quietly, slipped out and closed the door again with the utmost care.

But as she approached the gate a voice from under the house called out.

"You kian' go home at this time o'night, Miss Genetha." It was Bigfoot, who was sitting alone, watching the road.

"Why're you up so late?" Genetha asked him.

"Is in the day I does sleep most, mistress," came the deferential reply. "I does watch the place by night."

"Oh."

"You kian' walk the streets alone now," he warned her again. "If you want I can take you home. That's if you want."

"I'd be glad," Genetha said.

"All right." He got up eagerly and joined her. "You living far?" he asked.

"Albouystown."

They walked for some distance without speaking.

"I did miss you, y'know, mistress," said Bigfoot, without turning towards her, and using the term of respect country people use when addressing their wives or women for whom

131

they have great respect.

"Ha," was all Genetha could reply, to hide her confusion.

"Why you don't come back?" he asked. "Everybody know how Madame does like you."

"She said so?" Genetha enquired, more at ease now that the conversation was on firmer ground.

"Yes, she say so. Is true she been a servant in your mother house?" Bigfoot asked, slowing his pace.

"Yes, but that was years and years ago," Genetha told him.

"Years and years?" said Bigfoot. "You talkin' as if you old."

Why did he have to mention her age if he did not know that she was no longer young? He knew and felt sorry for her, she reflected. She had never met such consideration from the men in her house. Even Fingers at his most tender never spoke to her like that.

"What happened to Shola?" asked Genetha, curious as to the fate of her chief persecutor at the brothel.

"Madame put her out 'cause she did get too big for she boots. And she find out she been takin' more money from the clients than the other girls. It was a big thing: the other girls threaten to stop work if Shola go. But Madame give them all twenty-four hours to leave the house. The nex' morning even Netta wouldn't show she face to Madame. An' when Shola leave Madame start taunting them an' asking them why they wouldn't go. She refuse to cook for them and at midday she alone sit at the dining-table an' eat. It wasn't till the nex' day they get food. You never see such a thing in you life, but it happen."

"So Shola's gone," Genetha said in a soft voice.

"Is it 'cause of she you go?" Bigfoot asked hopefully.

"No, I wanted to go anyway."

"Madame say you goin' come back again," Bigfoot remarked. "She say she know you too good, an' that you goin' come back."

"Oh, yes?" said Genetha angrily.

"Why you vexed? I thought she did know something we din' know . . . . So you not comin' back then?"

"No, definitely not."

Bigfoot would say no more, fearing that he had offended her.

What Esther had actually said was, "She'll come back and kiss my feet and repay me for everything her mother did do me."

"I can't come back, you see," explained Genetha. "I wasn't cut out for that sort of life. I knew one man before I started. I

132

can't explain what I mean. It's not only that I knew just one man. It's the guilt and the feeling that one day I'd have to pay for everything."

Bigfoot gave Genetha time then began to speak.

"I uses to own a launch you know, mistress. I uses to be a decent man. Then in 1946, when the yankee air base close down and nobody had money no more, I had was to sell my launch for what I could get and come to town to look for work. When I meet Madame and she tell me she would like me to work for she I grab the opportunity. I tell you, if you come back I would look after you good."

"I'm not what I look like, Bigfoot. And if you got to know me you would take what you could from me and let me down. . . ."

"I wouldn't, mistress," Bigfoot hastened to assure her.

"No, you wouldn't," said Genetha. "I haven't got anything left for you to take."

"All right. That's what I did mean. I don't want nothing."

They walked at a leisurely pace, neither wishing to hurry. But Bigfoot believed that he had offended her and longed to make amends, while Genetha, unaware of his concern, was glad of his company and the discretion of his words. She wanted to ask him whether Esther had a man friend. And Bigfoot himself had never shown an interest in any of the other women in the brothel. Did he have a woman friend outside? Being married and having a wife in one place while working in another was a common condition. The men often started another family in the district where they worked. Bigfoot almost certainly had a woman in Georgetown, but was successful in hiding her existence from the others.

"You vex with me, mistress?" asked Bigfoot, without turning to look at her.

"Me? No, Bigfoot. I was just thinking how I enjoy walking when everybody else's asleep." Then, to reassure him, she went on. "I'm going to go and live with my aunts."

"Where they living, mistress?"

"Near Vlissingen Road." Then, after a while, "I haven't told them yet, but they won't say no."

"I think that would be good," he said simply, imagining that his words bore the weight of his sincerity.

If Bigfoot had put his arm round Genetha she would have done nothing to repulse him, for the need to be protected by someone was now strong, as if her abortive visit to the brothel had robbed her of the little confidence she had left.

What did women need men for? she reflected. If she worked and lived at her aunts' would she not have the security and protection of a home? Her body had no more need for a man's embrace. In the end was she not free now? Were not her father's death and her brother's going away a deliverance?

Finally she and Bigfoot stood in front of the near derelict building where she lived. Connecting it to the street lamp-post were two wires from which an abandoned kite hung, quivering with every gust of wind. The two solitary figures faced each other under the lamplight with no idea of the remarkable picture they made standing on top of their round shadows.

"Well, thanks," said Genetha.

"Remember what I did tell you," said Bigfoot.

She nodded to show that she understood, although she was not certain what he had said to her.

"Goodnight, mistress. I goin' stand here till you go inside. Just in case."

Genetha crossed the bridge and disappeared into the shadows of the house.

## 19. Aunts of the Blood

Genetha moved in with her aunts who, appalled at her appearance, granted her request to come and live with them. She gave up her job at the cake-shop, knowing that if she left for work every morning they would eventually enquire where she was working and, on finding out, demand that she stopped.

She recovered her strength quickly, her face filled out, her breasts and hips grew round and firm again. During this period she was encouraged by her aunts to do as little as possible around the house. But as she grew well again she relieved them of the sweeping and dusting, then of the ironing until she was taking her full share of the household work. Genetha did not mind, for she now felt stronger than she had ever done.

She came back to find that her grandfather had become senile and spent the greater part of the day in his bedroom, emerging in the afternoon to look out of the window across the trench to Vlissingen Road and at the crowds waiting to get into the cinema. From time to time he would say out loud, "Oh, my!

Oh, my!" This occurred with greater frequency as the weeks went by, until no one took any notice of him any more, even when he accompanied these outbursts with cupping his head in his hands.

In his periods of lucidity, when he saw and recognized Genetha he would make her sit down and tell her how his brother died while still in his thirties, "wrenched away after stepping on a rusty nail and contracting tetanus". Otherwise he ignored everyone, although frequently calling for their help, and spent the mornings contemplating the vast desert of blue beyond the eaves of the back-house, and the evenings out front.

His wife, Genetha's maternal grandmother, fell into a long silence as her husband became more confirmed in his senility. She had long ceased going to church, after the foreign minister went away and was replaced by a local man, and had also stopped taking her evening walks, as her husband was no longer fit to go out. His senility was the final blow and, fearing that her daughters could not grasp the seriousness of her plight, she withdrew into her implacable silence.

Genetha's elder aunt, Deborah, stubbornly refused to believe that her father was permanently afflicted and kept saying that he would soon pull out of it. She reproached him for his table manners, once impeccable, she often reminded him. And the morning she caught him urinating out of the back window it was all she could do not to raise her voice. She had noticed the stain on the painted white-pine boards beneath the window and was mystified as to its origin. He denied knowing anything about it, claiming that bats often left stains from their droppings. And the more he tried her patience the more she insisted that he would get well again.

As Genetha gained in strength, the old desires came back to plague her body. She decided that it would be best to work again and set about looking for a job in an office. But her first interview was disastrous for no sooner had she been called in to be questioned than she was recognized by one of the men.

"Excuse me," he charged bluntly, "weren't you working at a certain place in South Road?"

Genetha fled rather than deny the accusation, cursing the need to live in a town where anonymity was impossible. She had not told her aunts about her application, partly because she felt they might be displeased at the prospect of her working again and being unable to help in the house as before.

Embittered by her experience Genetha thought that she ought to go and see her paternal aunt and confess everything. But as the weeks went by she was overcome by a sort of torpor. Her only problem was that of renewing her wardrobe which, with care, would last another two or three years, she told herself. Until then, she would live as she had lived, sharing the food and shelter of her relations.

Genetha was now careful to go out only at night. She insisted that, though she was prepared to do all the work given her in the house, she would go out whenever she wanted. Her aunts gave in, seeing in her defiance a quirk that harmed no one. After all, the cook did the main part of the shopping in the morning, while the East Indian woman came round every day with her tray of greens. Only the bread had to be fetched and that had been the younger aunt's duty for a long time.

One night while Genetha and her younger aunt were out walking on a moonlit night, chatting like two young girls who had escaped the constraints of a supervising adult, Genetha saw a young man approaching them. She could not understand why her attention should be drawn to him because, at that distance, she was unable to make out his features. As he went by she smiled at him and he smiled back, an exchange that passed unnoticed by her aunt. Then on reaching home she said she was going out again, offering as an excuse that she did not get enough exercise.

She saw the man waiting in Anira Street and went boldly up to him, smiling but saying nothing.

"I didn't think you'd come," he told her, and they walked off together.

The young man was unable to make conversation, so taken aback was he by his unexpected success. He walked her along Albert Street and along the old highways, until they came to Palpree Dam, a haven for lovers.

When he saw that Genetha did not object to being taken to this road of shadows, where the light of the moon was shut out by the canopy of massive tamarind and saman trees, he became more confident. He put his arm round her waist, drawing her closer to him. Then, unopposed, he fondled her small breasts. Encouraged by her passive manner he bent down to pull off her

136

panties. She lifted one foot then the other and saw him put her undergarment in his pocket as he would a handkerchief with which he had just wiped his face. Half-naked, bathed in a cool film of moisture, she walked with him, sometimes trampling wild flowers on the parapet, sometimes exposed to the gaze of the moon where the canopies did not meet.

The young man laid her down in the grass and her skirt became covered with pollen and the clinging seeds of the sweetheart plant. She did not even know the stranger's name or if he was . . . . What did it matter when all her woes melted in the wonder of creation? Did anything matter? Who was she and her self, struggling against the perpetuity of things? Her transitory longings, her vain words? Then her body shuddered for the third time and the light of a fourth candle began to burn before her eyes, as if he had just lit it. When she was at secondary school a friend once explained to her how these soft tapers could be used to provide the most delicious of forbidden sensations. So struck had Genetha been by what she heard that the sight of those countless candles in Brickdam Cathedral and their shuddering flames never failed to intimidate her. Yet on Old Year's night she always accompanied her best school friend to Midnight Mass, where they met other acquaintances, Catholics and non-Catholics, who used the mass as a pretext to get away from home and mingle with the crowd of worshippers.

At last the young man collapsed on her with the same long gasp Fingers used to utter, like the panting of a dog. Then she would have preferred him to leave her there; but she knew he would be calling on her to follow him and that he would lay claim to her affection, as if by giving him something she owed him something more.

On the way back she asked him if his name was Glen, one of Fingers's formal Christian names.

"Why should my name be Glen?" he asked.

"Nothing."

"But why?"

"I tell you, nothing," she replied, irritated by his interest.

"You did know somebody name Glen?" he asked.

"Don't take me all the way," she said, anxious to see him go.

"Why?"

"Because my people don't like me having men friends."

He left her two corners away from Laluni Street.

But every night after that he came walking or riding by in the moonlight like a dog in dog season, when the whole family save Genetha's grandmother were assembled at the front of the house, on the porch and at the windows. One night she turned and followed him with her eyes as a sign of her interest.

When she went out on her own about ten minutes later he was waiting as she expected, round the corner in Anira Street in front of the church.

Genetha recalled the admirer who used to prowl round the brothel in South Road until one of the girls chased him away.

"What you want with me?" she threw at him.

"Don't you want to see me again?" he enquired.

"No. I thought you understood!"

"Aren't you in love with me?" he asked.

"No, I'm not."

"But you let me . . . the first time," he almost pleaded.

"How could I explain?" she thought.

"You're so decent," he said. "Decent women don't carry on like that. I *know* women." He came round, on the other side of his bicycle, to be nearer her.

Genetha stared at him indignantly, exasperated at his persistence. "Please leave me alone," she said. "You don't know me. If I'd passed you on the road that night you wouldn't have come here. Leave me alone, please. I don't know you."

He made a gesture of bewilderment, but could answer nothing.

As he started to move off Genetha held the handlebar of his cycle. But instead of saying what she had to say she turned away abruptly and made for the house. One day, she thought, she would take her younger aunt into her confidence.

Genetha walked away, impelled by an unreasoning fury, and when she reached the house she did not go upstairs right away, but remained under it.

"He knows women!" she said to herself. "He knows women. The same arrogance as Boyie and Father."

She recalled the conversation of one of her father's acquaintances, an assistant to a land surveyor, whose job it was to cut survey lines in the jungle. He often talked of his experiences in the forest, of being unable to see further than a few yards above his head into the upper reaches where most of the army of animals lived and, even farther above, where eagles soared.

That represented for her the state of her self-knowledge; only in her dreams did she glimpse that swarming world within her and a partial understanding of her nature that the men she knew claimed to have. Only Fingers seemed free of this masculine conceit and it was he who had brought her to this pass!

Gradually Genetha's anger subsided and her thoughts turned to her conduct on Palpree Dam. Had her life in the brothel made her depraved? Or did the brothel uncover what was already there? She felt no shame at her conduct, only curiosity that it was in contrast to the behaviour of the women from her social class. She remembered her disgust for her work at Esther's establishment, which, even now, made her head grow to think on it. But in retrospect there was something heady about the depravity, the wanton disregard for the regulated life of the family. Some of the girls openly admitted this, especially the East Indians from the country.

It was curious that everything she did seemed to be in relation to men. The problems of her freedom, of her depravity as well, were all reflections of her life with men. Even her rejection of male companionship was an admission of her preoccupation with them. Had she not been maltreated by Fingers she would not have treated the young man so harshly tonight. What was certain, however, was her resolve never to be hurt again. Every month she would seek out a stranger and entice him to Palpree Dam to assuage her own longings and then return to the house of women, where the once all-powerful male was dying a slow death and the elder aunt was becoming more authoritarian every day.

That night Genetha's grandfather took a turn for the worse and everyone sat up late, lit by the rays of two night-lights, watching and waiting. Genetha's elder aunt was staring straight ahead, while Alice's chin had fallen on to her breast.

The next day they took it in turns to watch, through the slow afternoon hours and throughout the night. When her turn came to relieve Alice, Genetha sat down at her grandfather's bedside, not daring to look at the old man lest he were already dead. At her father's wake she had sought refuge in sleep. This was the first time she had stayed up long after midnight and known the silence of those hours, broken only by an incessant chirping of crickets. The Old Year's night when she and Zara were on the way to her house came back, with its dance-hall sounds, the strident call of trumpets and the thud of stamping feet.

What was Death, in truth? She had heard so many stories of its coming. According to some, it arrived accompanied by a demon animal, while others said it came alone, invisible to all except the dying person and small children. Her mother, as it seemed, had been wrenched away; her father just went, discreetly, when she and Rohan were out at work, yet with the same effect, a terrible emptiness or an accumulation of some special misery. But on neither occasion did she see anything to confirm the hundred tales about death. Perhaps Death was silence, encompassed by night and its dark winds. Long ago, she believed that anyone who survived beyond the age of sixty was indestructible. Long ago, long, long, long ago, in the time of mask-makers and jumbee-band dancers of great reputation, when old things were revered and therefore indestructible.

Genetha turned to look at her grandfather, stretched full-length, with hands placed across each other at the wrists, like a corpse laid out. He was wearing his slippers, though uncovered by a blanket, an eccentricity her aunts allowed him on the grounds that his feet were perpetually cold, only to explain away an indulgence which had grown out of their respect for him. He wore his slippers even on the warmest and most humid nights, when sweat blinded the eyes.

Alice had said it was bad luck to interrupt the watch, and here, because the advice had been repeated when she arrived to take her place, she felt the urge to urinate. That was a portent, too, as was the inordinate silence. If only she had company she would listen to any trifling conversation. Words that seemed arid in Georgetown had been, in Morawhanna, like ripe-bursting fruit. "Who with you?" "Is me one." Or, "Where he is?" "Some place." And Ulric – who surely withdrew again after Fingers abandoned her – with his stories of keeping watch during war, and his halting way of speaking.

The old man made an unexpected movement, which gave Genetha such a fright she almost fell off her chair. At all costs she must concentrate and pray for him, she told herself, not only because it was her duty, but because the love he bore her shone even in his decrepitude. "Dear Genetha, no one is ever alone . . . everyone must love you, dear child." He was all her own father had not been, who never sighed nor wasted terms of

140

endearment.

Death was the end. And Time was its vahana, the drive to decrepitude, new leaf, old leaf, the precondition of perpetual renewal. Or an old East Indian man crying the hours on a sugar estate, "One bhaja, ohhhhhh!" "Two bhaja, ohhhhhhh!" Or simply a mathematical rate of ageing and decay.

"Almighty God," she prayed inwardly, so as not to disturb her grandfather, whose hands had become separated from one another when he moved. Genetha prayed for his recovery, using all the formulae she had learned since her church-going days and her childhood Sunday-school classes and the night services on the radio.

It must have been during her prayer that she dropped off with that abruptness that defies recollection.

Suddenly the shrill cry of an owl caused the younger aunt, Alice, to wake up with a start and the elder to make the sign of the cross on her chest, for there were no owls in the area.

Genetha's grandmother came out of the bedroom where she was sleeping.

"Was that an owl?" she asked. "I heard an owl."

"Yes, Mamma," answered Aunt Deborah, speaking over the partition. "It was an owl. It probably just flew over."

"Yes," said the old lady. "But why here?" She went back inside without an explanation.

"Genetha," said Deborah, who came to join them, "make us some chocolate. It's turned chilly. We're all imagining things."

"Yes, Aunt," Genetha said, getting up to go into the kitchen.

They watched for nine nights, Genetha and her two aunts, taking turns to stay up until dawn broke. But despite the omens, the dark dreams and their conviction that death had installed itself at his bedside, the old man recovered. And in the days that followed Genetha's elder aunt's irritation with him increased. The scent of bay-rum from the sick room, his constant demands made in a surprisingly loud voice, disturbed her music students' lessons, she claimed. Even when he could walk about again he behaved as if he required attention and, what was worse, wandered about the house in his pyjamas, to the amusement of the students doing their theory of music at the large table in the drawing-room. Genetha then detected for the first time flaws in Aunt Deborah's exterior.

In one of the old man's lucid periods she suggested to him

141

that he go to a lawyer and have all his possessions made over to those who were likely to survive him, so that they would have access to his bank account and government bonds after he died. He agreed, on condition that Genetha came with them. Genetha could not refuse, even though all the lawyers' chambers were in or near Croal Street, a stone's throw from Esther's establishment. Besides, she reflected, they would be going in broad daylight, and she would have to linger by the car while her aunt shepherded him from the vehicle to the office, an operation that was bound to attract the attention of passers-by.

The morning planned for the visit arrived. It was eight months since Genetha had been living with her aunts and this sortie was to be her first in daytime for nearly a month. With trepidation she stood on the porch while Aunt Deborah accompanied the old man down the stairs. He was dressed in a suit more than thirty years old which, though eccentric in cut, might have been made no more than a few months ago, so well-kept it was.

"Come on, Genetha," her aunt urged, with that new irritation that soured the atmosphere in the house.

"I'm coming, Aunt," she called out, deliberately going inside to fetch something imaginary.

Genetha came out when she was certain that her grandfather and aunt were already in the car.

"Why you don't want to go?" enquired Aunt Alice, who was leaning out of the window to watch the departure.

"I don't mind," Genetha protested, hurrying down the stairs.

Not a word was spoken in the car, and when it stopped in front of the Lawyer G's chambers Genetha's elder aunt helped her father out and beckoned Genetha to take his arm on the other side. Here, in the bustle of town, amidst the honking of cars and the continuous roar of traffic, she felt as if she were being observed. Fighting the impulse to rush back to the car in which they came she turned round to look at the passers-by.

A woman came out of the lawyer's chambers, staring at the threesome as she went by, much to Genetha's dismay. And so it was throughout the time of waiting in the chambers, in the company of three clients whom they met there, and of others who came in after them.

At last Genetha's aunt and the old man went through the open doors and disappeared into the room where the lawyer saw his clients, leaving Genetha in the company of four others.

Though her chances of being recognized as a prostitute were small, in the confines of the office, Genetha sat rigid on her chair, imagining the worst and not daring to look round her. Then the typist addressed her and she started from her seat.

"Me?" she asked. "No, I'm with the two people inside. Remember? I came in with them."

The young woman did not look away at once.

After what seemed an interminable period of waiting, Genetha's aunt and grandfather came out, accompanied by the lawyer, who followed them solicitously as if they were his own relations. The old man looked exhausted, while Deborah, relaxed and triumphant, patiently walked with him back to the waiting car.

"What a nice day," she said, to no one in particular, as the car drove off. She then lowered the window glass, so that the wind came in.

"He's a pleasant man, isn't he?" Deborah said to her father, hunched in his seat. But either he did not understand her or he did not care to answer.

For her, Genetha was still a girl, to be ignored or ordered about. She had no idea that the niece was sizing up the aunt, that for the first time since her return she was seriously asking herself whether the increasingly authoritarian régime in the house was worth bearing with, in return for three square meals a day and a roof over her head. Had she been able to earn a living, matters would have come to a head before. Now that her aunt was in charge of the source of the household income – apart from the old man's pension – things would certainly not improve. The prospect of a more severe régime, the anticipation of what might not even come to pass, set up Genetha's defences and disposed her to a hostility that, in the light of her older aunt's character, could only be to her disadvantage.

Genetha edged away from her and pressed herself against the side of the car. It occurred to her that, although the car followed a route that took them past Esther's establishment, she had not even noticed the place, so preoccupied she had been with reflections about her aunt's growing power in the house.

Now they were rushing past the cottages in upper South Road in the reckless manner that distinguished Guyanese drivers from those elsewhere. Almost thwarted in his headlong rush by

143

a car emerging from a side street, the driver pressed his horn in a long, angry reminder that his vehicle had right of way.

Aunt Alice came to the front to meet them with a smile which seemed to ask if everything went as was planned. Genetha and Aunt Deborah helped the old man up the stairs and into the house and he made for the back, to spend the rest of the day with his wife.

## 20. The Hinterland

Almost a month had passed since Genetha's encounter with the stranger and their walk to Palpree Dam. She had taken to going out in the daytime again. Since the trip to the lawyer's chambers she felt that, if she took great care in leaving the house, no one who recognized her on the road would be able to connect her with her aunts. It was on one of these morning outings to the bakery that she came face to face with Michael in the company of a woman and three small girls the image of him. In utter confusion at the unexpected encounter Michael made as if to go by, but Genetha stepped in his way and greeted him.

"Michael?"

"Good Heavens!" he exclaimed. "Genetha!"

He introduced her to his wife while the three children looked on, left out of the formalities.

"Joyce, this is Genetha . . . Genetha, my wife. I used to know Genetha at the church."

Michael's wife was a small, nervous-looking woman, who listened to her husband as if she expected to be beaten when they got home. She smiled, but said nothing, only occasionally turning to look at her brood anxiously.

"Look, I've still got the hymn book you lent me so long ago. Why not come and get it? I live in Irving Street with my aunts. . . ." She gave him the lot number and said that she would have the book ready for him.

Michael said goodbye, enjoined on his wife and each of the children to do as much, and took leave of Genetha with even more confusion than he had shown in acknowledging their acquaintanceship.

"Michael . . ." thought Genetha. "Well, well, well."

But he did not come, as she expected he would. Then the night when Genetha planned to go out alone, in the expectation

144

of a new passing encounter, after she had spent three-quarters of an hour in front of the looking-glass following a shower and wash with her aunts' bath salts, she was taken aback to see him at the gate as she opened the front door to leave the house.

Michael was his old self, composed and priggish, professing to have the right to call her Genetha after all that time.

She hurried down to meet him before one of her aunts could come out, and in a flash saw him as her husband and his three children as her own. She was about to go down to meet her husband who had taken her visiting and had now come to accompany her back home. She was clean and honourable, had known only him intimately, as her mother must have known only her father. Genetha experienced such an access of joy at his coming that she completely forgot herself and shouted, "Michael!" And he stood at the foot of the stairs, surprised by her extravagant greeting, having no idea that she was transported by her own anxiety to a time that never existed, to a place that was neither her old home nor her present abode in her mother's father's house; that the cry of his name was a call for help, and the laughter in her cheeks the banner of her desperate need.

"Hello, Genetha," Michael answered soberly.

The tone of his voice brought her back to her senses more sharply than an unexpected blow with his hand could, so that her laughter became a smile.

They went off in the direction of the sea and crossed the wall that ran along the beach. They talked of old times, while kicking the seaweed underfoot, and thought of what the next hour would bring.

"When I saw you with the children I had a wrench," she told him.

"So you didn't get married after all?" he asked.

"No," she replied.

"And what about that man living in the house?"

"We broke up," she said simply.

Michael fell silent, relishing the discovery that she had been abandoned by a man and that she had remained unmarried.

Genetha took his arm.

"Things weren't easy after we broke up," he told her, unwilling to let her off so lightly.

"I want you to kiss me," she declared, stopping abruptly.

145

After he had kissed her she led him towards the pavilion with the long staircase and seduced him there, enveloped in darkness, with the sea sounding far away.

He wanted to rush off, but she would not let him go.

"No, stay and talk to me!"

Thereupon Michael took out two five-dollar notes and gave them to her, "For old times' sake," he declared.

Genetha began to laugh softly.

"What's wrong?" he enquired.

"Nothing."

"Don't laugh like that. Someone might pass and hear you."

Genetha stopped laughing as he ordered. "I suppose you see this as a kind of revenge," she told him.

"I . . . it gave me a certain satisfaction," he admitted.

"You got your revenge on me a long time ago. But why you should need revenge I don't know. . . . Never try to avenge yourself on your wife or your daughters. Wait till you get sons. You all men lurk behind trees for one another with knives and guns and sticks and hit one another with all your might, even though you're avenging things done years ago. . . . And to think I still feel attached to you for old times' sake, as you say."

"I didn't wrong you," he declared. "It was you who did me wrong. But I don't want revenge at all. I just felt that you owed me something. We were all but engaged, weren't we? I can't stay here talking. I've got to go."

"You don't have to go right away, Michael."

Believing that he detected a threat in her voice he decided to remain. But being too embarrassed to speak first he allowed silence to settle between them.

"You wouldn't have me when I was pure," Genetha said at last. "Now I'm a slut you behave like an animal —"

"I . . ." he broke in.

She allowed him time to continue, but he had nothing to add.

"I'll tell you two stories, Michael. My younger aunt is nice. She's always telling me family stories. A few days ago she told me about their brother. I didn't even know I had an uncle; but they're not supposed to talk about him. When he was still at school he was always saying, 'All I want is a gun and a dog.' My grandfather doted on him and wouldn't shut him up when he talked like that, although Grandmother and my aunts were frightened at his threats to run away as soon as he could afford to buy a gun and a dog. He passed all his exams with distinction, and at eighteen left school to go abroad to study medicine. But during the holidays he went off into the bush – just as he said he would do – with an old hunting gun he bought from the vet who lived next door, Mr Bruce. The last my grandparents and aunts heard of him was that he had married an aboriginal Indian. It's not an exciting story, but it keeps haunting me: a gun and a dog. Do you know Georgetown has more stray dogs. . ."

". . . than any other town of similar size in the world?" Michael mocked her.

". . . and the biggest cemetery in the world?" she went on as if he had not interrupted. "And best of all, the country's got a huge mental hospital and the biggest wooden church in the world. Yes, Michael, while your priggish wife and your priggish children walk about with their noses in the air we are —"

Michael broke into her monologue, protesting. But Genetha replied sharply:

"We are a distressed people, but we know all about pleasure, don't we, Michael? Half the population dance through Old Year's night into New Year's morning, until they all but drop from exhaustion."

Michael made as if to go, but Genetha, with a short, malicious laugh, ordered him to remain with her.

"If you go now I'll follow you home, Michael, and tell your wife what we've been up to."

He stared at her, terrified at the implication of her words. Inwardly he began to go over different plans to slip away if she did carry out her threat.

"What was the second story you were going to tell me?" he asked, in order to appease her.

"Oh . . . the gun and the dog didn't appeal to you. Yet that's what most of you men want. When all is said and done that's what my father wanted, and Boyie. . . . Anyway, you'll like the second story, Michael. My aunt said that a man went abroad and returned with a European wife. Every day she came out with him to his work-place by cab. She then took him home again the same way. And you know what she did while he was at work?"

"What?"

"She waited in the cab all those hours while he was at work,

147

with only the cabbie for company."

"I don't believe it," Michael said. Though his protest was prompted by a need to placate Genetha there was genuine interest in his voice.

"I knew you'd like that one," she told him. "You find that kind of sacrifice exciting. But it doesn't appeal to me. It's the gun and the dog I like in a way I can't explain. Hundreds of porknockers take to the bush in search of gold, yet those who make a fortune hardly ever come back to town. They don't get further than Issano, where they spend their money on the whores. And they go in search of the very gold and diamonds they squandered at Issano. You know why they don't return to town? My aunt thinks that once they've tasted the freedom of the bush there's nothing to come back to. The hinterland, she calls it. To me the question is not why they remain in the bush but why they go at all. What draws them to that wilderness of trees and all the dangers? There's never been a single woman porknocker. Have you ever heard of a woman porknocker?"

Michael shook his head.

"You understand, Michael, for me that's the problem. Freedom and the secret of a settled mind. Because I was 'up there' for six weeks, I can't get a reference and have to take whatever job I'm offered. When I took up with Fingers, Boyie went away. And you wouldn't be content with my friendship: I had to love you. I'm not up to all these rules."

"I didn't abandon you," put in Michael, who did not care to find out what she meant by "up there". "It was you who showed me the door."

"My young aunt," said Genetha, "tells stories, kisses my hand to show how much she cares. But she'd never put herself out to help me. . . . Do you know I used to be a whore, Michael?"

Michael, despite his resolution not to offend, changed his expression involuntarily.

"I used to pick fair in doorways and worked in a whore-shop, undressing for men I'd never seen in my life. After a time I noticed nothing about them, except their teeth. And I'll tell you something. Some of the girls I worked with enjoyed fairing. Like the porknockers they'd never give up the life for the security of marriage. You think if your priggish wife came into a fortune she'd be so docile? My younger aunt is quiet and affectionate, but dangerous. She'd kiss the inside and outside of your hand but she wouldn't lift a finger to help you."

"You were always rebellious," Michael said softly, sensing that her resentment had drained away.

"One day," she said, turning to face him, "I'll discover my hinterland, Michael. And all the wild demons rushing by in their phantom carts wouldn't stop me from travelling there."

They went down the stairs of the pavilion together, she a little behind him, dwarfed by his stature.

Two streets away from the house she asked him, "Why did you offer me the money? Is it because you knew?"

"Knew what?" he asked, even now pretending to be puzzled.

"Oh, nothing. You needn't feel sorry for me. I'm happy with my people."

"Yes," he observed, "you're not as thin as you used to be."

"You see?" she said with a smile.

They took leave of each other, and despite the need she had for him Genetha had no intention of seeing Michael again, while he had already calculated how often he could afford to meet her in future, notwithstanding her threat.

As she skirted the grass verges the most unlikely thoughts passed through her mind. She must hoard the empty jars of night-cream she used to keep the furrows on her face at bay. There was a secret of great importance lying in those jars of soft, cool cream, something that chased away old age and remained in the thin film that lined them when empty.

The first thing she noticed on approaching the house was that the light in the gallery was on. Usually it was left off in order to save money. On coming closer she saw her elder aunt sitting at the window. As soon as Genetha opened the door the aunt said:

"I want to talk to you, Genetha."

Genetha hated being left alone with her older aunt and asked, "Where's Aunt Alice?"

"She's inside. Earlier she got hysterical when she saw the cat trying to deal with a centipede which had come out of the corner and was running across the floor. She's so squeamish! Listen to me, Genetha. It is not seemly for a young woman of your background to go out so heavily made up. And those long earrings! They —"

"I'm sorry, Aunt. I'm a grown woman," Genetha declared.

"If as your aunt I'm not permitted to tell you my feelings about the way you dress then who is?"

"Aunt, I'm a grown woman. I don't need advice on my clothes any more."

"So you're defying me!"

Genetha did not answer, and her aunt, enraged at her unexpected opposition, decided to bide her time.

"Very well, Genetha, I've done what I consider to be my duty." And she spoke with an ominous detachment.

"I'm sorry, Aunt . . . ."

But her aunt got up with a false smile and excused herself.

Genetha waited for the first opportunity to confess to her younger aunt what she had done on Palpree Down and in the pavilion by the sea, and when she did she was surprised at her horrified reaction. She had overestimated her Aunt Alice's broadmindedness and thanked God she stopped short of telling her about her way of life in Tiger Bay and at Esther's establishment.

The estrangement from her Aunt Deborah had brought with it the need to get closer to the younger aunt, who herself was suffering from her sister's growing power mania. Although according to the old man's recently made will their father's property would belong to the two sisters jointly after his death, Deborah had managed to persuade him since to sign a power of attorney in her favour, as he was incapable of going out to draw his pension or cash the coupons on his debentures when interest fell due. The possession of that piece of paper had accelerated the process of the growing authoritarian manner in which she managed the house.

Genetha did not again make the mistake of confiding in Alice, and whenever she went out to still the hunger of her flesh she pretended that she was going to visit her paternal aunt. And as time went by she and Aunt Alice grew even closer, to the chagrin of her Aunt Deborah, whose dislike for her niece, aroused by her defiance, waxed into hatred.

Genetha learned a good deal from Aunt Alice about her sister. Soon after Genetha's mother got married she took up with a gentleman who, like Genetha's father, came to visit her at the house. But Genetha's grandfather found fault with him, especially with the shoes he usually wore.

"Who ever heard of a decent young man wearing two-toned shoes?" he used to say.

She gave up the young man, only to take up with another

who was promptly criticized by her father as being too small in stature for her. The elder aunt decided to have it out with her father, but he declared that she could marry "who she damned well pleased". Yet when a third young man came visiting, he ignored him completely, causing Deborah the most acute embarrassment. No man ever came to see her after that and she, out of pride perhaps, never broached the subject with her father again.

Genetha, in time, learned many things from her Aunt Alice, only because she too was suffering at Deborah's hands, and gained satisfaction from reducing her sister in the niece's estimation. In her opinion, it was a good thing that her sister had never married, because she had been as demanding with young men as she was with everyone else. It was possible that she was afraid of marrying, knowing that she could never yield to a man's authority. After all, she responded all too readily to their father's criticisms of the male visitors.

Genetha also learned things about her grandfather; that, for instance, he had been contributing to the Burial Society for twenty-five years, since he was fifty, so that when he died he would be given an expensive funeral.

And so things went, the rift between Genetha and her aunt Deborah widening while her relations with the younger aunt were being cemented with the passing months.

## 21. Gold Bangles

One evening when the scent of the last August rains was in the air, Genetha's elder aunt settled in a rocking-chair with her crochet basket a few feet from the piano, where Alice was playing a piece by Granados. So peaceful was the night and so apt the music that Deborah put down her work and lay back in the chair. Outside, the occasional thud of the coconut-seller's cutlass opening up a fruit came through the window, or the hum of a car engine from Vlissingen Road.

"I think someone's outside," Alice said, stopping in the middle of a phrase.

"I didn't hear anything," rejoined her sister, who nevertheless got up and went to the front.

"Can I come up?" a woman standing at the gate asked.

"You want to see someone?"

"Yes, Miss Genetha Armstrong," came the reply.

"I see . . . . She isn't here; she's gone out.".

"Will she be long?"

"No, I suppose not," Deborah said, reluctantly.

"Can I wait?"

"Yes, of course."

The woman, dressed with a certain ostentatious elegance, came up the stairs and through the door opened for her.

It was Esther, who recognized Deborah at once, recalling her stay at the house in Agricola after Rohan's birth, when she and Genetha's father fell out.

Alice got up from the piano and excused herself, while Deborah offered Esther a chair in the gallery, after turning on the electric light.

Esther was wearing a ring on every finger of her left hand while on her right arm were several gold bangles; and Deborah, at once repelled and fascinated by her attire, could not resist asking who she was.

"You don't know me. I'm sure you don't."

"Do you mind excusing me?" Deborah asked. She got up to join her sister in the kitchen.

"She knows Genetha," said Deborah to her sister. "You see how she makes up lately when she goes out. I'm not surprised, if she consorts with women like that. She's wearing a fortune in jewellery . . . a woman like that."

Alice shrugged her shoulders. She was as intrigued as Deborah, but afraid that her interest in the visitor might be detrimental to Genetha.

The two sisters stood watching Esther from the kitchen; but if Deborah hoped that Genetha would come back soon so that she could hear them in conversation, Alice prayed that her niece would stay away until the stranger left.

"Go and keep her company," Alice suggested to her sister, who declined.

"You go, I'll make her something."

Dutifully, Alice joined Esther in the gallery and began talking to her, avoiding any mention of Genetha's name.

It was while making sweet chocolate for the visitor that Deborah hit upon the plan to follow her if she left before Genetha came home. After putting a pan of milk on the fire she came back and went into the bedroom she shared with her

152

sister, where she took out a hat to wear as a disguise in case Esther saw her.

Deborah could not explain to herself the extraordinary effect the woman made on her, and even when the chocolate was ready she stood watching her from the kitchen, across the intervening space of the large drawing-room with its open piano and abandoned crochet basket.

On bringing Esther the drink Deborah said, "She should be back any time now," her normally supercilious manner replaced by a nervous uncertainty.

But an hour passed and Genetha had still not returned. Alice would have liked to go back to the piano, for the visitor, uncommunicative and even haughty, intimidated her. But she could not leave the gallery unless Deborah was prepared to take her turn with the stranger.

Another hour passed and when Alice repeated that she had no idea what had happened to her niece Esther got up and declared that she would not wait any longer.

"Tell her for me," Esther said, "that Netta's friend came to see her and invited her round to the house."

"Of course," Alice promised, and accompanied her to the gate, which was "not easy to close", she told the visitor.

Alice came upstairs to find her sister with her hat on and looking out of the window after the visitor, who had turned into Laluni Street.

"What's the matter with you?" asked Alice.

"I'll tell you when I come back," said Deborah, who hastily left the house to follow Esther.

The mild evening hour had given way to a gusty night and Deborah cursed herself for not securing her hat more firmly on her head. Her right hand holding down the incongruous-looking head-gear she swept down Laluni Street as quickly as she could, so as not to lose the stranger, who was walking more briskly than she anticipated and had already crossed the next road parallel to Irving Street.

Esther did not turn again until she came to Foreshaw Street and then Deborah had to increase her pace so as not to lose her. Finally, in Regent Street, she could follow at a much closer distance, protected from the possibility of detection by the large number of pedestrians on the pavement and the noise of the cars on the road.

Once in South Road Deborah allowed Esther to increase the distance between them, for the street was practically deserted; but as soon as the latter turned into a yard she hurried up, even at the risk of being seen.

To her surprise the house was large and well-kept, and its bottom-house enclosed by lattice work. But her suspicions about Esther were aroused once more when there was a burst of loud laughter, followed by the appearance at the window of a young woman with a cigarette in her hand. Deborah only had time to note the lot number on the gate before she went past the house.

She turned east at the corner and made for home, where she found that Genetha had not yet returned.

Deborah told Alice of her suspicions and of the house where the stranger appeared to live.

"The young woman at the window was definitely not her daughter," Deborah observed.

"Why you're so anxious to find out?" Alice asked her.

"Where does Genetha go at night? Why does she make up like that and put on those earrings?"

"But she does everything you tell her to," Alice protested, fearing for her niece.

"She is a disgrace! And what about this woman?" asked Deborah. "I'll ask cook to find out who lives in the house. We'll see," she added.

Genetha came back home at half past midnight, later than she had ever done before. No one, apparently, had been concerned about her absence and so she stayed up to listen to the mysterious sounds of night-time and wonder what strange processes were at work within her, driving her on to a state of such utter indifference that she cared nothing for the elder aunt's veiled allusions to her position in the house.

When it became evident that Deborah was pursuing a vendetta against her she no longer minded to appease her, and even Alice's sympathy and her grandfather's affectionate ways were not enough to make up for the other's hostility.

In any case, if her elder aunt had done nothing, she, Genetha, would be obliged to break away from the family. Whatever her needs were – and she herself was uncertain what they were – they could not be satisfied in that house. Neither her grandmother, withdrawn and aloof, nor her Aunt Deborah were the real cause of her feeling of estrangement. It was rather

154

a desert-like bareness, on which their very lifestyle was grounded, an absence of joy, of quarrels and reconciliations. Her younger aunt's affectionate spirit quailed before her sister's sternness, while her grandfather's whimsical nature was never allowed to flourish.

Perhaps Esther had suspected all this when she told Bigfoot that Genetha would come back to the brothel. Or perhaps she knew that any woman who set out on that road would have to travel along it to the very end.

Whatever happened, though, Genetha was determined never to return to the brothel. Somehow she must travel another road and if this was not possible she now had the will to end her life; and the only impediment to this course was her belief that such an act would be sinful. She knew that there was an after-life and believed that in another world she would be reunited with her parents and Boyie. Turning her hand against herself might rob her of the chance of such a reunion.

It was hard to believe that her dear mother had grown up in that house, had endured the punishments meted out by a vindictive sister and learned to shape her gestures to a sterile tradition.

So silent was the night that Genetha could hear the sea pounding the shore nearly a mile away, a shore she imagined littered with debris brought down by the rivers from the great forests of the interior and from the Amazon river, a thousand miles away.

She got up and glanced on the gloom of Laluni Street, its parapet littered with the cast-aside shells of empty coconuts, its houses floating in the shadows like birds in a mist.

Early the next morning Genetha's younger aunt told her of Esther's visit and of her sister's anger; and for the rest of the day the two women waited for the storm to break. But Deborah said nothing and Genetha noticed no change in her behaviour.

Then, just before the evening meal, Genetha saw her carrying in her parents' fare on a tray, and, on glancing at the table, noticed that it was only set for three.

When she and her two aunts sat down to table the air of expectancy was almost palpable and Alice forgot to say grace.

"We haven't said grace yet," Deborah observed icily.

Grace was duly said, and then the sound of the knives and

forks against the plates was so loud – in the absence of conversation and the awareness of a tense atmosphere – it appeared to be deliberately made.

In the middle of the meal the elder aunt, with great ceremony, wiped her mouth with her napkin.

"You had a visitor yesterday, Genetha," she said, having judged the timing of the remark to achieve the greatest effect.

Genetha did not answer.

"A person who refused to give her name," she continued. "And, if my suspicions are justified, had every reason to be silent. Do you know an extravagantly dressed *person* who lives in South Road?"

"I do, Aunt. Her name is Esther and she is very close to me."

"Really? Close?"

"Yes, Aunt. In fact since Mamma died she is the person closest to me, apart f—"

"Never!" exclaimed Deborah. "Never you speak of that *person* in the same breath as your mother. *She* was a lady."

Genetha hung her head.

"I haven't yet found out," Deborah pursued, almost bursting with rage, "what goes on in that house in South Road. . . ."

"It's a brothel, Aunt," Genetha answered without defiance.

"A. . . ."

"Yes, Aunt. I used to work there, and it was my home for —"

"Be quiet! You . . . creature! You're no niece of mine. O Lord in Heaven! To think we're harbouring you. . . ."

"Aunt, I'm looking . . . ." But she, in turn, was not allowed to finish.

"Your mother —"

"My mother!" screamed Genetha. "You never even came to see her once. None of you!"

And Genetha broke off to look at her other aunt.

"It's you who mustn't call my mother's name," she continued. "My name is Armstrong and that was my mother's name!"

"I won't compete with you in shouting," Deborah said with a smile of triumph. "But I must correct you. Your mother was no Armstrong. That was your father's name. We are forced, when we get married, to bear the names of men a whole lifetime . . . . And I *did* come to take care of you when your brother was born and you were two years old and not yet so impertinent. But your father insulted me. That's why neither I nor your Aunt

156

Alice ever came again. But ingratitude is a vice that becomes you. . . ."

Genetha was looking past her aunt, vacantly staring at the wall behind her, as if she were alone and reflecting on a problem of incalculable weightiness. She began to weep, silently, crushed by the torrent of reproaches heaped upon her and the ignominy she had brought to her father's name. All the nights she had left the house to seek the company of strange men, enveloped in a kind of numbness that protected her from the enormity of her conduct, came back to her vividly: the moonlit night on Palpree Dam, the encounter with Michael, the fleeting, secret meetings with other men assaulted her memory, and the way they behaved afterwards. Some cursed her for not wishing to see them again; others offered her money, while others fled from her as if she was possessed of a score of devils. Genetha recalled how rapidly she had matured after leaving school and starting work, her preoccupation with the idea of marriage, and her desire to have girl children so that she could dress them up.

Suddenly her elder aunt's hectoring words broke in on her reflections and she heard that she was obliged to leave by the weekend. Genetha held it against Aunt Alice that she did not speak up for her. All her attentions, all her protestations of affection had come to nothing in the face of her sister's harshness. Her weakness had rendered her incapable of loyalty.

"As I've said," declared Genetha, "I've started looking for a place. At least that's what I wanted to say."

Deborah, as if that assurance had been the object of her tirade, got up and left the table to her sister and niece, who found nothing to say to each other, for all the affectionate exchanges of the long months Genetha had stayed in the house had been erased with the silent betrayal.

Genetha carefully placed her knife and fork together, as she had been taught to do, with that involuntary action that informs all acts inculcated in the minds of young children as the indispensable equipment of gentility.

Nothing was said between them, and, urged by an unspoken understanding, they got up simultaneously and started to clear the table.

Genetha's grandfather came out, as was his custom, when the heat of the day had settled and the trade winds blew in from the sea over the warmer land. Genetha helped him to his armchair;

but as she was about to go off he asked her to sit beside him.

"When my grandfather died," he said, "the pictures were turned to the wall and all the mirrors in the house were covered. We were sitting in the drawing-room, all of us except my younger sister. Suddenly there was a scream from inside. We rushed in and saw her – she was nine then – in hysterics on the floor; and when we asked her what had happened she couldn't answer. But the cloth that covered the mirror on the chest-of-drawers had fallen off and the mirror was left exposed. I don't know why, looking back now, but we stood staring at that mirror as if it was a gateway to somewhere. I'll never forget that. Oh! I could tell you scores of stories like that. . . . Do you know? Last night . . . I saw my death. It came out, emerged from a dense wall of smoke and started coming towards me. I shouted, 'Halt!' But it kept coming on until it was so near I couldn't see it any more . . . . I am dead and grateful for the respite, for the chance to look at familiar things for the last time. . . . One day you will marry and have children. He will marry you for your gentle eyes and make you happy. There's no doubt that *you* will make him happy."

He fell back into his usual silence, the same silence which his wife inhabited like a home. Genetha and he sat alone in the gallery, framed by the casement windows and walls. She felt that a part of her had never grown up; that some people were still capable of inspiring awe in her, an almost physical reverence that small children have for grown-ups, who tower like giants above them.

He nodded off and Genetha quietly got up and went to sit alone on the stairs.

## 22. Rats

At the end of the week Genetha moved out, taking her grip to her paternal aunt's flat. She had been promised her old Albouystown room when the man who now lived in it went home to Truly Island; and the landlord, who could not say whether he was to leave in a week's or a month's time, said he would let her know when she could move in.

Mercifully, she was able to move in less than a fortnight afterwards; for if life at her maternal aunts' house had its harsh side, here there was no pleasantness whatsoever. Apart from the eternal complaints of Genetha's neglect, there was little to eat.

The dilapidated condition of the house in which her aunt lived was accepted as a fact of life by the tenants, so that Genetha's aunt's objections to living in a building with a leaking sewage pipe and a yard infested with rats appeared excessive to them. Most of the tenants, with but a toehold in the capital, saw the quarter as a stepping-stone to a more desirable life.

But after moving out Genetha went back to see her regularly, whether in recognition of the fact that she was the last blood relative whose home was open to her or impelled by sympathy for her, she was unable to say. Yet from then on she went to see her aunt every Friday night until her death many years later, when all the goodness had been extracted from her by the pressures of her solitary existence and all that remained was a crabbed view of life and those around her. And Genetha never discovered the extent of her aunt's degeneracy, for she had learned to close an ear to everything she said about what she owned – knowing that they would end with her father's misconduct – even to the tales of her once magnificent house in the country.

When Genetha was back in the hovel in Albouystown she asked herself if she had not been hasty in crossing her Aunt Deborah, whose table overflowed with good things. The week before she left she and Alice had baked bread, and as a joke had spread it with the cheapest butter, a pink, salted fat that was used in cooking and making nut-butter. They had laughed while eating, as if the thought of cheap butter was a hilarious artless joke.

Genetha bought a second-hand lamp, trimmed the wick and set it up in the old place on the table. She disposed her meagre belongings in the room as before, reinforced the defective lock on the sash window with a piece of wood and swept out the room with her little hand broom. And bit by bit she settled into her old life, often thinking of Zara, whom the room called to mind.

The following day she tramped the town in search of work, but things seemed to be worse than ever. Even the jobs in cake-shops, which were once there for the choosing, were hard to come by, though no one could live solely on the income they brought in. More women than ever were moving from the country to seek work in town and competition for what was going had become fierce. And when night came and she had found nothing she went to lurk in the vicinity of the South Road brothel until Bigfoot came downstairs to act as watchman during the late hours.

"Eh, eh, mistress! Is you?"

"Hello, Bigfoot. I don't want anyone to know I'm here. I came to borrow some money until I get work."

"Of course. How much you want?"

"Ten dollars, if you've got it. I'm sure I'll find work this week."

"You stay here, mistress. I'll be back in a minute."

Genetha listened for the footsteps of anyone who might be coming down the back or front steps, ready to hide behind one of the brick pillars. Bigfoot seemed to be gone for five minutes or more, but there was no sound of anyone moving about upstairs. Then Genetha remembered that she needed much more than ten dollars, for by the end of the week she had to pay the rent and it was not certain that, even if she found work tomorrow, she would be paid at the end of the first week.

She heard the back door close and took refuge behind a pillar near the back stairs, where it was pitch black.

"Mistress!"

Genetha came out to find Bigfoot carrying a cloth bag. He gave her an envelope and explained that there were fruit in the bag, and bread with cold beef.

"I thought that after I hadn't got in touch with you you wouldn't want to help me," she said.

"But I told you, mistress."

"I thought. . . ."

"I can't come with you tonight. Madame in a bad mood. An' if she know I gone out is going to be the licks of Lisbon."

"I'll be all right," said Genetha. "It's the money I was worried about."

Bigfoot opened the gate for her after checking that no one was at the window. And as Genetha slipped through the half-opened gate he bowed slightly and whispered good-night.

On her way home Genetha recalled how Bigfoot was feared by the girls and his uncompromising attitude towards them. Esther had told her more than once that he was kind. The role he was forced to play in front of them suited his huge frame so well, as did his tone of voice, that Genetha had never really come to terms with his inordinate respect for her.

She recalled, too, the night she and Zara hurried to the latter's home in order to get her parents' consent to go to the Old Year's dance and their disappointment at her father's refusal. She had come back to her room and fallen asleep to the faint sounds of a closing year.

The next day when Genetha had begun to despair of ever finding work she went and sat down in a cake-shop in Werken-Rust, where she ordered a soft drink and a pine tart. The fierce heat of the midday sun had abated somewhat, but the interior of the poorly ventilated cake-shop, which was on the western side of the road and therefore exposed to the morning sun, was oppressively close. Genetha rolled the lump of ice from the drink round her mouth, then took it out to pass it over her lips before drinking the sweet liquid slowly. Afterwards, she felt as thirsty as before and, on an impulse, asked the young woman for a glass of water. She complained of the heat and like that the two got to talking, exchanging bits of information that told them little about each other. Their conversation was interrupted by a young boy who came in to buy a packet of cigarettes. When he went Genetha remarked in the most off-hand manner that she envied the young woman her job.

"You can have it if you want," she remarked with a wave of the hand, not taking Genetha's remark seriously.

It turned out that she lived over the shop and was only helping out her uncle, who had been looking for someone for more than a fortnight. Nobody wanted work like that now, she said, at least not for the money he was prepared to pay. He was stingy and, knowing that he could always count on her to stand in whenever a girl left, he sacked his employees on the slightest pretext.

"But I'm serious about the job," Genetha insisted.

The young woman looked at her in some surprise, but then shrugged her shoulders and suggested that she wait. Her uncle could be back at any time, in a few minutes or at midnight.

After that the young woman was reluctant to talk and Genetha could only sit and wait for her uncle to return. Clients came and went, until it began to rain; and then only the odd child ran in to buy cigarettes or a cake or a soft drink. Opposite there was a shop whose front was open along its entire length, and from the interior of which the faint click of pool balls came.

161

Opened only in recent months it had enticed the young men of the district, who had taken rapidly to the American game.

Soon after the rain began to fall a car drew up in front of the shop and a man stepped out, slamming the door behind him. It was the proprietor.

The salesgirl promptly introduced him to Genetha, who was hired with little ceremony for a derisory wage.

"You not goin' complain!" he exclaimed, anticipating a protest. "You'll eat my cakes and open the drinks when my back's turned anyway."

And with that the proprietor lifted up the flap of the counter and went into the back shop where he rummaged about among the boxes before coming out again to drive off in the rain.

"When am I to start?" Genetha asked the young woman, disconcerted by the rudeness of her new employer.

"Tomorrow!" she exclaimed in surprise.

"What time?"

"Seven. He does open at six o'clock, but you don't got to come before seven."

So Genetha came back to step on the treadmill from which she descended when she went to live with her maternal aunts.

Nearly all she earned the first week went to pay back Bigfoot, who would have refused to accept the money, had she let him. And this time she stayed to talk to him for more than an hour, no longer afflicted by the embarrassment she usually felt in his company. Esther had been ill and was now convalescing in her room on the top floor. Shola was now married and was living in Houston and came to Georgetown daily to follow a course in hairdressing, on completion of which she intended to set up the first hairdressing establishment in her husband's village. Bigfoot thought she was not really married, but the news did not fail to impress Netta, who had been sulking ever since she heard it.

Bigfoot wanted her to go up and see Esther, but Genetha decided against it.

"You don't understand," Genetha told him. "I want to cut myself off completely. In the end people'll forget I was in the business and I'll be able to work again. I can't take the chance."

And she told him what happened when she attended the interview for the office job.

Above her head she heard the windows being closed and bolted and the jalousies being secured with their metal pins, and the sound of footsteps crossing and re-crossing the spacious drawing-room. The ray of light that fell on the boards of the house opposite disappeared when the last drawing-room bulb went out, and after the girl who was responsible for locking up went upstairs to the top storey a long, homely silence fell on that area of night. In Vlissingen Road the cinema must long since have emptied, and the hoardings advertising their East Indian films under the street lamps must now dominate the entrance to New Town, with their fleshy heroes and voluptuous heroines.

In the end Genetha went home alone, refusing Bigfoot's offer to accompany her. There was a danger in his obligingness, the beginning of a sort of dependence that did not accord with her bid for self-sufficiency.

From the very beginning of her move back to the area Genetha knew that the itch that had taken her in her aunts' house – the irresistible urge to sleep with strange men, which somehow seemed connected with that house – had gone. In retrospect the episodes were incredible, and in them she no longer recognized herself. In any case the old feelings of impotence crept back with the lack of the diet she could not afford and the sweet cakes she ate at the shop.

Occasionally, after twelve hours at the shop and a meal cooked on a kerosene burner her aunts had allowed her to take away, Genetha would go down to one of the new eating places in Albouystown. There she felt less conspicuous among the new wave of East Indians arriving from the sugar estates than among her own people, one of whom sooner or later would point a finger at her; sometimes she even ate there, at a cost not much greater than her own meal.

After a time she gave up cooking for herself altogether and appeared in the cook-shop at about a quarter past seven, when her plate of rice and curry was promptly placed before her on the uncovered metal table with its plaques of rust.

And the old signs of malnutrition began to reappear: first the brittle nails, then the lack-lustre skin, and finally the white corners of her mouth, offensive-looking slits associated with the diseased and underprivileged.

In the old days there was Zara, and even after they became estranged, a memory of friendship and the belief, unprofessed though it was, that one day it would be repaired. Now she walked the street, head down, haggard and overcome with an indescribable fatigue. All her liaisons were strewn in the wake of the present like jetsam, becoming smaller and smaller with the increasing distance. Even Boyie, the most enduring memory, no longer crossed her thoughts or, if he did, only like the swift flight of a small bird.

Sometimes, overwhelmed by her loneliness, Genetha would think of joining the church, not the Methodist – her mother's religion and her own in the early days – but the Catholic, with its scent of incense, its mysteries and above all its weeping candles. But something held her back, a vision, as it were, of a kind of degradation, as irredeemable as her years as a prostitute. She would sometimes lurk in the shadows of the brothel, in search of something, some part of herself perhaps, or of her family, or even Michael, who once believed that without her life would be unbearable.

At other times she would take her Bible from her grip and read a part that she had been in the habit of reading to her father when he was ill and began to stink like a corpse:

"For that which befalleth the sons of men befalleth beasts; even one thing befalleth them: as the one dieth, so dieth the other; yea, they have all one breath; so that a man hath no pre-eminence above a beast: for all is vanity.

"All go into one place; all are of dust, and all turn to dust again.

"Who knoweth the spirit of man. . . ."

The first time she looked at herself naked in the mirror – she was thirteen – she had done, it seemed to her, a secretive thing, for which she ought to have asked her mother's permission. And the next time the minister spoke at church of sin she trembled with dread that he somehow knew what she had done and that she was the object of his sermon. Was she now alone because of her past? Was there the possibility of atonement?

One evening in the middle of her meal in the cook-shop Genetha made up her mind once and for all that she would go and see the priest at the Brickdam Cathedral, the same one who had irritated her so much. She would wait a full week and if at the end of that time she was oppressed by the same questions she would see him.

And with that decision came the sensation of excitement

164

experienced before a long journey to another country. She ordered a beer and then another, and to the proprietor's question about the state of her pocket she laughed and made a humorous reply.

"First time I see you laugh," a middle-aged man playing cards at another table observed.

Genetha laughed again without turning round.

"Gi'e the lady another beer, Josh," ordered the middle-aged man, when Genetha had emptied her glass.

"No, no. I'm not a drinker," she protested.

The proprietor took no notice and in a trice he had opened a bottle and was pouring it out into a glass over her shoulder.

Intrigued by Genetha's unexpected sociability the card-players plied her with beer, and after her fifth joined her at her table.

"We thought you was too great to talk to, lady," said the one who first ordered her a beer.

"I thought you didn't like women," she retorted, her remark raising a guffaw among the men.

Genetha dared not confess how overwhelmed she was by their attention. At first the effect of the alcohol was to make her drop her mask. But as she drank more she exaggerated her companions' kindness in a way that was all too apparent to the proprietor.

"A'right, a'right, ease up. She in' from the Punt Trench, you know," he said, referring to an East Indian settlement of tenements and hovels.

But Genetha, under the increasing influence of the beer, was laughing and talking with the men as if she had known them for years.

Protesting when the proprietor refused to serve them more beer she got up and fetched the bottle herself from the counter and brought it back to the men, who had ceased drinking. When she faltered at the table one of the men got up and pulled out her seat for her, winking at the others as he did so.

"Is who goin' take you home, eh?" the proprietor asked, concerned lest he offended her companions.

"I only live down the road," Genetha protested. "No one . . . ."

"I goin' see you home, missie," the middle-aged man said gravely. Sweat was pouring from his face and, as the proprietor saw it, he had only stopped drinking with one aim in mind.

The proprietor washed his hands of the matter and settled into his chair, his head disappearing behind the assorted bottles on the counter. His wife had retired when meals were no longer sold, leaving him to serve and shut up shop after the customers went home. Women hardly ever stayed so late, so that Genetha's presence disconcerted him, especially as he believed that the three men had planned to follow her home. The district was full of East Indian men without women, and for whom the prospect of marrying was remote.

More than an hour passed, during which time the footfalls of passers-by became rarer and finally ceased altogether. The proprietor stood up behind his counter, impatient to close his shop, but at the same time unwilling to offend his regular customers.

"I want shut me shop!" he burst out in the end, unable to impress them with his stares.

Genetha was sitting, head bent over her arms, which were stretched out on the table in the posture of someone engaging in exercises. The three men looked at her, exchanged glances and then got up.

"You t'ink we goin' interfere with she or somet'ing?" asked the boldest of the East Indians.

They filed out of the shop without another glance at Genetha.

"You better wait a lil bit, lady," said the shopkeeper. "They does live at Ramsaroop house, so you never know."

Ramsaroop was the owner of the Dar'm Saala, a doss-house in Albouystown where beggars and the homeless put up for the night. The proprietor had been told that one of the men had at some time in the past put up there, and it was on this information that he based his remark that they were all living there at the moment.

A little while later he went and peered out of the window, but saw no one in the mist which had descended in the last couple of hours, and through which an empty dray-cart and a row of palings could barely be seen.

"I think they gone," he said, without turning round, "but you better wait a lil bit more."

Genetha was now sitting up, just able to concentrate on the proprietor's words and the bearing they had on her short trip down the road.

A faint odour of damp came through the open front of the

shop, and the muffled yapping of stray dogs which broke the stillness from time to time sounded like echoes from another place. No one was about in this late hour of night and the lamplight, usually visible as a yellow patch on the bridge, was sucked up by the dank mist, leaving the boards in darkness. At best a sombre quarter, this portion of Albouystown now presented the aspect of an entrance to an eerie land.

"I shutting up now," he reminded Genetha. "If you want me advice, don' mix with them people any more."

She got up with the assistance of the proprietor, who, before he could ask how she might manage was told, "I know the way home, thank you. I don't need any help."

Once out in the damp air, she shuddered and folded her arms, then looked around her to take stock of her position in relation to the street which she had to walk. She then set off in the gloom, guided more by her instinct to make for the street-lamp a hundred yards away then by the houses along the road.

With each step the mist rolled away before her, unveiling now an empty cart, now a garbage square littered with vegetable peel and paper, and continually the thick, uneven grass of the parapet. Genetha walked slowly in an effort to counteract the slight swaying of her body. About halfway to the house a light in a house on the other side of the road came on and almost at once was put out again.

"Missie?"

Thinking she could hear someone calling in the mist she looked about her, but could see nothing. The street lamp in front of her house was now only about thirty yards ahead and, nudged into action by a sudden fear, she took it into her head to run for it, only to find that she was not even in a condition to walk more quickly.

"Missie!" came the voice again, in an insistent, threatening tone.

This time she stopped.

"Where're you?" she said, just audibly enough to be heard by anyone within a few yards of her.

"Over here," the voice came again. "On the other side."

"I'm home now, thank you," Genetha called out, trying to be conciliatory.

"No, missie, you live further down there," came the voice again.

And with that the three men from the shop appeared to climb out of the gutter on the other side of the road.

Genetha set off again without answering.

"Me friend want fo' ask you somet'ing," the one who had said nothing to her all night now declared.

They surrounded her, preventing her from going any further.

Now that Genetha felt that she was capable of running, her way was barred by the burliest of the three.

"Hold she," one said aloud, "then I goin' hold she for you."

The one behind Genetha grabbed hold of her from the back, but then, without warning, she let out a shriek so terrible that within a few seconds lights began to go on in houses on both sides of the street.

Only the man in front of her reacted at once: he took to his heels in the direction of the shop, leaving the other two momentarily dazed by Genetha's reaction. Then they too made off almost immediately behind their friend.

"Is wha' happen?" the unseen head of a woman called from an open window.

But Genetha started off again for her house, trembling violently, yet anxious not to be found out as the cause of the disturbance. She only looked back as she turned into her yard and saw the shaft of light from a torch sweeping the road.

In her agitated state she went straight to bed without bothering to take off her clothes. Her head was throbbing violently. Had one of the men struck her? She got up, put on the electric light and looked in the mirror, then, feeling the back of her head, she examined her hand for any trace of blood; but there was nothing.

As she lay back and fell into a doze she heard a voice say: "My child. . . ."

"I was coming to see you, Father."

"Only when you're alone you come," he said kindly. "How can I take you seriously if you only come when you're alone?"

"When I'm alone there's so much I would like to ask you, Father. But now you're here. . . ."

"I know what you want to know, my child. You want to know about purity, don't you? You soil yourself and the more you do so the stronger your interest in purity becomes. A roof cannot be repaired without much hammering. You must go back the same way you came, my child. You must travel the way of suffering."

"Haven't I suffered enough, Father?"

"Can the measure of suffering ever be filled?" asked the priest.

"Can I be loved, Father?" enquired Genetha timidly.

"Loved?" exploded the priest, his benign expression disappearing under a terrible anger. "Did you not see what love was a moment ago, in the street? Only God's love is worthy of that name. You were sent that experience as a warning, but far from heeding it you still persist in your passion for the flesh, calling it by a name you do not understand."

"I can't go on living like this, Father," Genetha pleaded.

"No, child," he replied, adopting his kindly manner again. "That is why you must join the church, where you will know the unending mercy of Jesus and the example of his mother, the Virgin Mary. As you have known suffering you will know joy, the joy of fulfilment in the bosom of Jesus Christ."

And with that he turned to go.

"Don't go, Father. Don't leave me alone."

The priest spun round, and with an evil smile said:

"Why do you call me 'Father', eh?" And with that he made an obscene gesture with his hands.

"Father!" Genetha exclaimed. "I'm not accustomed to that kind —"

"What? Didn't you entice those poor men in the shop? Didn't you accept their beer, knowing perfectly well why they were offering you it?"

"I didn't —" she began to protest.

"If they had been caught you would have testified against them when in fact it was you who led them on."

"You're not a priest!" she exclaimed. "Are you the Devil?"

He smiled his benign smile again. "Do I look like the Devil, my child?"

"No, no, Father," Genetha hastened to assure him. "But just now — your hands. . . ."

"My hands, child?" he asked, raising both his hands with the palms turned towards her. "These hands are used to bless people, to baptize children and close the eyes of the dead. You were never kindly disposed towards me. Can you remember the first time you came to the cathedral? Your insolence? The Church demands utter subservience, nothing less. Didn't Christ submit to the will of God? How can *you* afford to be insolent?

169

All around me I see nothing but vanity, insolence and upheaval; impossible demands are made by working people, political parties challenge authority. . . . No, my child. The way to salvation is through subservience, not strength of will."

"There's another way, Father," Genetha declared.

"Which?" the priest snapped."

"I dare not say it, Father."

"Do you see how ensnared you are in your insolence?"

"You know, Father, when I was a girl my brother and I used to have identical dreams. . . ."

"Don't babble on like a heathen! Before you seek God you must rid yourself of all superstition."

Genetha burst out laughing in an uncontrollable way and was only brought to her senses again when the priest raised his hand to display the sexual sign.

"Listen to me, you heathen! I'm here to *teach* you, and it is I who should be laughing, not you with your ignorance."

Put out by his violent reaction to her laughter, Genetha suddenly thought she saw him facing and backing her at the same time, and rivulets of water running down the nape of his pale neck. Once she had witnessed a fight outside her parents' house in Albertown and now she remembered the white bubbles oozing from the cutlass-wound one man had received.

"Father, are you all right?" she asked involuntarily.

"Yes, my child. The first time you came to the cathedral . . . the first time. It's never the same again after the first time. . . . We are humans, you know, and no vows of chastity can ever change that. Your insolence that first time was like a whiff of some forbidden drug."

"I was not a Catholic, Father."

"You're still not one now, my child," he reminded her.

"But I *want* to be one, with all my heart," Genetha declared, roused by a strange yearning. "I want to serve God and be near to him . . . and touch him."

"Will you come to the cathedral then?" the priest asked, betraying his eagerness. "On Monday?"

"Yes, Father."

"Very well, my child. I will be expecting you."

And, with an ambiguous gesture, he vanished.

# 23. A Mountain of Food

The following evening, Genetha cooked for herself. So shaken had she been by the experience of the previous night that she made up her mind to avoid the cook-shop for a couple of weeks. After that she intended only to eat there and leave immediately after the meal.

It was Friday and the proprietor of the cake-shop where she worked did not pay her her full wage. She had to wait until Monday for the rest, he told her, Genetha was in the habit of taking a loaf of bread or a bottle of stout for her paternal aunt when she went visiting on Friday nights. But tonight she would have to go empty-handed, she thought. She recalled the mist of the night before and wondered whether it would be like that on her way back home.

It was a cool, starless night, its silence broken by the occasional voices of passers-by or the clinking of harness as a late donkey cart was unhitched. Genetha looked out of the window for any sign of mist or rain, but the only indication of an unfriendly evening was a thin veil of cloud over the sky. The blind of the single window on the front of the house opposite was down to reveal the profile of the old woman who lived there, puffing away at a tiny clay pipe. A figure of a well-dressed woman appeared from the direction of town and slowed down to survey the houses on Genetha's side of the road. Genetha made up her mind to leave at once and come back as soon as her aunt would allow her.

Having changed into her only other decent skirt she was about to pick up her bag when there was a knock on the door. Immediately Genetha thought of Zara and she rushed to open the door. It was Esther, taller in appearance, with a tasselled shawl round her shoulders.

"Well, well," she said. "You don't come to see me, so I've come to see you."

"You're the last person I expected to see," Genetha told her.

She let the older woman in and cleared the bed so that she could sit on it.

"You were going out?"

"Yes." And Genetha explained how she was in the habit of looking up her paternal aunt every Friday night.

"I'll only stay a while, then I'll come with you to her gate.

You don't mind?"

"It's just that I. . . ."

"What?" asked Esther.

"Nothing."

Esther fingered the bed-covers, passed her hands over the table next to Genetha's bed and examined the wretched furniture with her eyes.

"You go to see Bigfoot, your aunts and everybody else, but not me," Esther complained.

"Who told you I was living here?" Genetha enquired.

"Your aunt."

"In Queenstown?"

"No. Them? They haven't changed. The one time I went to see you there they made me feel like a leper. They kept staring at me and asking all sorts of foolish questions. What do I care? I can buy them out. . . . It was your other aunt."

"So you came to seek me out, Esther, and flaunt your jewellery. You can buy me out, as you can see."

Genetha cast her eyes round the room.

"I came to see you, not to seek you out," Esther protested.

"My life," Genetha declared, sitting down on the bed next to Esther, "is nothing. Look!" she exclaimed, roused to anger by Esther's manner. "Don't misunderstand me. I have nothing, but I'm free. All I need is a full stomach. I've forgotten my family, and my aunts mean nothing to me. You'll never understand what I mean, Esther."

"I. . . ."

"You'll never understand! You spent your life serving other people. Even now your establishment's owned by a stranger living abroad."

"And how do you intend filling your stomach?" Esther asked sarcastically.

"I will. In a couple of months I'll be working again."

Esther contemplated the wasted, pathetic figure of her former mistress's daughter, the sunken eyes and premature lines in her dried-out face and made up her mind not to quarrel with her.

"Try getting a job looking like that and you'll see what'll happen to you!"

"I know why you came to see me," Genetha said resentfully.

"I came to see you for the same reason I came years ago . . . . I used to undress you when you were a girl. And even when you

172

were old enough to comb your hair I used to comb it for you. I'm not made of wood. I'm not your mother."

"You can never forget that, can you? You'll carry your resentment to your grave. I bet you take it out from time to time and examine it like a hoard of jewellery. . . . It's the sign of a mean soul."

Esther remained silent, angry that the enormity of Genetha's mother's conduct should be dismissed in such a way. She, Esther, was mean in Genetha's eyes, while there were no harsh words for her mother. It was this arrogance in the Armstrong women that routed her. She recalled the visit of Deborah to Agricola, when Genetha was a little girl. Mrs Armstrong accused her sister of behaving arrogantly towards Mr Armstrong, failing to understand that it was a trait shared by her whole family. Deborah's contempt for her brother-in-law's words and her conviction that even in his own house he should know his place had angered her sister beyond measure.

Unable to quell the flood of resentment Esther said:

"One day you'll come to me after you've done the round of your good aunts, your blood relatives. And I'll take you in as if your mother had never misused me and. . . ."

"That's what Bigfoot said," Genetha broke in. "But you'll never have that satisfaction."

Genetha's anger gave her face the appearance of a grotesque mask and Esther, remembering the child's soft skin and affectionate nature, felt an immense sympathy for her.

"This is for you," she said, bending down to pick up a cloth bag at her feet.

Esther, seeing that Genetha did not intend opening the bag, got up and emptied it of its contents. Fruit, salt, tinned food and other foodstuffs were piled in a corner on the floor.

"Put it all back," said Genetha quietly. "I don't want it."

"No, it's food," objected Esther.

"Put it back. I don't want it."

"No!" exclaimed Esther. "It's food."

"Put it back!" Genetha burst out. "Food! Food! I'm not obsessed with food. Put it all back in your dirty bag and get out of here! Leave me in peace. I never came and sought you out. What do you want with me? My mother sent you away and you keep coming back like a dog. Get out of my room, you stray dog! Everything about you is vulgar. You dress like a whore;

173

you drink wine, even though you don't like it. You think that dressing me as a girl gives you the right to follow me around? Take your hatred and old resentments to the men you've gone with. Take them to Bigfoot, who'll do whatever you ask him because he's got to eat. I don't have to drink wine and eat brown bread!"

Esther waited until Genetha had finished, then began replacing the mountain of food in her bag, carefully and deliberately, to ensure that it should all fit. Meanwhile Genetha stood with her back turned to her, in an attitude which indicated that she would have her finish as quickly as possible, so that she could go out on her business.

In the end everything was put back. Esther picked up her bag and went out and as she closed the door Genetha started weeping in that undemonstrative, uncontrollable way which took her as a girl when, overcome by frustration, unable to assert herself as Boyie used to, she would succumb to the need for tears. Her humiliation at Esther's restraint in the face of her outburst, her intense loneliness and the belief that she was beyond redemption were too much for her.

As soon as she was certain that Esther was out of sight Genetha left to visit her aunt, without any thought of the weather she would encounter on her way home or the possibility of being molested.

Once out of Albouystown and she could feel the pavement underfoot and could see her own shadow lengthen and shorten between the street lamps, placed at more frequent intervals than in the quarter where she lived, she shed her depression as a garment that was unsuitable in a certain place, or on a certain occasion. Cars rushed past her, their headlamps like beacons, their engines roaring momentarily, only to fade in the distance. She turned down the street that would take her to her aunt's house, hidden behind two other, more presentable cottages. The city was growing not outwards, but in its back yards, in its bowels as it were, at the expense of fruit trees and yard space.

## 24. The Cathedral

The day came for Genetha to go to see the priest. She had informed her employer that she was feeling unwell and that if

174

she did not come to work on Monday he should understand. Genetha had set so much store by her "confession" on Monday that she was ready to run the risk of losing her job.

To make certain that there was no hitch she waited for the same hour as the last time she went to the cathedral.

As she walked by the eastern façade with its well-maintained flower-beds she brushed a finger lightly against the iron railings, wondering the while what would come out of her visit. If there were a number of women waiting to confess he would probably dismiss her with the minimum of conversation.

The pavement came to an end at the corner to give way to the pitch road, glistening from a recent shower and from which a vapour rose as from the vent of a laundry. Across the way the pillar-box stood like a strange red growth in the broad grass verge.

Genetha turned into the avenue of shade-trees, then into the grounds of the cathedral. An old woman was coming down the concrete steps, sideways, as if afraid that she might slip on the wet stairs. Apprehensive about her visit, Genetha asked the woman if the priest was there; and learning that he was she hesitated, filled with the urge to turn tail and flee.

"It's so hot outside," the old woman remarked. "But inside it in' warm up yet."

The woman went on her way, leaving Genetha standing on the stairs, looking backward for no reason at all.

The church was indeed cold and the few worshippers were almost all wearing raincoats. The music from the organ appeared to be rising from beneath the church, while the cubicle seemed smaller than the last time and smelt faintly of sweat.

"Do you remember me, Father?" asked Genetha.

"I do, I do. But you come only when you need us, my child."

And then, unaccountably, as if she had been directed to speak by someone whom she dared not disobey, Genetha became offensive.

"I don't need you," she declared.

"Pride does not suit you. You are not by nature a proud person. Why do you pretend to be what you're not?"

Genetha did not answer. She had no slip on and the thin material clung to her body.

"Can I ask you a question?" she said.

"You're here to confess your sins, not to ask questions," the priest answered sharply.

"Then why didn't you send me away the last time?"

"I felt sorry for you . . . and I hoped you would become a Catholic."

"Can I ask you the question?" Genetha persisted.

"Go on."

"Why are all Catholic priests foreigners?"

A long silence followed.

"There are local priests in some countries. But if there were local priests here would you respect them?" he answered finally.

"I respected my teachers, and my father and my mother," Genetha retorted truculently.

"A priest is not your father or even your teacher. He is God's representative."

"I'm sorry I came," Genetha told him. "The last time I left feeling you had given me something. I didn't want to admit it to myself then. . . . Last night I dreamed you were the Devil."

The priest stiffened, astonished at her hostility. His face was pink, marred, as it seemed, by a permanent blush.

"I feel sorry for you," he said.

"You can't feel sorry for me, Father. You don't know me."

"You are one of God's creatures," he said.

"When I'm alone," said Genetha, "I long for my mother and father and a man I once knew. He was handsome and strong. But I didn't know how to keep him. He walked all over me and took away everything I had. . . . If I had a child I'd teach it all about the pleasures of the flesh, and especially how to survive in your world."

"You measure survival by material standards," said the priest.

"I've got to eat or I'll get sick and die."

"And then?" he asked, his self-satisfied manner again beginning to come to the fore.

"And then I don't care."

"It's not food you need," he declared, shaking his head in sympathy for her.

Genetha noticed that his eyes were continually sinking.

"You see how thin my knees are?" she said, lifting her skirt two or three inches above the knees.

The priest closed his eyes and said, "You don't understand, my child. I'm beyond temptation."

Genetha pulled down her skirt.

"God sent you to test me," he observed. "There is something disturbing about your presence. I don't think ill of you, my child. You're sick and need help."

"I told you so, but you wouldn't believe me."

"Will you join the church?" he asked kindly. He was himself again.

"I don't know, Father. I want to, but something's holding me back."

"Confess that you didn't mean what you said about the way you'd bring up a child," he invited.

There was a long pause before Genetha answered.

"I meant it," she said.

"I don't believe you. It can't be true."

Genetha got up and left the cubicle, disgusted by her own behaviour and by her futile conversation with the priest.

Outside, in the street, a dray-cart pulled by two donkeys with their heads down made its way through the drizzle which had begun to fall while she was in the cathedral. Genetha, dogged by an overwhelming fatigue for the last few months, wanted to sit down but was not able to return to the empty pews. She would have been obliged to pretend that she was praying or meditating, and the thought that the priest might have caught her made her put the idea out of her mind. She leaned against the wall and watched the rain, overcome by a feeling of aloneness that she had often experienced as a girl when her parents went out and left her at home. A young woman standing on the other side of the doorway was also looking out on the street. She wanted to go over and speak to her, but did not know how to.

Did she come to church because she had troubles? Genetha wondered. Her dress was shabby, but well cut. What did it matter?

The young woman turned and caught Genetha staring at her, but she looked away just as the stranger smiled.

The organ stopped. Suddenly the rain began falling more heavily and gradually the porch began to fill with worshippers who could not get away.

Genetha, on a sudden impulse, stepped out into the rain and was drenched before she reached the corner. As she was crossing the road a passing car had to swerve to avoid her. She walked as in a dream, taking corners instinctively.

177

On reaching home she took off her wet clothes, changed into her nightdress, then drew the worn blanket over her and fell asleep soon afterwards.

At about two o'clock in the morning she was awakened by a knock on the door and when she got up and called out, "Who is it?" a voice answered, "It's me, my child."

It was the priest's voice.

Opening the door she saw him standing on the step. She hesitated a moment before letting him in, then sat down on the bed without a word. The priest, uninvited, sat on the only chair and looked at her as she instinctively arranged her hair.

"How did you get my address?"

"You gave it to me the first time you came, do you remember?"

"I didn't," Genetha replied.

"I never lie, my child."

"Why did you come?"

"I came to apologize," he said. "I didn't realize you were living like this."

Genetha did not answer. She made no attempt to button up the top of her nightdress.

"The women nowadays," he said, "have bold smiles and a partiality for indecent jokes."

"If you're staying, I'll light the lamp," Genetha offered. "The electricity's not working."

"No, it's all right. My child, will you let me help you?"

"How?" Genetha asked.

"In God there is security and salvation."

"I need money."

He took out a bank note, which she accepted without a word.

"You don't call me 'Father' any more," he protested.

Genetha did not answer.

"It's too late for you or anybody to help me," she said, unable to bear the way he stared at her.

"I know you have relations in Queenstown. Why don't you let. . . ."

"How d'you know so much?"

"You told me about them," he replied, as if he were talking to a forgetful child.

"I don't like asking my relations for anything. Even my brother."

"And your brother, what's he done for you?"

Genetha did not answer. As at the time of her last visit to the church he kept looking at her legs. Genetha pulled her nightdress down over her knees. The priest got up and sat beside her on the bed.

"My child, my child! Don't torture me!"

Then, trembling violently, he put his hand under her nightdress and placed it on her knee. He explored the upper reaches of her leg until he touched her pubic hair.

"You pig!" she exclaimed, yielding to the pressure between her thighs.

The bed creaked mercilessly. Outside, the night silence pressed upon the house, broken occasionally by the distant sound of a car in Sussex Street. She remembered her lover, the asylum and the things that had gone for ever. Even now, what she had desired most of all gave her no pleasure. Her chronic malnutrition prevented her body from responding.

Then there was silence in the room. Turning her face to the wall, Genetha heard the rustling of his garments. Then she heard the door knob turn and knew that he was leaving.

Jumping up from the bed, she called, "No! You've got what you wanted so you're slinking away."

"I . . ." he began.

"Stay and talk to me! Tomorrow I'm going to do something terrible. I want to talk to someone tonight."

"All right."

He sat on the edge of the bed, staring at the floor. There were no words, until, in the end, looking round him he asked her:

"Don't you eat?"

"There's nothing in the house," she replied.

"How can you live like that?"

"Hundreds of people've confessed to you, yet you don't know how to make conversation."

"Listen, my child. . . ."

"Don't 'my child' me!" Genetha exploded. "One day we'll run you all out of the country."

"When? In a hundred years? All these political speeches are going to you people's heads. In any case. . . ."

"Just sit there," Genetha said, "you don't have to talk. It's enough to have a human being in the room. I can't bear to be alone. I had a dog, a puppy. But he got run over the day after I got him."

"You said you were going to do something terrible tomorrow," the priest said.

"I was only talking," Genetha answered. "There must be talking . . . . Is it true that if you taught everyone to play at least two games well the crime rate would fall?"

"Hm," said the priest. "And where would you get the money and the facilities?"

"You could use the churches as games rooms. . . . I feel as if my life is drawing away from me. Here, you see, is my life . . . and here I am. They're attached like the engine and carriage of a train. And I feel as if my life is drawing away from me. It's odd. How different you are now from the figure of authority listening to my confession."

"I've got a confession to make. From the first I admired your defiance. It's a quality the early Christians had. . . ."

"I'm not defiant," said Genetha, as if all fight had gone out of her. "I'm submissive. I enjoyed being ruled. If I'm —"

"Then why don't you join the Catholic Church?" he asked.

She was silent for a long time before saying, "I don't know."

Suddenly a thumping from the floor above made them realize that they had been raising their voices.

"I'd better go," he whispered.

"If you want to. It doesn't matter after all."

"Promise — no, you'd better not. Do me a favour . . ." he said.

"No, I won't tell anyone."

"Thank you," he said, looking at her with an odd expression.

Genetha opened the door and he went out into the night. She looked up at the low, fast moving clouds and, feeling afraid, closed the door. Then she lit the kerosene lamp before lying down; but she could not fall asleep. She tossed from one side of the bed to the other and every time the bridge creaked she thought than an intruder might try to enter the house. Each outburst of barking announced a prowler. When, finally she fell into a fitful sleep a wind rose up and she awoke and drew the blanket over her scantily clad body. She could hear the branches of the coconut tree in the back yard and the wind rushing down the street.

Genetha was awakened by a knocking on the window. The

kerosene lamp had gone out and the wind had fallen.

She got up, cautiously drew the blind aside and saw the priest standing on the bridge, half-turned towards the road, but looking back at her room. He must have knocked and withdrawn to the bridge at once.

She was uncertain whether to go and open the door or pretend she had not got up. Raising the window she stood before it without a word, and the priest returned hesitantly.

"You weren't expecting it was me."

"No," Genetha said harshly.

The gutter in front of the house was overflowing and the street was empty under an ashen sky. Looking down at the priest's feet Genetha saw that he was wearing a pair of galoshes.

"Can I come in?" he asked.

"What for? If I stand here talking to you they'll hear upstairs."

"Well, can I come in for a few moments then? I promise I won't be long."

Without answering, Genetha went and opened the door. She followed him into the room. He sat down without being asked, as on the previous visit. Genetha slipped under the blanket, lay full length on the bed and looked up at the floorboards above her head. She had eaten nothing since the day before, but the pain of hunger had given way to a dull sensation in her stomach.

"You're still angry?" he asked.

"That's what you came to ask me?"

"Look," said the priest, his eyes blazing as if he had suddenly come to life, "I'm alone. It's just that I can't talk about myself. The last time I tried to talk to you, but you seemed to be mocking me. I know what annoys you about me, but I can't help it. You can't help what you are. This room – the dirty blinds, the floor, the wooden partition fascinate me. It's hard to explain, but I feel drawn to this room. Don't you want to know how I got your address? You know, I became. . . . You live in a country bursting with love. But instead of reaching out and grabbing it you cut yourself off from everybody. . . ."

"I'm going to do a terrible thing," she interrupted him.

"What? Tell me and perhaps I can help you. I respect you, you know, as I respect the Virgin Mary."

"My brother was murdered in the Essequibo," said Genetha.

"What are you saying? Are you trying to frighten me?" asked

181

the priest in a pleading voice.

"My brother was murdered in the Essequibo," she repeated.

"Why didn't you tell me?"

"What for? You don't listen."

"But you don't know what you're saying. I've spent my life listening."

Then, seeing that Genetha did not want to say anything more to him, he got up. Without warning he threw himself on her and began kissing her fervently on the lips. She struck him in the face with both fists and when he persisted scratched him with both hands. Drawing back he put his right hand to his face.

"Is there a mark?" he asked, alarmed at the thought that she might have left some evidence of their struggle on his face.

"If you don't go. . ." she began.

"All right, all right," he whispered, "I'll go. I'll go, my child."

Genetha turned her head away from him as he passed and then slammed the door after him. She went to the window to watch him walk down the road in the direction of Sussex Street, where the street lamps had already gone out and the morning glow brightened the ridges of the roofs. Someone came down the stairs and left by the front door, closing it gently so as not to disturb the occupants of the house.

She heard the noises of the awakening day, the carts, the stray dogs, the banga mary seller, the bicycle bells, the kiskadees; and the bustle of morning and the silence of afternoon and the falling of day and the gathering night succeeded one another.

She got up at about midnight, took a shower in the corrugated-iron bath in the back yard, dressed and packed her clothes into a cloth bag.

On approaching South Road there was a certain exhilaration in the air. She stopped under a street lamp, took the small mirror from her handbag and looked at herself. Then she patted her hair into place, put back the mirror into the bag and resumed her way. As she crossed the bridge she impulsively threw her cloth bag into the trench, looked down into the water and watched it float for a while, then sink slowly.

Esther's establishment was brightly lit. She could hear music, while shadows appeared and disappeared at the window.

When she opened the door it was Esther who saw her first.

The man to whom she was talking turned round to look at Genetha as well, while Esther came forward and embraced her friend.

"You've come back," Esther said, trying to sound detached.

"Yes."

"I'm glad."

"Eh, eh! Is where you come from?" Netta shouted out across the room. "Eh, eh! You come back!"

"I come back," replied Genetha.

The band was playing a popular tune and the girls were dancing. Salome, despite the violence of the rhythm, was dancing slowly with her partner who at the same time was kissing her on her neck.

There were new girls, who seemed more vulgar than the others. Everyone, apart from Salome, was caught in a frenzy induced by the music, the dancing and the alcohol.

Esther was dragged off by a middle-aged man and Genetha went to sit on a chair against the wall. She knew none of the men, but surveyed them one by one.

"Cigarette?"

The cigarette was offered by a man in his early thirties with a pock-marked face, whom Genetha hardly looked at while stretching her neck to accept his light. They smoked together without talking and when a slow piece was struck up Genetha put her cigarette out and fell on his shoulders. He led her through the crowd of dancers to the middle of the floor where they swayed gently.

The music stopped as the Stabroek Market clock struck one, and the cool air rushed in through the open window and the lattice-work.

Genetha and her friend sat down by the window, then she accepted another cigarette, before looking outside on the empty street and up at the stars. For the first time that day she felt the pain of hunger.

# Epilogue

The years went by; and the only major event in Genetha's life – apart from the racial riots that set East Indians against Africans and Africans against Indians and spawned a breed of fire-raisers who threatened universal conflagration – was her grandfather's death, the news of which she heard over the radio. It came eleven years after she went back to live in Esther's establishment. She attended the funeral and saw the diminutive coffin – he had shrunk – being lowered into the grave, and the spadefuls of clay falling and obscuring the lid, and finally its disappearance under the indifferent earth. She called to mind her father's funeral and her ride back with Boyie in the mourners' carriage. Her grandfather's remains had been transported in a motorized hearse, an abomination, Genetha reflected.

No one recognized her, although here and there she picked out, apart from her aunts, well-known townspeople and others she had known. The anonymity she had prayed for years ago was now complete, for in her seclusion she now hardly saw anyone from the outside world.

Genetha brushed past her aunts, both dressed in black, both incredibly gaunt, and between them, a frail, veiled old woman with a pronounced stoop. The austerity of the three women set them apart from the crowd, like the remnants of a singularly striking species that was no longer capable of breeding and so was doomed to extinction.

Genetha herself was grey, her hair yellowing in parts, like the colour of dead leaves. The slight stoop of her back, although pointed out by Esther, could not be detected by looking in the mirror. Besides, she had lost her vanity and even the memory of it. Making her way among the crowd to the hired car that was waiting for her she gave no thought of her appearance, only to the confirmation of her belief that she was indeed nothing in a town where she had once had mother, father, brother and grandparents.

Back at the brothel Esther, by way of an indulgence, invited Genetha for a drive. She only accepted reluctantly and the two women drove down to the ocean where Esther sat on the wall looking out over the beach, while Genetha went walking on the corrugated patterns of sand until she came to the retreating sea. Here and there jellyfish bobbed up and down on the waves,

Portuguese men-of-war with indigo crests. The sea had left behind masses of seaweed, like the hair of drowned women, wet and limp. Above, gulls were wheeling over the empty expanse of beach and grey water, occasionally diving low to recover just before striking the waves. Genetha, far from reflecting on herself, was thinking of Bigfoot's cedarwood bird-cages, hung out from the back and side windows, on nails hammered into the boards. He had bought her a field canary and a blue saki, whose azure wings soon faded to a lustreless grey.

That night she ate with the household, after which she went up to her room to conjure up the past and the future, before her birth in Agricola and beyond her death in another time of streamlined hearses and small funerals with two cars and the indifferent faces of their occupants. And she heard the drunken voices of children crying out and saw a vast forest of pillars stretching like trees to the unanchored peaks of Akari.

Came July, the season of mangoes, and August, when the plums are ripe. The months passed like leaves from some ill-used picture book, glimpses of a dimly perceived time. And one December evening she sat on the ornate porch that looked out on Croal Street where barristers' chambers stretched in a row, her eyes fixed obsessively on a fine persistent rain that had been falling for most of the day, and which curled and folded in the distance like drifting wreaths of smoke.

The servant was now the mistress, the former mistress's daughter a dependent friend with a room on the upper floor and, for the succession of girls who came and went, an obscure connection with Esther's past.

Genetha woke up on the porch and saw the houses and offices opposite smeared with the colours of morning. She found a shawl round her shoulders, a tasselled, multi-coloured cloth she had never seen before. It must have been Bigfoot who had put it on her while she was sleeping; and she wondered at his devotion.

The sound of birdsong had awakened her, the warbling of canaries singing from their cages as if they were free. Observations floated around in her head, remarks unconnected to one another. "We'll never dance again in Wakenaam!" "What's your direction?" as a young woman once enquired of her address. She smiled and got up from her seat; and at the sight of a shutter of a cottage opposite being pushed open she recalled her own home that had been closed to her, and the woman and her son living next door, hardly ever seen, like polyps in an underwater garden.

Genetha saw the hues of the sun changing by the moment and felt that she had come to the end of a long journey, arriving at a place where she was to be cleansed, to be freed from all notions of happiness and unhappiness, pain or exhilaration. The sun and the smell of grass from the verge were like the broom that swept the house after a corpse had been taken away and the merriment of the wake had been forgotten. Here was the root of all awareness, the knowledge of death, the mystery of time and insights into the unexplored countries of the heart.